MaryJanice Davidson has written in a variety of genres, including contemporary romance, paranormal romance, erotica, and non-fiction. She lives in Minnesota.

Visit her website at www.maryjanicedavidson.net.

Undead and Unfinished

MaryJanice Davidson

piatkus

PIATKUS

First published in the US in 2010 by The Berkley Publishing Group,
A division of Penguin Group (USA) Inc.
First published in Great Britain as a paperback original in 2010 by Piatkus

A CIP catalogue record for this book
is available from the British Library.

ISBN 978-0-7499-0925-3

Printed and bound by Clays Ltd, St Ives plc

Papers used by Piatkus are natural, renewable and recyclable
products sourced from well-managed forests and certified
in accordance with the rules of the Forest Stewardship Council.

Mixed Sources
Product group from well-managed
forests and other controlled sources
www.fsc.org   Cert no. SGS-COC-004081
© 1996 Forest Stewardship Council

FSC

Piatkus
An imprint of
Little, Brown Book Group
100 Victoria Embankment
London EC4Y 0DY

An Hachette UK Company
www.hachette.co.uk

www.piatkus.co.uk

For Sarah and Sherrilyn and Jen and Lisa
and Vicky and Marissa,
who helped me bring my bad self
back to my bad self,
and never once asked me for anything.

Acknowledgments

Okay, so, at the end of the day, when it's time to write a book, it's just me and the computer . . . me, glaring balefully at same; computer refusing to make eye contact in the childish way it has.

(I should probably rewrite that: it should be *the computer and me*, right? Cuz I'm tryin' to write good n' stuff. Enh. I've already lost interest.)

But! For me to have the time to sit my big white butt down in the seat and get the work done? Tons of people help with that. And since I willfully ignore them most of the time, when I'm not figuring out how to frame them for felony assault, I'll go on ahead and drop a few names.

First, many thanks to my valiant yet self-effacing assistant, Tracy Fritze. The poor woman no doubt assumed, well over a year ago, that it'd be a typical office job. Working for a writer was probably like working for an accountant: it sounded important but was ultimately mind-numbingly dull.

Sure, her workplace was my very own home, but how much different would it be from driving to an office three days a week?

Tracy likely assumed her duties would fall along the lines of word processing, setting up meetings, arranging interviews, proofing ARCs, booking speaking engagements, working with copyeditors, and occasionally running tornado drills.

Instead, the poor woman has been forced, in pretty rapid succession, to endure: being greeted by my pantsless son on more than one occasion, being interviewed by a German magazine (them: "How terrific is it to work for *the* MaryJanice Davidson?" Tracy: "Um . . . "), fighting off our overly affectionate dogs, enduring the smells of McDonald's chicken nuggets and pots of chocolate Malt O'Meal when she's trying to eat like a grown-up (and set me an example of same), and ceaselessly trying to encourage me to sit down to make decisions (on PR products, on book signings, on answering reader questions, on turning in interview questions the day I agreed to do so, on why I shouldn't wolf down a half dozen Reese's Cups at 9:30 a.m.) like a grown-up.

Not to mention being locked out of my house when I've crawled back into bed with a migraine (see above: greeted by pantsless son: "Hi, Tracy. Mom's sick. Can I have some Malt O'Meal?"), and holding her ground when I ruthlessly set the dogs upon her (I found my dogs are especially fond of her if I rub bacon grease into her shoes while she's hard at work in the office).

Tracy is an assistant as the dictionary defines it: she contributes to the fulfillment of a need; she assumes some of my responsibilities. She rescues me from the minutiae that nearly everyone has to endure if they want to be a functioning member of society. She's smart, she's quick, she never has to be told anything twice, she's discreet (nobody knew about my pantsless son or Malt O'Mealgate until I stuck it right in my acknowledgments page). Also, she smells terrific.

Thanks are also due, as always, to the awesomest of awesome husbands, Anthony Alongi (he also cowrites the Jennifer Scales series with me). He tirelessly reads, suggests, edits, mocks, enrages, inspires, and annoys. Without him, there's absolutely nothing for me.

My folks and sister, for being completely unwavering in their support, one hundred percent of the time. They wouldn't abandon that stance if I stuck a gun in their ear. Do not ask me how I know that.

The Magic Widows, who have endured me for years and pretend that I'm worth the trouble.

The best of agents, Ethan Ellenberg, who paid me the ultimate compliment of calling me low maintenance. That was a wonderful lie for him to tell!

The always terrific Cindy Hwang, who reads my book suggestions and synopses, edits my manuscripts, exudes copious enthusiasm for same, and doesn't smack herself on the forehead when I can see it, or hear it. (Though I do occasionally hear odd background sounds when I'm on the phone with her.)

And to Leis Pederson, kick-ass assistant editor, who is repeatedly forced to track me down and corner me like a rat to get edits out of me, but does it with such style I feel wanted, not stalked.

Thanks also to the Yahoos, my fans on Facebook, the readers kind enough to write to me, and the readers who don't go near Facebook or the Web, who don't have computers but who write to me, care of my publisher, with real pens on real paper. (I feel bad I received one such snail mail and instantly assumed, as comedian Jim Gaffigan suggested, that someone had been kidnapped.)

I write for myself—I always have. I think if you write for other people, the end result is something of a cheat, for you and for them.

But you guys make the writing that much more fun, for which I am continually humbled and slavishly grateful.

—MaryJanice,
Winter 2009

Author's Note

I've got nothing against Claes Oldenburg or his wife, Coosje van Bruggen. And I've got nothing against the Minneapolis Sculpture Garden.

But at the end of the day, it's just a giant spoon.

A spoon!

The Story So Far

Betsy ("Please don't call me Elizabeth") Taylor was run over by a Pontiac Aztek almost three years ago. She woke up the queen of the vampires and in dazzling succession (but no real order), bit her friend Detective Nick Berry, moved from a Minnesota suburb to a mansion in St. Paul, solved various murders, attended the funerals of her father and stepmother, became her half brother's guardian, still avoids the room housing the Book of the Dead (Book of the Dead, noun: the vampire bible written by an insane vampire, which causes madness if read too long in one sitting), cured her best friend's cancer, visited her alcoholic grandfather (twice), solved a number of kidnappings, realized her husband/ king, Eric Sinclair, could read her thoughts (she could always read his), found out the Fiends had been up to no good (Fiend, noun: a vampire given only animal [dead] blood, a vampire who quickly goes feral).

Also, roommate Antonia, a werewolf from Cape Cod, took a bullet in the brain for Betsy, saving her life. The stories about bullets not hurting vampires are not true; plug enough lead into brain matter and that particular denizen of the undead will never get up again. Garrett, Antonia's lover, killed himself the instant he realized she was dead.

As if this wasn't enough of a buzzkill, Betsy soon found herself summoned to Cape Cod, Massachusetts, where Antonia's Pack leaders lived. Though they were indifferent to the caustic werewolf in life, now that Antonia was dead in service to a vampire, several thousand pissed-off werewolves had just a few questions.

While Betsy, Sinclair, BabyJon, and Jessica were on the Cape answering these questions, Marc, Laura, and Tina remained in Minnesota (Tina to help run things while her monarchs were away, Marc because he couldn't get the vacation time, and Laura because she was quietly cracking up).

They hadn't been gone long before Tina disappeared and Marc noticed that devil worshippers kept showing up in praise of Laura, the Antichrist.

In a muddled, misguided attempt to help (possibly brought on by the stress of his piss-poor love life . . . an ER doc, Marc worked hours that would make a union-less sweatshop manager cringe), he suggested to Laura that she put her "minions" to work helping in soup kitchens and such.

As sometimes happens, Laura embraced the suggestion with tremendous zeal. Then she took it even further, eventually deciding her deluded worshippers could help get rid of all sorts of bad elements . . . loan officers, bail jumpers, contractors who overcharge, and . . . vampires.

Meanwhile, on the Cape, Betsy spent time fencing with Michael Wyndham, the Pack leader responsible for three hundred thousand werewolves worldwide, and babysitting Lara Wyndham, future Pack leader and current first-grader.

With Sinclair's help (and Jessica's cheerful-yet-grudging babysitting of BabyJon), Betsy eventually convinced the werewolves she'd meant Antonia no harm, that she in fact had liked and respected the woman, that she was sorry Antonia was dead and would try to help Michael in the future . . . not exactly a debt, more an acknowledgment that because she valued Antonia and mourned her loss, she stood ready to assist Antonia's Pack.

Also, Betsy discovered that BabyJon, her half brother and ward, was impervious to paranormal or magical interference. This was revealed when a juvenile werewolf Changed for the first time and attacked the baby, who found the entire experience amusing, after which he casually spit up milk and took a nap.

Though the infant could be hurt, he could *not* be hurt by a werewolf's bite, a vampire's sarcasm, a witch's spell, a fairy's curse, a leprechaun's dandruff . . . like that. Betsy was amazed—she'd suspected there was something off about the baby, but had no idea what it could be.

Sinclair, who until now had merely tolerated the infant, instantly became proudly besotted ("That's *my* son, you know") and began plotting—uh, thinking about the child's education and other requirements.

Back at the ranch (technically the mansion on Summit Avenue in St. Paul), Laura had more or less cracked up. She'd fixed it so Marc couldn't call for help (when he discovered their cell phones no longer worked, he snuck off to find another line, only to be relentlessly followed by devil worshippers, who politely but firmly prevented this), and she and her followers were hunting vampires.

Betsy finally realized something was wrong (a badly garbled text secretly sent by a hysterical Marc), and they returned to the mansion in time to be in the middle of a vampires-versus-Satanists smackdown.

Betsy won, but only because Laura pulled the killing blow at the last moment.

People went their separate ways, for a while. And nobody felt like talking.

Three months later, there still has been no real discussion about the ominous events over the summer.

I'm here on the ground with my nose in it since the whole thing began. I've nurtured every sensation man's been inspired to have. I cared about what he wanted and I never judged him. Why? Because I never rejected him. In spite of all his imperfections, I'm a fan of man.

—SATAN, *THE DEVIL'S ADVOCATE*

Can you imagine what it was like? Ten billion years providing a place for dead mortals to torture themselves? And like all masochists, they called the shots. "Burn me." "Freeze me." "Eat me." "Hurt me." And we did. Why do they blame me for all their little failings? They use my name as if I spent my entire day sitting on their shoulders, forcing them to commit acts they would otherwise find repulsive. "The Devil made me do it." I have never made any one of them do anything. Never. They live their own tiny lives. I do not live their lives for them.

—LUCIFER MORNINGSTAR,
DEVIL IN THE GATEWAY

It's not easy being the Barbra Streisand of evil, you know.

—SATAN, *BEDAZZLED*

Undead and Unfinished

Prologue

Archived audio files of Elizabeth, the One, Queen of the Vampires, circa 2010

Okay, so, here are various yucky excerpts from the Book of the Dead. Gawd, I hate that thing.

"The Queene's sister shalt be Belov'd of the Morningstar, and shalt take the Worlde."

That'd be my sister, Laura. She's a great kid—a college student at the U of M. Also, she's the Antichrist.

"And the Queene shall noe the dead, all the dead, and neither shall they hide from her nor keep secrets from her."

Yeah. That fun tidbit translated to, "Zombies will lurk in

your basement, and ghosts will follow you around and bitch. Lots."

". . . and the Morningstar shalt appear before her own chylde, shalt help with the taking of the Worlde, and shalt appear before the Queene in all the raiments of the dark."

This? I have no idea. Could be the end of the world, could be a visit from Boy Scouts selling wreaths. And it's maddening, really maddening, because I can't read too much of this fucking horrible tome from hell (probably literally from hell) in one sitting because I go crazy. Anyone who reads it for too long at a time goes crazy. Also? I can't get rid of the damned thing.

It finds me. It always finds me, sometimes via the nefarious operators of the United Parcel Service. As Ferris Bueller put it, "How's that for being born under a bad sign?"

"And the Queene shall noe the dead, and keep the dead."

Yep, got that one figured out. I live with vampires and talk to them, and I'm having fabulous sex with one of them. Also we're filing joint tax returns, a good trick for dead people.

As for keeping the dead—I have a zillion roommates, none of whom I asked to move in, in case anyone's keeping track.

"And the Queene shalt noe a living chylde, and he shalt be hers by a living man."

Score another one for the Book of the Dead. My half brother, BabyJon, is now my legal ward due to the recent grisly deaths of my father and stepmother. I had pretty much given up on the idea of being a mom—I no longer sweat, never mind menstruate—when BabyJon landed splat in the middle of my (undead) life.

What's worse, that I can't read the thing long enough to make sense of it, or that it's always right?

"To challenge the Queene, thou shalt desecrate the symbole."

At least this isn't getting weird.

"The Queene hath dominion over all the dead, and they shalt take from her, as she takes from them, and she shalt noe them, and they her, for that is what it is to be Queene."

Now it's getting weird. See, um, one of my superscary evil vamp powers is that I can pull energy from other vampires, then boost it and slam it back into them. I only did it once. It sucked rocks, and nearly killed me (again).

Please God, I never have to do it again.

Do a lady a favor, okay, God?

"The Queene shalt see oceans of blood, and despair."

Now, that one? That's the one that really scares me.

Chapter 1

I would never have gone to hell in the first place if the Antichrist hadn't been fluent in Tagalong. Talk about your perfect storm of paranormal weirdness . . . and on Halloween, too.

Okay, so, I'll back up. This whole mess started simply enough (they always, always do): Bloomingdale's was having a shoe sale and for once, the retail time warp worked in my favor.

Okay, I'll back up more. You know how stores are actually about four months ahead of the actual calendar? Like Halloween decorations on sale the day after Easter (pardon me while I embrace the horror)? Like that. So anyway, even though it was Halloween, they were having their spring shoe sale (because when there's a foot of snow on the ground, everybody wants to buy sandals, right?). And the Antichrist asked if she could tag along, so I said okay.

I . . . said . . . okay! You'd think I hadn't been paying attention the last four years. Okay, I haven't been. Still, how could I not see the coming disaster? It shouldn't have mattered that the Antichrist needed a new pair of sandals. I should have realized that an innocent quest for fine leather footwear would have ended up with me in hell and the Antichrist freaking out. Again.

Right. The Antichrist. I should probably explain that, too. My half sister, Laura, was fathered by my, uh, father. Dear Old Dad was banging away at my stepmother, the wretch formerly known as Antonia and whom I had always called the Ant, and Dim Old Dad didn't notice she was possessed by Satan. I'm betting devil-possessed Ant isn't any worse than non-devil-possessed Ant, which is a sad commentary on my father's taste in second wives.

The thing is, Satan hated pregnancy, delivery, and breast-feeding. So she did the whole baby-on-the-doorstep thing and beat feet back to hell.

So my sister, who was raised by a minister, is not only the Antichrist, it's been foretold she'll take over the world. Possibly between donating blood and teaching Sunday school.

But! I will be the first to admit, the Antichrist is nice. Works in homeless shelters, runs blood drives (kind of hilarious, given that her sister is a vampire), makes cupcakes for church bake sales. Chocolate ones. With real buttercream frosting. *Buttercream*, not the colored Crisco grocery stores try to pass off as frosting. Ummm.

God, I miss solid food.

Of course, Laura's got a temper. Who doesn't? And occasionally she loses it and then slaughters anyone she can get her hands on. That gets awkward, kind of. And she's totally conflicted about the undead. Which is actually a pretty normal reaction to vampires.

Her temper and occasional forays into psychopathic rage were why we were meeting tonight at the Mall of America. Laura had sort of tried to kill me a couple of months ago, and still felt crummy about it. She detested conspicuous consumerism and also shopping, which is why her offer to go to my personal Graceland was an olive branch.

I had risen from my unholy grave (bed, actually, with navy blue flannel sheets from Target—it was a day away from November, and I'm not a savage), devoured an innocent for breakfast (a triple-berry smoothie; a perk of being the queen of the undead was that I didn't have to suck down blood every day, though to be honest, I always want to), then commandeered my sinister chariot (a Lexus hybrid) and was mall-ward bound.

I parked in the east parking lot, second floor—lots of my favorites were on that side, including Williams-Sonoma and Coach—not that I'd ever cough up four hundred bucks for a knapsack that looked like it was designed by a bright second-grader. Also, Tiger Sushi was there, and Laura was seriously addicted to their Tiger Balls.

So I forced a smile as I marched toward a restaurant that sold seaweed, rice, and raw fish for a profit margin of several hundred percent. The sushi thing. I didn't get it and I never would. I'd been fishing too much as a kid; I couldn't make myself eat bait. No matter how fresh it was.

I spotted Laura while I was still thirty feet away, and it had nothing to do with my supercool vampire powers. Laura was just ridiculously gorgeous, all the time. So annoying.

Look, it's not envy, okay? Well, not extreme envy. I'll be

the first to admit I'm not one of those girls who pretends they have no idea they're mega-cute. I'm cute; I freely confess. Tall and blonde (big surprise in Minnesota . . . we're about as rare as yellow snow in the dog park), pale skin, light eyes. Never really had to fight the fat, and being undead means I'll be slender forever. The phrase *I'm at my winter weight* no longer has power over me. My senior year I was a contestant in the Miss Burnsville pageant and went home with the Miss Congeniality sash, sort of the you're-not-the-prettiest-or-the-most-talented-but-the-other-gals-thought-you-were-nice consolation prize. I don't exactly drink my water out of a dog dish.

Laura, though . . .

Breathtaking. Gorgeous. And, as my friend Marc put it, "mouthwatering."

My *gay* friend Marc.

And there she was, standing with someone I didn't know, gesturing wildly in the manner of the native Minnesotan (or, perhaps, The Omen). And as I approached I remembered the *real* reason the spawn of Satan and my dead stepmother made me so uneasy.

She was just annoyingly stunning, all the time. One of those (vomit) natural beauties. Elbow-length hair the color of corn silk. Big blue eyes. First-day-of-spring blue. Cloudless-summer-day blue. Really, really gorgeous blue. Oh, and thin—did I have to tell you that? I probably didn't have to tell you that.

Great tits, of course, and always primly secured in a 36-B bra. Long legs—she was just a hair shorter than me, and I topped out at six feet—clad in truly faded blue jeans. Not prewashed and faded blue jeans . . . Laura's mom bought them new (yeah, her adopted mom still bought most of her clothes, though the girl was a student at the U of M). Then Laura wore them and wore them and wore them until they were actually faded, ripped, et cetera. Waste was a sin, after all. Oh! And let's not forget the spawn of Satan's flawless creamy complexion, courtesy of Noxzema.

And faded running shoes, I realized as I got closer. Also by Target. Running shoes! Who wore those to go buy sandals? She'd have to sit down and pull off her shoes *and* socks each time she . . . argh, it was going to make me nuts just thinking about it, so I thought about something else. Like the woman she was waving at.

It wasn't a surprise the Antichrist was talking to someone; it was a surprise she wasn't followed around by packs of men and women and small children, all the time. In addition to being gorgeous, people just naturally flocked to Laura. Like I said—for the Antichrist, she was pretty nice.

Except, I realized as I got close enough for her to notice me, she wasn't talking to the woman. And she wasn't waving at her, either. Both sets of hands were flying—Laura had either gone deaf or recently become fluent in American Sign Language.

Chapter 2

"Oh, and here she is!" Laura's hands, with their long, slender fingers and bluntly short nails, flew as she introduced me. "This is my sister, Betsy. Betsy, this is Sandy Lindstrom." A short, plump woman in her thirties, Sandy brushed her shaggy bangs away from her dark, tip-tilted eyes and smiled at me. "She was wondering when Macy's was having their next sh—"

"November second," I replied automatically. "It starts at eight a.m., an hour before their store usually opens. Park in the west ramp."

Laura's hands moved in translation—I was always amazed at how cool and mysterious sign language looked—while I jabbered shoe-sale tips like a crazed robot.

"Okay, thanks," Sandy Lindstrom mouthed while signing.

"No problem," I said, but she was already turning away,

so I started to raise my voice, then realized I was getting
ready to shout "No problem!" at a deaf person. Not too lame.
Instead, I turned to my sister. "Who was that?"

"Eh? Sandy Lindstrom."

"Oh. You mean you didn't know her, or—"

"No, but I knew *you'd* be the perfect person to answer her
question." Laura grinned and linked her arm through mine.
The Antichrist was a toucher and a hugger, did I mention?

"So she was just some random person?"

"Sure." A frown creased Laura's perfect creamy brow.
"Why?"

"Nothing's wrong," I assured her as we began marching
past Crabtree & Evelyn, arms linked like half of the cast from
The Wizard of Oz. The brainless and clueless half. ("This isn't
the Burnsville Mall anymore, Toto."). "I just didn't know you
knew sign language, is all."

"Oh." That short reply was completely unlike Laura; so
was the shutting-up period that followed. In fact, we were
passing Daniel's Leather before she said, "So is this the way
to Payless?"

"Payless?" I nearly screamed, coming to such an abrupt
stop the Antichrist nearly brained herself on a nearby pillar.
"What foul mouth speaks that filth?"

"Mine," the spawn of Satan replied, straightening up and
making sure she hadn't dropped her purse in the near colli-
sion. Laura was a terrific fighter of the undead (weapons of
Hellfire, daughter of Satan, etc.) but not so much a shopper
of retail. "You know I'm on a budget, Betsy. We can't all be
married to millionaires."

"Undead millionaires," I reminded her, just to see the
flinch—and it came, just as I expected. Which is what a lot
of people did when mention of my husband, Sinclair, king of

the vampires, came up. Hell, half the time I still flinched, but usually in irritation instead of fear. "And be fair—you know damn well I bought designer shoes on an admin's salary." Like my precious, precious Burberry rain boots, a steal at two hundred bucks, and it took me almost nine weeks to save up for them.

"Yes, well." She fussed a bit, then spotted a mall directory. "Um . . . Payless Shoes . . . You could pay more, but why?"

Now it was my turn to flinch at the sound of the dreaded slogan. You could pay more, but why? *But why?* How about because quality costs, nimrods? How about—

"Here it is! One Fifty North Garden."

"Barf Garden." Sure, it was childish. Sue me.

Can dead people be sued? The way the last three years had gone, I was likely to find out by Thanksgiving.

Barf, don't get me started on Thanksgiving.

"Oh, come on." She grabbed my arm again—ugh—and lunged toward the escalator. "You might see something you like."

"That's about as likely as you fretting about what to buy next Mother's Day."

She gasped and wilted, and I had to clutch her arm to keep her from slithering to the bottom of the escalator. "Too mean," she reproached, while people heading up stared down at us with polite midwestern curiosity.

"Oh, please. Since when do we pretend she isn't your mom? Think that's shameful? *I* admit your other mom is my stepmom."

"Your dead stepmom."

"Yeah, well, I'm seeing her as often as I ever did." Disadvantage Number 235 about being queen of the vampires: I see annoying dead people.

"Insinuating I would ever buy her a Mother's Day card *ever.*"

"Yeah, well, that's why it was a joke, because I'm not likely to find—hey!"

Laura had just as abruptly unslithered and spotted . . . something, because she was now dragging me off the escalator and hauling me toward . . . a crying child of about three, dressed in typical kid gear of jeans and a MoA T-shirt.

Oh, for—not again! Laura was always finding/sensing/communing with lost children. It was one of her superpowers, along with never having a pimple, or bad breath, or eye boogers.

Look. I've got nothing against children. I even have one of my own, sort of. He was my half brother, but also my ward, so I was his sister/mother. Mine and Sinclair's own little tax deduction. I *liked* kids, all right? But I didn't find them like a booger-seeking missile. Laura always did. It's why I wouldn't go to the zoo with her anymore.

Now she was kneeling in front of the dark-haired tyke, chattering away in—um—another language I didn't know. Jeez. Probably shouldn't have dropped out of the U back in the day; they apparently had a fierce foreign language program for sophomores.

Ah! Now, predictably, Lost Tyke Number 32 had forgotten all about crying and was now babbling at my sister, who was listening and nodding at every unintelligible word, and would—ah!

The cry of happiness/stress from Lost Mom Number 32, who had either spotted Laura the Gorgeous and was drawn to her beauty while forgetting about her kid, or had heard her kid's mumbling and zeroed in like—well, like another booger-seeking missile.

Now Lost Mom and Lost Tyke were Reunited Family Number 6, chattering in response to whatever Laura was chattering, now came the handshakes, now came the sticky but earnest hug from the kid, now came earnest and tearful gratitude from the mother, and now . . . they depart!

"What *is* it with you?" I asked as the Antichrist bounced up to me.

"Only you could make helping a lost child sound like a character defect." She smiled as she said it, so I wouldn't take offense. Laura tried very hard not to offend vampires when she wasn't trying to kill them.

"No, but—and what was that?"

"What?"

"How you were talking to them. What was it?"

"Tagalog." Another curt report, and now she was tugging me toward the hated Payless Shoe Source.

I'd do anything to avoid being immersed into that retail Hellmouth, so I asked, "Tagalong? What's that?"

"*Tagalog*. It's a language."

"Well, I didn't think you three were doing an impromptu play. What language, specifically?" Not only did I not know the language, I'd never heard of it, either.

"It's spoken in mmpphhheemes."

Now she wasn't tugging; she was yanking. This was a girl who wouldn't yank if a garbage truck was bearing down on me because she thought startling people was rude. Curiouser and curiouser.

I set my feet, hoping I, intrepid vampire queen, wouldn't actually get into a tug-of-war contest outside Payless Shoe Source with the Antichrist. My reputation! Not to mention my sanity. "I didn't catch that. You want to stop mumbling? And pulling?"

"It's spoken in the *Philippines*," she almost shouted. "By about twenty-two million people."

"Twenty-two million and one," I joked. "And seriously. You're cutting off the circulation to my wrist. If I still had any." Then it hit me. Why the conversation was making her so uncomfortable—when usually only one thing made her uncomfortable. "Wait. You didn't learn Tagalong, did you?"

"Tagalog."

"Or sign language, right? Oh my God. You didn't learn them; you already knew them. I mean, you just know them. You know them all. Every language . . . you know every language in the world, don't you?"

Chapter 3

She shrugged sullenly at me and tried to haul my undead carcass toward the retail Hellmouth, but I wasn't having it. And not just because of the obvious reason.

"Speak, Laura! You don't mind doing it when strange children are around. Why clam up now? It's part of what you can do, isn't it? You don't like talking about your mom, you don't like other people talking about your mom—and you sure don't like talking about what you *got* from your mom. You just—you know every language. On earth."

Oh, the deals she could haggle in Paris! I was momentarily dizzy at the thought. *Every* language. On earth. Every spoken language on earth . . . so she was fluent in Latin and all sorts of other dead languages. Zow! And typical of Laura, she'd never said shit. In any language.

"Just like in that movie!"

"What movie?"

"*The Devil's Advocate.* That one where Al Pacino is the devil." The awesomest devil *ever.*

She looked away. If it was possible for someone so gorgeous and nice and smart and occasionally insane to look ashamed, she was pulling it off. "I never saw it. My parents wouldn't— and then I didn't want—it was about—you know."

Her! It was about her—or her if she'd been Keanu Reeves in that movie. She didn't just dislike movies about Satan, she disliked movies about spawn of same. She disliked movies starring . . . herself! "So you haven't seen *any*—"

She shook her head, making shiny blonde waves obscure her face. Her demonically pimple-free face.

"*The Omen? The Omen II? The Omen III: The Final Conflict?* Or *Rosemary's Baby?* Or *Little Nicky?* Or *Bedazzled?* No, you're not in that one, just your—"

"No, I haven't!"

Except she didn't sound mad. Well, she did, but she also sounded . . . interested?

I peered at her. I knew that look. That was a my-God-those-Pradas-are-on-sale! look.

"Well, you're gonna," I decided, clamping down on her demonically clammy palm and hauling her—praise Jesus!— away from Payless. "I've got at least half those, and we'll Netflix the rest. You're gonna learn all about your heritage—at least, what Hollywood thinks it is. Which, given that they greenlit sequels for *Speed, Teen Wolf, Legally Blonde, Dumb and Dumber, Jaws,* and *The Fly,* you should totally take with a ton of salt."

"Have you seen all those—"

"One of my many superpowers," I assured her, hauling her away from the Hellmouth.

Chapter 4

I have to tell the truth," the Antichrist said through a mouthful of popcorn. "Al Pacino is a terrific Satan."

"Tell me about it." I was on my seventh strawberry smoothie, furtively slurping because my snobby fink husband thought frozen berries were worse than early morning Mass. In the summertime that was fine; all the good stuff was in season. In the winter, I had to be stealthy with my smoothie fixins. "Although tell me anything Al Pacino isn't terrific at—ah! Cool, I love this part. Look, he's gonna jam his finger into holy water and make it so you could boil an egg in there."

"What is the purpose of that?" Laura asked, aghast and amused.

"Who cares? He's Al freakin' Pacino!"

Munch. Crunch. "He *is* Al freakin' Pacino."

We'd gone through *The Omen* ("Have no fear, little one.

I am here to protect thee."), *Rosemary's Baby* ("We're your friends, Rosemary. There's nothing to be scared about. Honestly and truly there isn't!"), and now we were coming in on the homestretch with Big Al.

Laura, after her initial resistance, was gorging on these movies the way I wolfed down chocolate shakes (or strawberry smoothies out of season). It definitely had the look of forbidden fruit. And whenever we heard a door slam in another part of the house, she'd jump a little, as though she were afraid of getting caught.

Her parents—her adoptive parents, I mean—knew she was the devil's daughter. Laura had told them. *Satan* had told them (she's a big believer in partial disclosure at the worst possible time).

And I think . . . I think Laura tried to make it up to them for being the Antichrist by pretending indifference or even dislike toward any pop culture Antichrist references.

Because she sure as shit couldn't get enough of these movies now. Presumably this wouldn't come back to bite me in the ass. Right? Right.

Sure.

"What's your favorite?"

"Elizabeth Hurley. *Bedazzled.* 'Most men think they're God. This one just happens to be right.' Also she was a great traffic cop. And candy striper! Giving M&Ms to the patients instead of their meds . . . it's kind of like belonging to a really sucky HMO."

"My mother . . ."

"Yeah? Your mother?" I tried not to sound too eager to prompt her; Laura *never* talked about this stuff. I was afraid to even move, sprawled on the love seat as I was with one of my shoes upside down on the floor and the other dangling from my big toe—I didn't want to break the spell. "Your mother, Satan . . ."

Laura shook her head so hard, I couldn't see her face for all the blonde strands whipping around.

"Come on! Laura, you're the Antichrist and I'm the queen of the vampires. You're still a virgin and I lost mine after prom to a guy named Buck. *Buck!* You beat a serial killer to death and I once passed off a knockoff pair of Louboutins as the real thing. I'm just as sick and evil as you are. I'm in no position to judge."

"Oh." Then: "Buck?"

"Well, jeez, don't judge *me*, either."

"Oh, never. Um. Really, your virginity? Well. I've been seeing her."

"Your biological mother."

Laura smirked. "I'm not even sure that's so. I wasn't born of her body; I was born of your stepmother's body. The devil fled back to hell after I was born."

I nodded. "Yeah, living with a newborn just must be so incredibly awful, if hell seems like a respite." Memo to me: be thankful you have BabyJon and quit bitching about never being able to get pregnant and force another human being through your uterus and out into the world.

"I'm not her biological child at all."

"Do I look like a genetics expert to you? Or a theology expert? It's just all kinds of supernatural fuckery. Who knows how it works? Not me; I'm still trying to get through the vampire queen manual. You'll drive yourself nuts if you try to force all of this—Antichrists, vampires, werewolves, ghosts, and half brothers who are wards, and weddings and funerals and suicides and kings and queens and coups—to make sense. So, your mom's been popping in a lot uninvited?"

"She's always uninvited."

"Yeah, tell me." The devil occasionally dropped in on me as well. Worse: the heartless cow tempted me with shoes! Wonderful, beautiful, sinfully delicious and hard-to-come-by shoes. Oh, she was a diabolical wretch. Also, she looked weirdly like Lena Olin: cougar hot, with sable-dark hair shot through here and there with gray strands. Killer legs. Great suits. And the shoes . . . let me not get started on the shoes . . .

"She's been telling me things."

"Eh?" Oh. Right. Laura was opening up about her mom. I should probably pay closer attention. "Okay." I was fairly certain this was going to be bad with a capital *B-A-D*.

"And I . . . I'm curious about her." Laura almost whispered that last. Like it was bad. Like it was shameful; like *she* was.

I laughed. "Oh, honey, is that's what's bugging you? Shit. What adopted child hasn't been curious about their parents? What, you think that makes you a bad daughter? Like it's disrespectful of your folks who raised you?" I laughed again. I didn't want to, but it was funny, and I was relieved. "Stop kicking your own ass for being normal, okay?"

My sister instantly loosened up . . . her shoulders lost the bowed-in look of somebody in the middle of a serious stress-out. She leaned forward and brushed her hair out of her eyes. "Okay. So, Baal keeps—"

"Whoa, whoa. I'm gonna have to ask the audience for a replay on that one. Ball?"

"An old name for my mother."

"Really old, because I've never heard of it. I guess it's slightly less offensive than *crack whore*."

"Slightly."

"I prefer Beelzebub, personally."

"Call her Old Scratch if you like. Call her the Lord of Lies. Call her Mrs. Tiggy-Winkle. Whatever name she uses, she wants me to visit her. To see her."

"Okay."

"See her world. Her lands."

"Your mom wants you to go to hell." I paused, chewing that one over. "Literally."

Yeesh. And I thought my mom was a pill when she made me come to the all-faculty cocktail party when I was seventeen. There's no group duller than a group of academics with inferiority complexes. So, not just any historians. *Bragging* historians.

"And I won't deny I'm tempted. I'd—I'd like to see it. I'd like to . . . I don't know. I'm just so curious, all the time. I have so many questions. And to think, if I hadn't met you, I never would have thought it was okay to—"

"Whoa, *whoa*. Nuh-uh. This is not my fault—it's not going to be my fault. Do not drag me into this."

"I'm not blaming you. I'm thanking y—"

"Well, stop it! Whatever happens after this moment, whatever happens the rest of November, none of it was my fault." Being dead the last couple of years had made me paranoid beyond belief. And I was starting to smell disastrous situations that started out cutely innocent and ended up with me almost dying, or my husband almost dying, or one of my friends actually dying. Or a parent dying, or a thousand werewolves out to get me.

What can I say? Fate likes me to keep busy.

"I just think it would be an interesting trip."

"Wrong, oh sweetly deluded sister of mine. Chicago is an interesting trip. The Boundary Waters is an interesting trip, if you don't mind hiding your food in a tree. Hell is a life sentence. More than that, actually." She opened her mouth, and I made a slashing motion with my hand. "Don't even. I'm not gonna talk you out of it—I know better than to try—and I am definitely not going with you. I've never done one thing in my life to warrant a field trip to hell."

This was a rather large lie. I could think of several reasons I might have earned a day pass to the Underworld, starting with burying my mom's purse in the backyard when I was five, figuring that with no driver's license, she wouldn't be able to drive me to Payless Shoes. As gambits went, it was risky. As punishments went, it was lengthy.

And we ended up going to *Wal-Mart* instead. Jesus, pity your humble undead servant.

Chapter 5

"Disgusting, horrible, wretched, tremendously evil, evil, yuck-o, poop-ridden *crap*!"

"I could hear your dulcet tones at the front door," my husband, Sinclair, commented as he came into our bedroom smelling like secrets and blood. "However, you seem more, ah, agitated than usual."

"Agitated is putting it mildly."

"Yes, my love, but *furiously foaming* is not romantic in the slightest. Was that Laura just now leaving?"

"Huh? Yeah."

"She did not seem inclined to chat."

"She's having mom issues."

Sinclair grimaced, his emotional equivalent of screaming hysterically and yanking out his hair by double handfuls. A taciturn man, the love of my life. "Laura's mother issues? A sobering thought." He shrugged out of his navy suit coat, stepped to our walk-in closet, and fussily hung it on a wooden hanger. "I missed you tonight, my own."

"Oh, yeah?" I was unmoved. Big, big perk of being the vampire queen: I didn't have to feed every day. So when I could, I drowned my thirst with gallons of iced tea and blenders-full of smoothies. It didn't help. Not really. But it made me feel better. Less freaklike. Not quite so movie-monster-ish. "I didn't miss you, not even one little teensy—*yeek*!" I collapsed on our bed, giggling, as the king of the vampires zapped me with his evilly wriggling fingers of death-by-rib-tickling.

"My understanding is that admitting to being ticklish is admitting you have no willpower of any kind."

"Oh, you I'm-not-ticklish thugs always fall back on that one. Like being some sort of weird genetic freak is, I dunno, proof of willpower or something."

"It is," he said with an absolutely wicked smile, and then his fingers were skating over my ribs again. I thrashed and kicked and yowled. Do other queens have to put up with this shit? Did Victoria? Did Anne Boleyn? Elizabeth II? It seemed unlikely. Not that I envied Anne Boleyn. But I'm pretty sure that, although Henry I'm-never-satisfied Tudor planned her legal murder, he never tickled her until she felt ready to pee her pants.

"No, quit, I've got a—stop that!" I wriggled and shoved and managed to extricate myself from his rubber-cement-esque grip.

Okay. Lie. He *let* me up. I'm strong for a dead girl, but Eric Sinclair was one in a million. Literally.

"I've got this humongous problem."

"Oh, so?" He, too, rose from the bed and kept methodically undressing and hanging everything up. I didn't blame him—I saw his AmEx statement once and nearly went into shock on the spot. I'd hang up everything, too, if I spent over a hundred bucks on a single necktie.

We were plenty rich—he was, I mean, and Jessica—my best friend—was, sure.

The most I ever earned was forty thousand dollars a year, and that was as an executive assistant with seven years of experience the year I got run over by a Pontiac Aztek. But we lived in a mansion on the supertony Summit Avenue in St. Paul. Our mansion, in fact, looked right at home on the street with all the other mansions. Our mansion could give some of the other mansions a run for their money. Our mansion could freely taunt the other mansions. (Our mansion wasn't very mature, though; it was built in 1860, I think.)

See, the way things happened was—you know what? I actually don't have time for the whole story. I'll sum up: woke up dead, kicked ass, became queen of the vampires, hooked up with Eric Sinclair and made him king of the vampires (I *still* get mad when I think about how his having sex with me was the beginning, middle, and end of his coronation . . . what kind of a sad-ass society planned for stuff like that?), moved into Vampire Central a couple years ago when my old house was teeming with termites, and have, at any given time, about half a dozen (uninvited) roommates, living, dead, and in-between.

See? If I'd coughed up the whole thing, we'd be here all month. The awfulest month. November.

(It was 3:18 a.m., November 1. The beginning of Hell-month. The awfulest month. November.)

"Does this have something to do with your unreasonable hatred of the Thanksgiving holiday?" Sinclair the Uncaring asked, carefully removing cufflinks (gold beans by Elsa Peretti, and yeah, you read that right, the man wears gold *beans* at his wrist and then mocks me for indulging in jewelry by Target) and placing them in his cufflink drawer.

Yeah. That was the sort of man I was condemned to live with for five thousand years.

"Dude! Unreasonable? Anything but, you ruthless putz. My Thanksgiving hatred is extremely reasonable."

"How is it I have known you for—"

"An eternity."

"—no, it only feels like that, dearest. I have known you going on three years—"

"Absolutely, completely an eternity."

"—yet I never cease to be surprised by your absurd prejudices, in particular your dislike of a basically inoffensive holiday."

"Inoffensive? Spoken like an old rich white dude." Annoyed, I swung my toe toward one of the bed legs and nearly fractured the thing for my trouble. Undead strength and speed did not mean invulnerable toes.

"I do not understand."

"Of course you don't understand; you're a *guy*. A rich white one, if you didn't catch that. All you've ever had to do for Thanksgiving is commit mass genocide, watch football, and wear turkey pants."

Sinclair blinked at me slowly. Like an owl. A big, pale, gorgeous, muscle-y owl. "Turkey pants?"

I waved his question away. "You know. Like sweatpants. Pants with tons of elastic so you can eat turkey until you vomit."

"Thanksgiving was somewhat different in my home," he said, looking amazed.

"That's the big lie, dude."

"Also, I loathe it when you refer to me as *dude*."

"Dude, like I care! Listen: from the first Thanksgiving up until three weeks from now, all the Thanksgiving pressure is on *women*. Cook, clean, stuff, eat—barely; we're too busy jumping up and down with more gravy and cranberry sauce—clean, fall on face and pray for the strength to make it to Christmas, rinse, repeat. It's inhuman. As an inhuman, I should know. Also it's a conspiracy to keep us chained to our mops."

"Do we have a mop?"

"We must." The kitchen was as wide as a football field; the counters were always shiny clean, the floors always gleaming. The place smelled like lemons and old wood. We probably had a dozen mops. A battalion of mops. And a discreet, over-paid housekeeping staff.

"But, my own, you need do none of those things: cook, clean, stuff—you recall the litany, I pray. Frankly, I am certain you have never had to do those things."

"That's not the—listen, I'm trying to strike a blow for feminism here."

"Feminism?"

"Yes, you know, that pesky mind-set that assumes women are the equal to men. Don't say 'feminism?' like you've never heard the word, you repressing bastard."

My husband had an expression on his face I knew well: he was amused, and annoyed, and thus looked as though he were coming down with a three-day migraine. "But I have heard the word, my sweet, and—"

Too late! I was hip deep in lecture mode. "We feminists had to invent it to stop all the rampant repressin' and stuff going on."

"How are you repressed?"

I gaped. "How am I—do you not see my boobs, which

perkily classify me as a member in good standing of the repressed people?"

"But you are not. You are wealthy—"

"It's *your* money." I paused. "And before you, it was Jessica's money."

"All right. You have access to money, shall we leave it at that? Your father made an excellent living, and you have always had access to funds. I have never seen you clean a window nor stuff a bird."

"Oh, so because Sinclair the Great didn't see it happen, it didn't happen?"

"My love, I shall swear obeisance to you and drop this entire line of discussion, provided—"

"Obeisance, awesome, I like the sound of that. I would like gobs of obeisance, but it's weird that you're giving up so early in the—"

"*Provided* you tell me where the mops are kept."

I stopped talking. I blinked. (Did I have to? I didn't pee, I no longer menstruated, I didn't sweat, and I didn't barf. Did I need to blink, or would my undead eyeball just naturally moisten itself, and why was I thinking about eyeball juice right now?)

"While I am grateful for the momentary silence, I will not deny that the thought of your rebuttal strikes terror in my breast."

"Dude, can we have one marital chitchat without talking about your boobs?"

"The mop, my own?" He adjusted the pleat on his Savile Row supersuit, then unbuckled his belt and, okay, major digression here, but I absolutely *love* the sound of Sinclair's belt unbuckling. It's sexy, yet practical. Yet clink-y!

Anyway, he was unbuckling his belt, *clink-clank*, pulling

his zipper, and now he was sliding out of his pants and yakking the whole time: "Do you know where said mop resides? Do you know how many we have? Do you know"—he folded the pants onto one of his fancy wooden hangers; _where a proud rain forest once stood, now there are holders for my husband's slacks_—"where the Mop & Glo is kept?"

"_You_ don't even know that," I guessed. It was a shot in the dark, but I was pretty confident.

"I will take that as a no."

"Okay, so I don't know exactly where the mops are. That doesn't mean I'm _not_ repressed."

"In fact, it does, dearest."

"Because I—" Because I had a brain full of thoughts, and they all wanted out at once.

Okay. Let me think about this.

I never had to make a meal or a bed. I hadn't sewn on a button since seventh-grade Home Echh. I didn't pay any bills. I didn't even have to grocery shop, though I still did.

But Sinclair was white, and old—in his seventies. Or nineties. I could never remember and frankly, never tried too hard. If I thought about the fact that I was gaily and frequently fucking someone old enough to be my grandpa, he could unbuckle his belt until the end of time and it'd still squick me out.

But! He was old, he was white. Sure, he'd grown up on a farm, but he'd been pretty rich not long after he died. I think not long.

Hmm. This was a little embarrassing. How much did I know about the love of my life, come to think of it?

Chapter 6

Let's see. He was born and raised in the Midwest.

His parents were farmers.

He lost his folks and his little sister in some awful accident—I was pretty sure it was an accident—and he met Tina (more on her in a minute) the night of their funeral.

I knew he favored Kenneth Cole shoes, in black.

I knew he loved strawberries.

I knew he loved me.

I knew he loved power most of all.

And that was pretty much *all* I knew. If this was a book, and not my life, what I knew about my husband wouldn't even fill up one page. How's that for humbling?

Chapter 7

"My own, you appear deep in thought. Or perhaps you are having a foot cramp."

"The former," I admitted, "and listen, remind me to ask you if you were a Presbyterian. And what your favorite meal was when you were a kid. And how old you were when you found out there wasn't a Santa. And how you lost your virginity. And if you opened presents Christmas Eve or Christmas morning. And—and other stuff, when I think of it."

Sinclair blinked again. "My love, are you taking a survey?"

"Eventually. But I gotta stay on track here, because white guys don't get to tell blacks or women or Lutherans that they aren't repressed."

"But they are not. Rather, you are not. I very much doubt Jessica has been repressed for even half a moment." He paused, then admitted, "I cannot speak for Lutherans."

"So I don't cook or clean. Or make beds. Or go grocery shopping except for funsies, or take my car to the shop. Or take it to get the oil changed. Or scrub toilets. Or—" Hmm. He might have a point. "But you're even *less* repressed than I am. Let's see you deny *that*!"

"This isn't a way of distracting yourself from Antonia and Garrett's death, is it, my own?"

I abruptly sat down on our bed. Shit.

And shit again.

Chapter 8

Scratch that—I sat down on *my* bed. Sink Lair had just bought himself six weeks on the couch. "That's not fair," I said, and cringed to hear that my voice actually shivered with hurt. I loved the lunkhead, but it wasn't much fun for me to appear vulnerable and lame to anyone, never mind someone I loved and wanted to impress.

He stopped fussing with his clothes, came to sit next to me, and carefully draped an arm across my shoulder, as if wondering if I'd jam an elbow in his gut. Or his teeth.

"I have wondered when would be an appropriate time to discuss this with you."

"Try never. That'd be appropriate."

"The events leading to their deaths were fantastically stressful and dangerous; there were few opportunities to ponder the consequences of their actions."

"Yeah, that's pretty much on the nose," I admitted.

"Our trip to Massachusetts was eventful enough that you did not have time to properly mourn."

"Eventful? Not the word I'd've picked."

"You have carefully avoided all mention of either of them, and now you're seizing on things like inoffensive holidays, feminism, and Laura wanting to take a—what did you call it? A field trip to hell."

"Well. These are issues I have to deal with. I can't help that. Wait. When did I tell you about the hell trip? I was working up to that."

"See how well I know you, my own?"

He was studying me so intently I could actually feel his gaze on my skin. "In fact, you can."

In fact, drop dead. I tried to squash my irritation. "They're dead. They're gone, and we couldn't help either of them. Then, for funsies, we almost had our heads handed to us by a bunch of pissed-off werewolves with Massachusetts accents." Tough to decide which was more frightening. I'd been called *wicked smaht* and it had taken a few seconds to decode the compliment. Their accents had sounded as strange to me as my midwestern twang had no doubt sounded to them.

I took a breath and kept griping. "Now I've got the devil bugging my sister every ten minutes and the worst holiday ever looming on the calendar."

"And you could not save them."

I rested my chin on his shoulder, so I was staring straight into his left ear. "What's that got to do with anything?"

"Everything, most charming of queens. It has everything to do with anything."

Chapter 9

The fink I married wasn't entirely off base. No, we hadn't really dealt with what had happened. And yes, I sure didn't discuss it with anybody—not even him. Not even my best friend.

That was because I knew something my husband and friend didn't: I was a coward.

I never looked at the stairs.

I never looked at the perfectly repaired spokes in the completely repaired banister.

I never looked at the tiles Antonia fell on, bled on, died on.

I never used the front door at all; the last time I had done so Antonia had caught a bullet in the brain and her lover, Garrett, had caught wooden spokes in the chest, stomach, and throat.

Never.

So, with all that never and all that ever, yeah, okay. I never think about it. On purpose, of course. Unlike some, I'll cough up: of course I never think of it on purpose. Who could never think of that by accident?

So Captain Buzzkill had a point.

But that didn't mean Thanksgiving didn't blow rocks because it absolutely did.

"What's your point?"

"That your responsibilities entail facing trouble instead of wishing it away."

With a bound I was off the bed. "Oh, here we go. Responsibilities of royalty. Leadership. Right. Never mind the fact that your average vampire is about ninety-eight years old. *They* should be leading *me*. In vampire years, I'm still a toddler."

Okay, huge pet peeve here. I could tell by Sinclair's expression that he'd heard this before and was unmoved. And yep, it's pretty childish to whine about circumstances I'll never, ever be able to change.

But I *hated* that I was expected to boss people around who were (a) old enough to take care of themselves, (b) old enough to know better, and (c) way, way old enough to not need a micromanaging vampire queen. I quit all that stuff when I got fired from my last admin job.

But here we were. And back again: my responsibilities. My, my, I certainly was fulfilling all my if-I-become-Miss-Vampire-Queen-I'll-work-tirelessly-for-world-peace vows. The Antichrist went nuts. My father died. My stepmother died and started haunting me. The devil liked to hang around. Garrett killed himself. Antonia caught a bullet with her brain . . . three times! My best friend broke up with the love of her life, who insisted she pick between him and me.

Oh my, yes. Everything was *aces*.

I was at the door by now, half hoping Sinclair was right behind me. He wasn't. He was still sitting on the bed. "I'm sick of discussing this."

"How is that possible," he asked coolly, "when we never have?"

Ouch! "If I go out this door," I threatened, "I'm . . ." Well. *Never coming back* was untrue, and he knew it. But *eventually coming back* didn't have the ominous ring I was hoping for. ". . . gonna stay really pissed at you!"

He yawned.

I went.

Chapter 10

I stomped down the *Gone with the Wind*-esque flight of stairs (carpeted in deep red plush, how positively Scarlett) and passed through a couple of hallways. (This place had more bathrooms than the White House, not to mention armoires, linen closets, dumbwaiters, parlors, bedrooms, and butler's pantries—I'd found three so far.)

For the hundredth time I wondered what I, Elizabeth Don't-call-me-that Taylor, was doing living in a mansion stuffed with paranormal oddities like my husband. For that matter, what was I, Elizabeth Taylor, doing *being* a paranormal oddity in the first place?

It hadn't been that long ago that I was footloose and fancy-free, living on my own, in my own house, not married, not babysitting the undead or the teething, just getting my shit done and occasionally indulging in the new Beverly Feldman spring pump.

Maybe that was my problem: I couldn't remember the last time I'd bought myself a new pair of shoes.

How . . . how could this have happened to my life? No wonder everything was fucked up! My God, it was all so clear . . .

I had wandered into the kitchen, not quite by accident. The room was as big as a stadium, but warm and inviting . . . big long counters, a couple of fridges always stocked with snacks, big bar stools and lots of magazines and newspapers spread all over the marble countertop Tina occasionally rolled out cookies on. (Which was funny, because she couldn't eat them. None of us could, except Jessica, who was always morbidly worried about gaining weight and edging up into the dreaded 102-pound territory. Where the hell did all the cookies go?)

As I half expected, Tina was already there. She was freshly showered—no surprise, because she smelled like blood. Just back from hunting, then.

Tina and my husband had to feed daily (nightly, I s'pose). The unwritten rule was, we fed on bad guys only. So if you were a mugger or rapist or killer or thief or embezzler, watch out. You were eligible for our nightly snack-'n'-go program. We'd snack, and you'd just . . . go. Where, we didn't much care.

She was standing in front of the freezer, hanging on to the open door, wearing her post-shower uniform of a neck-to-toes nightgown of gorgeous, heavy cream-colored linen. With her cascades of blonde hair and her big brown eyes, she looked like an extra from *Little House on the Prairie*. A hot extra.

I suddenly realized something I knew about Tina—you know how you don't know you know something until you realize you *do* know? (Shut up. It makes sense if you think about it.) What I now knew was that Tina always dressed as modestly as a schoolmarm. The most daring ensemble I ever saw her in was a pair of linen walking shorts topped with a long-sleeved T-shirt.

She favored skirts and long pants. Turtlenecks and long nightgowns—never anything frothy or revealing. I remembered she once told me she'd become a vampire during the Civil War (or was she born during the war? Couldn't remember . . .); apparently old habits of modesty died hard. Or, in Tina's case, didn't die at all.

She was, I knew, eyeing her vast and weird vodka collection. Like any vampire, she was continually compulsively thirsty. Like me, she occasionally tried to drown it with stuff besides blood. Also like me, she failed every time . . . but enjoyed the trying.

Here she was pulling out a bottle—ugh, chili pepper–flavored vodka. Like a drink made from potatoes wasn't yuck-o enough.

Nope, she didn't want pepper-flavored. Back into the freezer it went. Here came cinnamon. Somewhat better, I s'pose, but nope, she didn't want that one, either. Here came—aw, no! Bacon! Bacon-flavored vodka! (I swear to God I am not making this up. Wikipedia it if you don't believe me.)

I was going to barf right now. Right here in the kitchen near the feet of one of my most loyal vampire minions. Nothin' was stopping the Vomit Express. Except possibly the fact that I hadn't barfed since waking up dead in that funeral home three years ago.

Concentrate. Think about all the nice things Tina's done. Think about what a crass, crummy thing throwing up on her feet would be. Think about . . . think about the fact that she wouldn't even let you clean it up!

Chapter 11

She was Sinclair's majordomo, which was a fancy word to describe the awesomeness that was Tina, super secretary and administrative assistant to the damned. But she was even more than that.

She knew where the bodies were buried—not an idle phrase in *this* house. She knew all the account numbers and passwords. She knew birthdays and death days. She knew favorite foods and allergies. She was practically a genius with firearms—a pretty good trick for someone who'd been born during the Civil War. Or turned into a vampire during same.

She had made my husband—turned him. And stuck with him ever since, and when she met me, instantly threw her loyalty right at me.

She was—you know. She was Tina. Tina, undead citizen

of the undead with a penchant for booze made from potatoes and flavored with cured meats.

Really, about all I knew about her was that she turned Sinclair into a vampire the night of his family's triple funeral, and I guess they'd never looked back.

Tina and my husband hadn't hooked up, which I found both a relief and weird—they would have made a gorgeous power couple. I was sort of amazed he'd resisted her, frankly. She was supremely gorgeous, and even better, massively smart. Like, Dog Whisperer smart.

No, the two of them had just calmly gone about the business of amassing money and property and . . . this is going to sound pretty damn conceited, even for me, but they basically spent scores of decades waiting for yours truly to show up.

Enter *moi*, recently deceased and pissed off (the latter nothing new; the former extremely new). The night I met Tina she saved my ass. I've managed to return the favor once or twice.

The point? I guess the point was, I loved and admired and lived with and depended on people I really knew very little about. Not that they were taciturn—I just usually couldn't be bothered. Who cared if Sinclair had been raised Presbyterian or Lutheran? Who cared if his grandmother ever made him eat lutefisk at Christmas time? Who cared if Tina had ever been married, ever been a mom?

Well. They did, probably.

And I should have.

Chapter 12

"Majesty, how long are you going to lurk by the door?"

Of course. She knew I was there, had known I was there probably before I knew I was headed toward the kitchen. I could be quiet when I wanted, but Tina was more ghost than vampire, and nothing got by her.

"Please don't pick that one," I begged, and she chuckled.

"No, I'm not quite in the mood for that . . ." I listened hard; did she have a southern accent? No. I was sure she never had—at least, not in the three years I'd known her. It's possible it had worn off after sixty-some years of living in Minnesota.

Wait. Was she even southern? Or was I just assuming because she referenced any time line with the Civil War?

I could have just asked her, but I was too embarrassed.

"I think . . ." A low *clink* as she moved bottles around.

"Hmm." She withdrew . . . root beer. Root beer–flavored potato juice.

"Now you're just torturing me."

"Never, Majesty. I live and die at your very command." *Clunk!* Back went the root beer bottle. And here came . . . gah, I was afraid to look . . .

Mint.

I exhaled with relief, a habit from being alive I hadn't dropped yet. Tina chuckled again—she had a great, low laugh, sort of like ripping velvet. "I think, yes," she said, setting the frosty bottle on the counter. "Join me, my queen?"

"Not on a bet." She drank it neat. "Isn't it cheaper to just guzzle rubbing alcohol?"

"Yes indeed, but much less satisfying."

"Good hunting?" As soon as I asked, I grimaced. Whoever Tina'd snacked on, they were human beings. Not the weekly deli platter from Rainbow Foods.

Except sometimes, that was almost the most they could hope to be. There were such *shits* running around, all the time.

I still remember a meal from over a year ago . . . I'd happened on a pedophile who was just lowering the pants of her victim. I'd meant to knock her out and save the middle-school boy. Instead, I'd nearly put her through the wall. The *brick* wall. The good news was, when she came to she was so rattled she started compulsively confessing to . . . everything. The bad news was, after it happened? I hardly ever thought about the useless cow.

It wasn't that I felt bad. I felt bad because I didn't feel bad. Not *too* migraine-inducing.

". . . but after, he promised to turn himself in and return

all the bootlegged copies of *Ironman Three* and *Spiderman Eight*."

"And the populace sleeps in peace. Bootleg. So, uh, that word. I bet it takes you back . . . to moonlit nights in the deep South when you ran moonshine for your many cousins . . ."

"Majesty?"

"Unless, of course, it doesn't. Take you back I mean. So does it?"

Tina's brow was knitted, so much so that for a scary moment she appeared to sport a unibrow. "I beg pardon, my queen?"

"Never mind. So, you're probably going to bed."

Tina glanced down as if assuring herself that, yes, she was clean and freshly tubbed, and also wearing a nightgown as opposed to, say, a cocktail dress. "Yes, I was, but if you require anything at all—"

"No, no. No. I'm—" What exactly? Sulking and wait-ing for Sinclair to cough up an apology? Worrying about my sister? Not using the front hall so I wouldn't think about Antonia and Garrett? "I'm using the door, that's what I'm doing!"

Tina had backed up until her (permanently shapely) butt was pressed against the fridge. "As—as you wish, Majesty."

"Damn right!"

Yeah! No one could accuse *me* of not using my own front door. No way, babies.

I was gonna use the *hell* out of the front door.

Chapter 13

I hate the front door.

Well, I do, and that was before The Thing. First off, it was practically the size and thickness of a redwood. Heavy as hell, even with hinges. No peephole . . . and given that most vampires knew where I lived, that was murderously stupid. Sort of like the asshats who occasionally came looking for me.

Plus, it opened onto an enormous foyer of marble and ancient furnishing and, on the housekeeper's off days, dust bunnies the size of orangutans. The house smelled like ancient wood, floor wax, and dead flowers. Everything was larger than life . . . Tall doorways. Marble everything. Tables that seated twenty. Chairs for the tables that looked like thrones. (Target doesn't carry chairs like that. I've looked.) Someone who didn't know a thing about the house's residents would instantly sense we were all up to no good.

Subtle, it wasn't. And when the mistress of the obvious

notices something isn't subtle? Brother, it's time to pack up and leave town, because the rain of fire was about to start.

Oh. Right. There was one other thing I didn't like about the front entryway. The library (one of the libraries) was just off said entryway, and the library was, in almost every way, worse than the front hall.

The Book of the Dead was kept in the library. Which was a lot like saying the bomb was kept in the garage next to the snowblower.

I crept toward the awful thing. And why not? It was barely November and the month already sucked rocks. What was the thing gonna do, give me demonically infectious paper cuts?

Nope. You needed paper for paper cuts. The Book of the Dead was written (in blood) by a(n) (insane) vampire, on human skin.

Collect the set!

I could feel my mouth trying to pull down into an unattractive frown as I sidled closer. Not that I had to worry about wrinkles. Only about turning evil and watching helplessly while roommates died. And, you know, taxes.

All the answers were in there. The Book of the Dead was never wrong. The thing was just sitting there on an old-fashioned, never-in-style book stand, mocking me. If my late stepmother were a book, she would be that book. All my questions could be answered. No more worrying . . . no more wondering, even.

Yep. All right there, if I didn't mind going insane. Now, I'm not the type to be picky, and one girl's insanity is another's too-many-daiquiris weekend, but the last time I'd over-indulged I'd scared (and bitten) my best friend and raped my husband. (I never did decide what was worse: that I'd aggressively molested him or that he didn't notice I'd turned evil over the weekend.)

Have I mentioned the horrible, horrible thing was fire-proof? And waterproof? Every time I tried to throw it away or destroy it, it came back. It was like being in one of those buy-ten-DVDs-for-$2.99 clubs except more with the evil and not so much with the weekly mailings.

Still, it was tempting. Sure it was. Even though I knew it was dangerous—or was that because I knew it was danger-ous? Because if I really had to give it some thought, I'd—

"What an unattractive frown. Since you can't rely on your brains, dear, you should try to stay pretty as long as you can."

My heart took a great big *ka-THUMP* in my chest and I actually staggered. I knew that sly-sweet voice. First the book.

Now the devil.

Chapter 14

I whirled. "You!"

"Me," Satan agreed. Against every instinct of self-pres-
ervation I'd come up with in thirty-some years, I instantly
glanced at her feet. And moaned.

"Ah," God's Problem Child simpered, batting her long
eyelashes. "You noticed."

Of course I noticed. She could have pulled mukluks over
them and I would have noticed. She could have been disguised as the Michelin Man and I would have noticed.

The devil was wearing a pair of Stuart Weitzman stilettos.
They were trimmed with 1,420 Kwiat diamonds (over thirty
carats!), which were set in platinum. Anika Noni Rose (the
other Dreamgirl) wore them to the Oscars in 2007. And they
were quite the bargain at half a million dollars.

"Tell me. How are things with my favorite dead thirty-
something?"

I was too overwhelmed to reply, or take offense. Or even really notice. I was . . . dazzled. The Book of the Dead could have morphed into naked Robert Downey Jr. and I wouldn't have so much as glanced at Hollywood's hottest new/old bad boy.

Satan smiled down at her beautiful, beautiful, beautiful, beautiful, beautiful, beautiful, beautiful, beautiful, beautiful shoes, and who could blame her?

While I was thinking about it, have I mentioned the devil looked like Lena Olin? Like the hottest cougar in the history of hot older women? A cougar who could seduce all your guy friends but then take you out for drinks and charm you into grudging forgiveness?

Pure evil stalked me in my own home, wearing stiletto heels and a severely cut suit with a high neckline. The suit, I knew at once, was made of vicuna wool, the most expensive fabric on the planet. It ran for about $1,780 a yard. I knew because she'd worn another suit in a different cut and color last year, a deep luscious black, and I'd been curious enough to look it up.

Severe suit in midnight blue, great shoes, minimal makeup, no perfume, no jewelry (who needed it with foot-gear like that?), and the sheerest stockings, more like silk webbing than something man-made. Satan preferred garter belts (I wish I didn't know that). And also tempting the bejee-zus out of your friendly neighborhood vampire queen.

"—a favor."

"Bluh?"

"I said you've got the look of someone who needs a favor."

"I whuh? Neh? Mem."

"You seem less loquacious than usual. Now then. I know you and my daughter had a nice chat over Al Pacino movies and microwave popcorn. I also know that you have a problem. Several, not least of which is your anemic IQ, but one in which I can be of some assistance. Even better, one in which I wish to be of assistance. And I *am* willing to assist you, but in return I must insist—"

" 'Scuse me. I have to lie down." I tottered toward the love seat (recently reupholstered in a deep moss green velvet after one of my roommates barfed buffalo grass vodka all over it) and tried to lie down. But I couldn't make it in time before my knees buckled, so I just . . .

I just sort of . . .

Um . . . sort of . . .

"Well smack my face and cast me out of heaven." Satan's face appeared above mine; the devil was about as concerned as she ever got. "You swooned. Do you know how rare an old-fashioned swoon is these days? It looked like a slow-motion belly flop. Would you like a pillow? I trust that carpet isn't as dusty as it looks. And smells."

"Those are just really very great and awesome shoes," I managed, blinking up at the Morningstar.

"And I got them for a song," she replied. "Or more specifically, a soul. But they can be yours for the low, low price of—"

"What the hell is going on here?"

Satan snapped her head around, and I heard a hiss of irritation. Or maybe she just had a leak somewhere. My best friend, Jessica, was framed in the doorway, arms akimbo. Which was pretty alarming, because she was beyond bony and her elbows could have been registered as deadly weapons. She could shatter car windows with them.

"None of your concern, Ms. Watson. Why don't you run along and spend more money you didn't earn?"

"And why don't you go back to hell?" Jessica was doing pretty well given that (a) she'd never met the devil and (b) she was, in fact, spending money she didn't earn. Daily, even. "Not that it's any of your damn business, but I bled for that money. Now, I don't know why you're here—"

"Most likely because I would never trouble myself to inform you."

"—but no way is it good news for anybody in my house."

"Her house," the Adversary snapped back, pointing a perfectly manicured, French-tipped finger at me. "The deed is in her and her husband's name."

"It is?" Oh. Right. I think Sinclair had mumbled something about that a few months ago. I was too busy avoiding the front hall and this room to pay much attention. "So we own the house . . . so? It's just semantics."

"Do you actually know what that word means?"

"It means Jessica's owned plenty of the places I've rented or lived. So if the deed's in her name or my name or Tina's name or the cat's name, it's just as much her home as mine."

"Except from a legal standpoint," Baal said, rolling her eyes.

"Out!" Jessica actually stamped her foot. Also frightening . . . she was a size nine, but her feet had, like, almost no width. It looked like she walked around on rulers. They were sharp like rulers, too. When she swung one into my shin, it stung like crazy. Undead superpowers could not prevent the stinging. "Right now!"

"Or what? You'll tell *Daddy*? He's fine, by the way, my dear, dull Miss Watson. Actually that's not true. He's damned! He is utterly un-fine."

Jessica's skin was too gorgeously dark to go pale when she was afraid. Instead, when she was scared, her face seemed to tighten. That broke the fog I'd been in since I'd eyeballed the demonic footgear.

"Knock it off." I'd meant it to sound like a tough command. But it came out weak. And feeble.

The devil didn't even glance at me. And she hadn't moved, hadn't taken a step toward Jess. But it seemed like she had. It *felt* like she had. With only her voice, she seemed to loom over Jessica. To . . . to blot her out.

Which really, really pissed me off.

"It's a dull pattern, isn't it? In your showgirl mother's shadow until she died. And now in Betsy's. Who, of course, will never grow old and ugly, just less and less intelligent."

"Hey!"

"Do you pick beautiful women to live with on purpose?" She sounded genuinely interested, which was just another way she lied. "Or do you only realize it waaaaay down deep, in the bottom of your brain where the serpents live?" The devil grinned. "And me, of course. I visit there." Pause. "I love it there."

"You get out of here," Jessica managed, and she sort of wheezed it. I think, in her head, I think *she* thought she was shouting.

"Of course! But before I go, did you have any messages for dear, damned Daddy? Or your mother, who chose her husband's money over her daughter's safety? She's still a showgirl in my realm, you know. And still can't get work. And still in your father's shadow! You should *see* her, Jessica, you should see them both. They hate each other. Almost as much as they hate you."

Satan threw back her long, elegant neck and laughed. The booming chortles filled the room like a swarm of bats—tried, anyway, because a crunch of wood and skull cut the laugh-fest off just when it was getting started.

Jessica smiled, but her lips were trembling. "Oh, Bets. That might cost you one of these days."

The devil was rubbing the back of her head and glaring at me. I'd managed to shake off my stupor, get off the floor, snatch up the book stand (the Book of the Dead went flying, but it wasn't like anything would happen to it), and crown Satan with it. Since I was moving at vampire superspeed, I'd been able to get some momentum behind the swing. And did the crunch sound feel good?

Hells yeah! Tax-refund good. All-your-tests-came-back-negative good. I-can't-finish-do-you-want-the-rest-of-my-dessert good.

"The next one," I warned, brandishing the broken stand like a jagged baseball bat, "goes through your teeth. Get your saggy ass out of our house."

Satan finished shaking splinters out of her perfectly coiffed hair. "My ass is not *saggy*."

"Yeah? You should check it out from where I'm standing," I sneered, which was total bravado. Her ass was awesome. "Now scat. Or do I have to get a priest in here to perform an exorcism?"

"Tempting. I haven't had a good laugh in eighty-seven seconds. An eternity with you people." Lucifer Morningstar folded her wool-clad arms across her perfectly shaped boobs and eyed the toe of her beautiful, beautiful, beautiful, beautiful, beautiful, beautiful, beautiful, beautiful, beautiful, beautiful, beautiful, beautiful shoes. "I shall scat, as you like. But Betsy, when you need to reach me, and you will, you will know what I require."

"What are you gonna require?" Jess asked, a suspicious scowl on her face.

"The queen will know," she said with Lena Olin's voice. "She need only think about temptation."

"Right now I'm only thinking about caving in your skull. Again. Ha! So take *that*."

"Oh, and Betsy? I've already forgiven you that little bit of criminal assault, so it will all be behind us tomorrow. You need not fear to call on me."

"Yeah? Wrong again, you loser devil-type fallen angel, because I *will* f—" Then she blipped right out of existence. There was even a sharp *pop!* which I realized was the sound of air rushing into the space she had been occupying. "I hate when she does that. Right in the middle of a sentence. She's like Batman that way. Except bitchier."

Jessica still looked dreadful, but her expression was relaxing a little and her eyes, while shiny, didn't drip tears. It hadn't exactly been the worst day of her life when her useless, disgusting parents had died. To paraphrase Stephen King, sometimes an accident can be an unhappy woman's best friend.

Put it this way: if they hadn't died, I would have eventually had to kill them. And who needs *that* on a to-do list?

"Jeez, Betsy." She eyed the book, the splinters, the bookstand-turned-limbo-pole. "You're such a badass."

"Hey. The only person who can belittle you and taunt you with family secrets until you almost cry is me. Besides, those shoes weren't even in my size," I lied, knowing *exactly* how the fox had felt when she couldn't snatch the grapes.

Chapter 15

Then she said mean stuff to Jessica, so I smashed a book stand across the back of her skull. Then she left. Then Jess left. Then I left." I took another gulp of my Orange Julius. Enduring November, and back at the Mall of America. Pattern? What pattern? "Oh, and I'm not speaking to the king of the vampires right now, but I s'pose I'll forgive him in a couple more hours."

I happened to look up and catch a pair of teenage boys openly staring at me. "What? Is there something on my face?" I furtively touched my nose, chin, and eyebrows. Was I dripping Orange Julius from somewhere? "Stop staring," I told them, and like testosterone-swamped seventeen-year-old robots, they both went back to their Big Macs.

It's not that I'm a sexpot, or even a Miss America type. I have this undead sex-appeal thing going on. It had nothing to do with me and everything to do with Why Being A

Vampire Takes A While To Get Used To. Yes, I occasionally made ruthless use of it to get out of a speeding ticket. But that was the extent of my evil. I swear!

"Aw, give 'em a break. You did say, in the middle of a public food court, that you made the devil your bitch and that you're not putting out for the vampire king. I'm surprised only two people noticed."

My roommate (one of the legions) lounged in his plastic chair at our tiny sticky food-court table. Marc was—I think I mentioned this—an ER doctor, though tonight he was disguised as a shave-needing, sleep-deprived cutie in faded scrubs that smelled like cotton, sweat, dried blood, and Mennen Speed Stick. (Alpine Force . . . and how dumb was that? Alpine *Force*? Who thinks this shit up?)

So, he was in disguise as an ER doctor. I saw Marc in scrubs so often, I didn't think I'd recognize him in jeans, or gingham.

He was also slammin' handsome if you liked the sharp-featured, compassionate, green-eyed, warm, hilarious, brunet type.

"I knew I shouldn't have covered Ren's shift." Marc groaned and raked his fingers through his schizophrenic hair. In the couple of years I'd known him he'd tried shoulder length, shaved, crew cut, short and messy, short and short, buzz cut, ponytail, the Caesar, the Beckham, the fauxhawk, the crop, the Keith Urban, the Josh Holloway, and even, during one ten-day period no one in our house ever talked about, the armadillo (complete with white spikes).

Today he was sporting the relatively benign Christian Bale. I was sporting my usual blonde-with-red-lowlights, which I was fated to stick with for five thousand years. Thank

God I'd gotten a touch-up a couple weeks before I died. Bad hair . . . forever. That's just mean. And so, so wrong. Nobody deserves that.

"But he was bitching about how his kid did the Heimlich on some other kid in the cafeteria . . . I guess the school's giving him a plaque for making a cheerleader barf up a French fry. Like the world would miss one cheerleader."

"Too mean," I commented.

Marc waved away my criticism. "Ren cornered me when I was weak from not having my fifth Coke, and I let him talk me into the switch. So where was I? Huh? Huh? Yeah," he added as if I'd said something. "Stitching scalps and fending off rash-infested babies, disimpacting a sundowner, getting puke on my shoes and *in* my shoes, and pretending I'm in a meaningful relationship so Dan-Dan-the-Ambulance-Man quits asking me out."

"It sounds pretty yuck-o," I acknowledged.

Marc took a swig of Coke. "*ER* lied to me, Betsy. *All* the TV shows about doctors lied to me. There's nothing glamorous about working in an ER. Not one thing. The only reason I even applied to med school was because I had dreams of being in a George Clooney–Eriq La Salle sandwich."

"Do I want to ask what disimpaction is? Or a sundowner?" About the sandwich, I could fill in the blanks. Frankly, I'd heard worse ideas.

He shook his head. "You know I'll answer you."

"Okay. So, not asking."

I had called his bluff on that once.

Once.

"Anyway," I continued, "you didn't really miss all that much."

He snorted.

"Yeah, okay, you missed tons. It was weird and scary and interesting."

"Like all of the devil's visits."

"Yup."

"Or a trial by jury." He shuddered. "How's Jess?"

"Oh, you know. Stressed. Missing Nick. And the holidays are starting up. Bad time."

"So her parents are burning in hell. Literally burning in hell."

I shrugged.

"Well, what did Jessica *say* about it?"

I shrugged again. I didn't blame Marc for loving gossip or being curious. But that didn't mean I had *Information* written on my forehead in purple Sharpie.

Marc leaned back, slung an arm across the back of the chair next to his, and gave me a long look. I slurped and waited him out. Gone were the days when a long, studied stare would startle me into blurting out my bra size. I was a stone of patience. A stone!

"Y'know, Betsy, there aren't a lot of dead black guys who lived in Minnesota and had one daughter, married a showgirl, and made a billion dollars before their thirty-fifth birthday."

Then I, the stone, nearly sicked up Julius all over my friend's cheese curds.

Chapter 16

"Don't let my gorgeous face fool you," Marc said, dabbing Julius out of his eyebrows. "I do occasionally have to resort to detective work. Even research. And that stuff—well, it made all the local papers at the time. The guy was the pride of Minnesota, the state's biggest philanthropist, proudly raised on a farm (so the yokels liked him, too), and had better press than Tiger Woods, pre-affairs."

"Yes," I managed through gritted teeth. I hated even hearing the fuck-o's name, never mind about his disguise as a dad who wasn't a perverted narcissistic egomaniac. "He got good press in life."

"Right up 'til his daughter made headlines winning her emancipated status. And his fatal car crash with his wife the same day."

I looked longingly into my empty Julius cup. Another four or five of these would go down great. Also? I felt remorseful *and* stupid, which I hate. I should have known Marc would have figured out all that stuff, probably about ten minutes after he met Jessica the first time.

He jabbed his finger in my general direction. "You should have known I'd figure that stuff out."

"I was thinking that very thing."

"I know why *you* hate November—and there was no need to knock over the entire Fine Cooking display at the Barnes and Noble."

"I couldn't take it. Sixty pictures of giant bronzed roasted turkeys. It—it *loomed,* practically."

"Still. If you hadn't mojo'd the manager, we'd be sitting in the security office right now. Anyway, I know you're anti-Thanksgiving and anti-family—"

"I am not anti-family!" I brought the flat of my hand down on the table, then winced when I heard the sharp crack. Stupid, cheap plastic tables. "I'm pro-family. I'm all for families. But our situation is not a family. It's a comic book. We've got the Antichrist, my eighty-year-old dead husband, my dead stepmother who gets off on popping into my room when I'm exploring the wonderful world of chocolate syrup with Sinclair—"

"Aw, God." Marc rubbed his eyes. "Do you know how long it's been since I got laid?"

"—my dead father who *isn't* haunting me for some reason—"

"Wait. Are you complaining that he's dead or that he's not one of the ghosts giving you to-do lists?"

"—my orphaned best friend who recently quit having cancer, my half-brother-slash-son who is immune to any and all paranormal weirdness—"

"Not the worst superpower to have."

"—a gay ER doc equally obsessed with sex, texting, and Beyoncé—"

"Which makes me completely normal, except with really good taste."

"—and a roommate-slash-secretary-slash-bodyguard who knows my husband better than I ever will—"

"Don't forget how awesomely hot she is. I mean, you're cute, Betsy, but Tina . . ." Marc whistled and glanced at the ceiling. "D'you think she'd cut her hair and give it to me?"

I flinched but kept on: "That's my family, okay? Norman Rockwell never painted this. Because if he did? Everyone would run screaming from the room. Sort of like I'm thinking about doing right now."

"Boo-hoo. You're in perfect health—"

"I'm *dead*, Dr. Doofus!"

"And rich—"

"But it's not my money."

"Community-property state, babe. And you're married to a gorgeous guy who adores you, and you have all kinds of cool Scooby-esque adventures—"

"Which occasionally end with a friend catching bullets with her frontal lobe."

"I'm just sayin'," he continued, unmoved by my rising hysteria. "Better find another shoulder to cry on, honey."

"I will." I jumped up. Time to get gone before I decided to see how often Marc would bounce if I threw him over the railing and into the amusement park. "I will do exactly that."

"See ya," he replied, admirably unconcerned.

I snatched his unopened can of Coke, taking bitchy

pleasure in his flinch—he probably hadn't seen me move. "*And* I'm taking this. Yeah! Reap the whirlwind."

I stomped toward the escalators, not acknowledging his, "Don't forget, you said you'd clean Giselle's litter box tonight!"

As far as parting shots went, it was a pretty good one.

Chapter 17

"All is well, beloved stud muffin o'mine. I have decided to forgive you."

I was smiling at Sinclair from our bedroom doorway. Yep, time to forgive him for whatever it was he did, and get laid. It had been—jeez, was that right? Four days? *Four?* No wonder I felt so bitchy and out of control.

"Mmm," the love of my (un)life hummed. His back was to me as he was sitting at the small shaker-style desk in the corner, working on his laptop. We usually had a please-no-paperwork-but-how-about-oral-sex-instead rule in our bed-room, but exceptions were made now and again. I mean, he was a rich powerful king-type guy. When we weren't putting our footprints on the ceiling, memos had to be read. Or writ-ten. Or whatever the hell he did on that thing.

"So, I didn't see you here last night when I came back."

Nothing.

"In fact, I haven't seen much of you in the last day or two. What with our little, uh, you know, and the devil dropping by."

Tap-tap-tap of his fingers hitting the keyboard.

"So, the devil. Dropped by. But I took care of it." Yep, never underestimate the negotiating power of felony assault.

"How fortunate none of your thoughtless actions will come back to haunt us. Or hurt us." *Tap. Tap-tap.*

"Uh . . . okay. Are you all right?"

Tap. TAP-TAP-TAP. I wondered if the tips of his fingers were going to punch through the keyboard. "No," Sinclair replied. "I am not. I have an inordinate amount of paperwork. I must clean up another of your messes. I have asked you no less than four times to be at my side for a significant social obligation—"

"What, this again? C'mon, Sinclair, teatime with vamps? Barf. And again, I say barf."

"I. Wasn't. *Finished.*" Still he wouldn't look at me. Why wouldn't he turn around and look at me? More: Why weren't we having sex right now? "You say you want our people to be more independent, less predatory, and—how did you so charmingly phrase it? Ah. 'Less sucky in all things, pun intended.' "

"Heh." Good one.

"But you resist any opportunity to give them positive reinforcement. You resist any opportunities to appear at my side as a show of our concentrated, combined ruling authority. You—"

"—are wondering who bit you on the ass." I knew it wasn't me, literally or figuratively. Could he have a headache? A fang-ache? Overworked, maybe? Hard to imagine . . . Sinclair lived for this shit. Grumpy because he was on the same four-day-sexless streak I was? Bingo.

I crossed the room and put my hands on his shoulders, surprised to find his muscles were thrumming like steel cables. "Yeesh, you're grumpy tonight. But I have a cure, which will entail you making that sexy-clinkey sound when you unbuckle your belt, and then I will make that oh-God-put-it-in-right-now sound, and—"

"Do not say that!"

"What? What?" I was astonished; he hadn't shouted it so much as roared it. Then I realized a *God* had slipped out, which felt to most vampires like a paper cut. On the genitals.

"Oh, jeez, I—oh, *jeez*! I mean, sorry. Uh, sorry. It just slipped out."

"It continually slips out. You have no interest in modifying your behavior even when it harms those closest to you. You have had years to implement this adjustment and have not troubled yourself. This, while those around you risk their lives. Or lose their lives. I find it . . . dishonorable."

Was it possible I never left Payless Shoes with Laura the other day? Instead of coming here for the Saturday Satanic Movie Fest, perhaps I'd passed out in Payless and everything that had happened since was some sort of crappy-shoe-induced fever dream brought on by lack of sex and impending November.

I guess he got tired of me just standing there with my mouth unsprung, because he put the final spank on his verbal cat o'nine tails with, "I require your absence."

"Uh. You do?"

"Remove your hands. Then remove the rest of you. Quietly, if you can manage such a feat."

I yanked my hands back as though he'd gotten lava hot. Then I took a slow step backward. Then another.

Something was seriously screwed up. Had I been that much of a brat the other day? Well, sure. But this was not new behavior. Certainly not new to Sinclair, who ran up against my self-involved brattiness about eight seconds after we met.

"You seem . . . um . . . upset. D'you want a smoothie?" Or a tranquilizer? I wondered if Marc had made it back from his AA meeting yet; I had the feeling I'd need his shoulder again, and there were only so many burdens I dared put on Jessica this time of year.

Marc had a love-hate relationship with AA. As he described it, AA was like a high school girlfriend who was hot, one you'd known for a long time, but who also cheated on you. So Marc and AA broke up at least once a year but always got back together. And why the hell was I thinking about Marc's easy-come-easy-go alcoholism now?

I wrenched my thoughts onto a more relevant track. "When did you feed last?"

I was surprised to feel my shoulder blades hit the bedroom door. I'd let him back me all the way across the room. Or, rather, I'd let *me* back me all the way across the room.

I had seen Sinclair enraged, despondent, joyful, horny, worried, irritated, tender, motivated, goaded, annoyed, terrified, ravenous, and provoked. But the stranger hanging out in my husband's suit? I'd never met him before. Cold and hateful were sentiments I never dreamed my heart's love, my only love, would use on me.

Also: he hadn't bothered to answer my question. For a weird moment I thought maybe this time, I was the ghost.

"Maybe I'll just . . ." What? Kill him? Kill myself? Race for Tina's vodka collection? Set the house on fire? Smack myself in the face until I woke up? That last was probably not the worst plan in the world . . .

"Why are you still here?" He didn't bother to raise his voice that time. And he sure hadn't turned around to look at me. He was re-engrossed in his work; I no longer rated strong emotion.

Then, a life preserver was tossed my way when I'd never wanted an escape hatch more: "Living Dead Girl" started blaring from my pants.

·My ring tone. My hands shot into the pocket of my cargo pants (hurrah for eighteen pockets of varying sizes even if khaki made me look like I recently escaped basic training!) as I clawed for the Rob Zombie–blaring lifesaver.

"Oh, thank God. I mean, hello?"

"Betsy?" A small, crumpled voice. A tearful voice. "Betsy, are you there?"

Sure, Laura, I just don't know where *here* is right now, what with my husband channeling Joey Buttafuoco. "What's wrong? You sound—"

"I'm naked!"

"Uh, figuratively, or—"

"I just woke up here!" she whisper-screamed. "I don't know how I got here. All I remember is going to bed last night in my room, and now I'm naked in the spoon!"

As someone born and raised within an hour's drive of the Walker Art Center in Minneapolis, I knew at once what the problem was and, even better, where it was.

"I'm coming," I told her, dropping the phone back in my pocket and all but diving out my bedroom door.

It wasn't running away. It sure wasn't a retreat. A family member needed help. I *had* to go, no matter what just happened with my husband, no matter how much I wanted to stay and thrash this out.

Yup. That was my story. It even had the advantage of sounding almost true.

Chapter 18

Hennepin Avenue wasn't too wretched—it was only ten at night—which made me wonder why Laura was waking up at such an odd hour (and naked, no less). She was a student at the U of M; she tended to stick to the typical daytime schedule of a nine-to-fiver. Time enough to pin her down on that one once I rescued her from the spoon.

The spoon was one of the things the Twin Cities were famous for (aside from subzero temperatures that would make a weasel squeal).

It was an enormous sculpture of a spoon with a cherry sitting in the bowl of said spoon, and was the pride and joy of the sculpture garden. The husband-and-wife team who created it were hailed as artistic geniuses, and gobs of people came to look at the thing every year.

Not me, though. Once was enough (ninth-grade field trip, which was made even more exciting when Jessica barfed her

Dilly Bar all over my new sweater). Okay, it was a very nice gigantic spoon. And a very vibrant, pretty cherry.

Uh, geniuses? The ones who thought this up were geniuses? The guy—the husband—even admitted that he sketched while he ate. He would get inspired. While he *ate*. No wonder he thought of doing a giant spoon. He was probably wolfing down ice cream at the time. Maybe even an ice cream sundae. With a big red guess what on top? I s'pose we're lucky he didn't sculpt a giant pudding cup. Or a giant tuna melt.

Okay, so, as a people, we midwesterners are easily impressed. All anyone has to do is eyeball the sculpture garden to figure that out. Don't even get me started on the guy who did the sculpture of a bench. He used three kinds of materials for his sculpture. Of a *bench*. Which people keep insisting is art. When it's a *bench*.

This was probably why my major had been Studies in Cinema, as opposed to Art History, before I dropped out. Never mind; I had stuff to do and Antichrists to haul out of giant cherries.

I parked (badly), then beat feet over to the sculpture garden. I was wearing good shoes, of course, but they were Dolce and Gabbana floral print sandals, which meant they were gorgeous, expensive, and flat. I could actually run in them.

For a wonder—at least it was a chilly night—there weren't any couples trying to sneak over to have sex in the spoon. So I found Laura alone, shivering, and—she hadn't exaggerated for dramatic effect, though I'd had hopes—naked.

"What happened?" I asked, already shrugging out of my jacket. I handed her a small, crumpled Target bag—no time to shop, or wrap—which held one of a thousand pairs of my leggings. (You know how, a couple years ago, everybody credited Lindsay Lohan with bringing back leggings? A vicious, damnable lie. I brought 'em back. *Me*.)

I didn't bother to bring shoes—she was two sizes bigger than me. "Are you okay? Are you hurt?"

"I don't know! I woke up in here. And I was cold and this thing—this spoon is *so* cold! And—"

"Wait. You woke up like this? *Just* like this?" I watched as she yanked on my leggings—should have remembered to bring underwear—and pulled the jacket closed over her breasts. "How did you call me?"

"There was a guy with a sketchbook—he said he'd quit sketching because it was dark, but was still hanging around—and he gave me his phone. He said I could use it. And then he—" She peeked around the spoon. "I guess he left."

"I didn't pass anyone." And couldn't smell or hear anyone. Enh . . . one worry at a time. "What's the last thing you remember?"

"Saying 'I guess he left' just now," the Antichrist snapped. A rare display of temper; I guess waking up in a big chunk of art made her testy.

"Before you woke up, I meant."

"I told you!" Her teeth were clacking together like ivory castanets. "I went to bed. I wasn't feeling good again—"

"Again?"

"Can I finish?"

"Don't bite my head off because you've got impulse-control issues."

"Sorry," she said, sulking. "I went to bed just before suppertime. I've been feeling kind of crummy, but nothing like—"

"Wait. You've been sick?"

She nodded, shivering and miserable. "I didn't tell you—it's just cramps. And headaches. I guess I should have . . ."

I laughed. "What? Predicted you'd wake up as the sculpture garden's newest exhibit?"

She smiled. It was teeny—no teeth—but it was a smile. "When you put it like that . . ."

I reached out and took her hand, which was as chilly as mine—a good trick, since my heart only pumped about four times a minute. "C'mon, let's get you—" I cocked my head.

"What's wrong? Does your stomach hurt, too?"

"No, but I think I know what your Good Samaritan's been up to." As I spoke, a tall, well-built blond stepped out from behind one of the clumps of trees. He was dressed in dark slacks, loafers, a white dress shirt, and a navy jacket. He was clean shaven, wearing wire rims, and smiling at us.

"Thank you for—" Laura began, then stopped when two other men stepped out behind the first.

"—the attempted gang rape," I finished. They didn't look the type—nice clothes, pleasant and open expressions. Recently showered. But then, one thing I've figured out: rapists didn't always lurk in alleys drinking hooch from brown paper bags. And killers weren't always shuffling around the fringes of things, playing God with handguns and rewriting their manifestos.

"I see your sister came," the first one said. Yeesh; he even *sounded* boy-next-door. "First her money. Then the party."

I snorted, and Laura said, "That's not nice, you—you cretin."

"Less talk," another one said. "More naked."

"Oh boy," I said. It was the perfect surreal touch to a late-night visit to the Walker. "You poor dumbass. Did *you* pick the wrong girls."

The one who had remained silent—a redhead, with the creamy freckled complexion of same—spoke up. "Why are you still dressed?"

I giggled, which was a surprise to everyone but me. I tried to muffle it, but before long it exploded into full-blown guffaws.

Laura went from shivering and almost crying to wide-eyed surprise. "What is it? Other than me being naked in a big spoon."

I hee-hawed louder. "Oh, that's—that's part of it . . . but these guys! Oh my God! They have no idea what we're going to do to them! I m-mean—they've been lurking in bushes—ready to jump us—except th-their victims—their v-victims are the queen of the vampires and—and the Antichrist! And I'm . . . I'm so hungry!"

While our prom dates from hell exchanged puzzled glances, Laura let that sink in and started to laugh herself.

"Listen, you twats, you—"

"Pipe down, B-positive. I'll get to *you* in a minute."

Hungry was an understatement. I hadn't fed in three days. Three stressful, weird days. Hungry? Try starving. But, and hooray for the petty criminal thoughts of well-dressed Neanderthals, my entrees were here.

I took them, one by one. Normally Laura would have left or looked away—she didn't like vampires, and she sure didn't like watching me chow down. But tonight she just walked around my entrees and me. The other two were too scared to flee, not that they could have gotten past the Antichrist in the dark. So she prowled around and waited for me to finish, occasionally checking her watch.

Afterward, I was full and sleepy. And Laura had been able to slip into the navy jacket—the one that showed the blood the least—on our way to my car.

Chapter 19

"How long has this been going on?"

Laura didn't answer. I couldn't blame her; it'd been a weird night. We were back at my place, thinking about making smoothies. I say *thinking about* because I was stuffed, and Laura didn't feel like hulling strawberries. The kitchen was a place we gravitated to even if we weren't hungry.

And the house was quiet, which was a mild miracle. Tina was pillaging somewhere—wait 'til I told her about my three-course meal of white-collar rapists—and Marc was using my half brother to troll for dates.

Yeah, I know. Ugh, right? Which I told him. But he remained unmoved, and unguilty.

"How else am I supposed to meet nice guys?" he'd asked. "When I'm not working, I'm running around town with the vampire queen. Or trying to prevent the Antichrist from taking over the world. Now, I've found a group for single parents who work odd hours. Tonight's mocktails-and-playdates night. I gotta have a prop. So hand him over—don't *look* at me like that. He'll be perfectly safe. I'm a doctor, and he's immune to anything weird."

I'd had my doubts at the time—not about Marc's babysitting skills, which were terrific. But we'd had weirder adventures spring up from even more innocuous events. I was getting sooo paranoid in my thirties.

Now, of course, I was thrilled the baby was out of the house, and would be all night. My mom was out of town, attending a Civil War convention in Virginia. Which was just as well—she disliked having her dead ex-husband's infant dumped in her lap.

As for Sinclair, I had no idea where he was—and didn't want to know. I wasn't up for another confrontation. Although I'm not sure *confrontation* was the right word, since most of the talking had been on my end. He almost couldn't be bothered to be in the argument with me. I'd never seen someone be distant and terrifying at the same time.

But fortunately—unfortunately, I meant; sorry, a minor slip, un, un, *un!*—unfortunately my sister needed my help. Marital woes would have to wait. I would quit wondering about everyone's convenient absences and be grateful for them instead.

"Laura? You said you'd been sick for a while. So, how long?"

"When I'm not sick, I dream. Sometimes both."

"Sorry?" I doubt I would have caught that, if not for vampire hearing. "You dream?"

"About my mother. About hell."

"When?"

"Mmmms prbbbl insll."

"Huh?"

"Almost every night."

I stared at her across the marble countertop. She'd started nibbling on her fingernails, when normally her hands were beautiful and her nails neatly trimmed and filed . . . how many other new habits had she picked up? What else hadn't I noticed?

Even a year ago, I'd be ass deep in this and still oblivious to all the danger. But I never realized that all experience could do for me was assure me, every day, that however bad things were, they'd get worse.

Experience wasn't keeping me out of a jam. It was just making me scared and nervous. So what the hell was it good for?

"You dream about hell. Every night."

She spit out a hangnail, which I took as an affirmative.

"And now you're waking up inside sculptures. When you aren't using your secret devil power to speak every language on earth."

"Mmmm."

I couldn't believe I was going to do it. I couldn't believe I was even thinking it. But this stuff was way over my head. Shit, *vampire* stuff was way over my head. And I wasn't smart enough to think of another way to go. I mean, you could take that one to the bank, pretty much every time.

"I think . . . I think we need to talk to your mother."

She sighed. "Yes."

"Now, before you freak out, just think about—what?"

"I agree. I think it's all we can do. I can't think of anything else, either."

Nuts. I was sort of hoping she'd send up a storm of shrill protests. Or hit me over the head until I blacked out.

"I think she can help you." Probably. "She can help both of us." Probably.

Question was: Would she?

The scarier question: *Why* would she?

I've already forgiven you that little bit of criminal assault, so it will all be behind us tomorrow. You need not fear to call on me.

Dammit!

"I'm not gonna lie. I don't like where this is going."

"It's good you didn't lie, then."

"Hilarious. But this has barely started and already I don't like the smell. I think it's gonna be one of those things that starts off mildly worrisome and turns into screaming, shrieking death for at least half a dozen people."

The Antichrist sighed. "I think you're right. Maybe you should have left me in the spoon and hoped for the best."

"No, no, no. I was glad to get out of the house. It was a pleasure. I needed some air. And to, uh, put more mileage on my car. So it was good that you called from a rapist's cell phone to tell me your ass cheeks were sticking to a giant spoon."

Laura laughed so hard she fell off of the bar stool in a tangle of long, graceful limbs, which made me feel better. I was pretty sure the hyuk-yuks were over for a while, so I was gonna take what I could.

"All right, it sounds like we're both on the same page. We'll go."

My sister looked relieved, which was an improvement over looking suicidal (or homicidal, come to think of it). "Right now?"

"Just a sec—let me go pack an overnight bag."

The Antichrist blinked. "Why?"

"Why? Laura, we're going to hell. Of our own free will. I can't think of a place where I'd need to pack a bag *more*."

"But—"

I was already off the bar stool and headed for the swinging door. "I'd bring a change of clothes to the gym, but not hell? Good God, Laura, what's the matter with you?"

"Many, many things." She was giving me the strangest look—probably because she hadn't thought of this stuff herself. Well, I could throw in an extra pair of leggings for her. But only if she was nice! And didn't take over the world in a sinister rain of blood and fire.

Packing didn't take long. I grabbed my new Burberry bag, which had been a just-thinking-of-you gift from my husband last month. I hadn't even taken the tags off yet, which I now rectified. I then randomly grabbed things until I figured I had enough to overnight in hell. And would look stylish yet practical while doing same.

I loved the bag's screaming red color, practical size, and quilted pattern. Not to mention the nylon material—I tended to wave drinks about excitedly as I talked, and had soaked more than one purse by accident.

I wasn't nearly as picky about bags and purses as I was about shoes—shit, the shoe thing was enough of a drain on my finances—so getting used to really nice bags was a new thing for me.

As was, apparently, a husband who was quietly furious with me a *lot*. I'd have to face that music sooner or later, and I didn't dare put it off more than a day or two.

I'd have to find out what had gotten into Sinclair—or what had gotten out. Apologize. Swear to God never to swear to God again.

I should probably work on that apology a little.

I took a last look around our bedroom, which is when I saw it: a cream-colored number-10 envelope (sorry; years of secretarial training sometimes kicked in when I least expected . . . I mean, a *business-size* envelope, the most common size) with my name slashed across the front in black ink.

Sinclair's handwriting.

Uh, no. I wasn't up for this tonight. Nope. Sinclair was either sorry or not sorry. Which meant I would then either be sorry or not sorry. Either way: no time for this right now.

I stuffed the envelope into my screaming-red bag and was as ready as I could ever be. I took another look around and realized I was stalling. Not too lame and cowardly.

Right! I was ready. Denizens of evil, look out: a former secretary was gonna kick your asses all over the Underworld.

And now: to hell! Which wasn't as cool as it sounded.

Chapter 20

Laura and I met in the library, which was interesting. We hadn't said in so many words, "After I pack and tuck away a probably angry missive from the dead guy I'm screwing when he's not coldly furious with me, let's meet in the library next to the hideous and smelly Book of the Dead." But here we both were. Ah, sisterhood.

The book stand was still broken, which was strange. Between the two of them, Jessica and Sinclair had a battalion of employees at their beck and et cetera. Things were usually fixed so quickly and efficiently, it was like living with elves. Elves who washed cars and kept the fridge stocked with fruit, yogurt, juice, vodka, and (for those of us in Vamp Central who breathed, ate, and shat) meat and meat by-products. Also half-and-half. I put half-and-half in everything. Tea. Milkshakes. Booze.

So it was a bit of a surprise to see something in the house that hadn't been fixed.

Anyway, long story short, the Book of the Dead had been unceremoniously dumped on the end table by the far window. It should have looked ridiculous, this big, smelly ancient tome written in blood and bound in (yerrrggh!) human skin, plunked onto an end table like a *TV Guide*. But it didn't. It looked ominous and weird.

"So." I glared in the book's direction, then glanced at my sister. She'd changed clothes, which was fine with me—the outfit she'd put together in the sculpture garden clashed, to put it mildly. No one should have to rely on the clothes of concussed rapists to accessorize. Luckily she'd been keeping a few outfits here ever since she recovered from almost killing me. "Call her."

"Who? My mother?"

"Yeah. Give her a holler. Or the secret devil password, or whatever."

"I can't."

I sighed. "Laura, we've been *over* this. We both agreed that it sucks, and we both agreed that we have to do it. So go and do it already."

"I don't know how to call her. What makes you think I'd know?" She shivered. "I don't even like to speak to her."

"Oh." I hadn't thought of this. "So . . . you're saying the devil comes when she wants, not when she's called. Like a cat. A very, very, very evil cat."

As if there were any other kind. I'd been stuck with Giselle the cat since before I died, and cordially loathed her. Our home was big enough so entire weeks went by when I didn't see her, though I was still occasionally stuck with her litter box. The elves eschewed dirty litter boxes.

Laura shrugged. "She just sort of—you know."

"Too well. Uh. Maybe a sacrifice?" My soul shrank from the words. Had I said I already didn't like this? I so so so didn't already like this. It wasn't even midnight and we were talking sacrifices. "That's how they do it in the movies. Some group of clueless horny teenagers sacrifice a virgin—"

"I am *not* going to let you sacrifice me."

"—and poof! Up the devil pops." I eyed my sister. "You're probably the only virgin in a fifteen-block radius."

She folded her arms across her chest. "I refuse."

"Yeah, yeah; don't get your borrowed panties in a twist. It sort of defeats the purpose, sacrificing you so we can get the devil to help you."

"There you go, then." Laura looked relieved.

I rubbed my forehead and squashed the urge to boot the book into the fireplace. "She said something, too. Something she prob'ly thought would be sinister yet helpful yet cryptic. Which of course I can't remember. Something about how I'd know."

"How you'd know what?"

"I dunno. I knew the devil depending on me to remember something weird and out of context was gonna be bad, bad news. The older I get," I added grimly, "the less I enjoy being right all the time."

"She wouldn't have given you a clue if she didn't think you'd be able to think of it."

Laura's faith was touching, yet insane and misplaced. "Ha! All I can think about are those beautiful, beautiful, beautiful, beautiful, beautiful, beautiful shoes she was—aw, shit."

"What?"

I sighed. "I know what to do. I know how we can get her here."

"There, see!" Laura sounded delighted. "I knew you'd figure it out! See, she was right to give you a clue."

"It's possible I hate your mom more than you hate your mom."

"That's so nice of you to say," Laura said, and squeezed my hand.

Chapter 21

l dragged Laura up to my room—still no Sinclair, hallelujah brothers—and walked into my closet with all the speed and urgency of the condemned sprinting to the noose. I knew exactly where *they* were, of course.

I went to the right rack at the back of the walk-in closet, in the right spot. I took the box and opened it. Pulled aside layer after layer of carefully folded tissue paper, and carefully withdrew—

"You sort of look like those guys who have to handle used fuel rods in nuclear plants. They use those big giant gloves and take all these safety precautions in order to—ohhh."

"This." I turned and walked toward Laura, cradling the box as I would my brother, BabyJon. "This is what I was looking for."

She followed me out of the closet, back down the stairs,

through several hallways, and back to the library, where I'd started a fire before galloping to my room.

"This is what I must do."

Laura whimpered and her hands flew to her mouth. Her blue eyes looked enormous as she stared at me over her fingers. "Oh . . . no, Betsy. Please no."

"I must sacrifice . . . my Valentino couture black-lace midheel peep-toe pumps."

"No!"

"Italian made. They cost almost a thousand dollars."

"Oh my God . . ." Laura reeled before me. "This isn't happening . . ."

"It took me three years of overtime to save up for them."

Laura moaned through her fingers.

"I have never worn them."

A muffled sob from the Antichrist. Or maybe I was the one sobbing.

"They are black. So they go . . . with everything. I can wear them . . . with everything!"

"Please! We'll think of something else! Betsy, you don't know what you're saying. You can't do this! There's no coming back from this!"

"I have no choice. You think the devil's gonna show up for a half-assed sacrifice of last year's running shoes?"

"I don't care, it's not worth it! Think about what you're doing! Please, don't do something you'll never be able to take ba-aaaaah!"

I had flung them into the fire. Laura shrieked. No—that was me. I shrieked, as though *I* were the one on fire.

Laura tried to dash past me. "We can save them! They can be repaired and good as new! No! Let me go, Betsy. *I can save them!*"

I was able to catch her by the elbow and swing her away from the merrily blazing high heels. "It has to be done." My sister and I clung to each other, sobbing. "The sacrifice has to be made."

"Wow," someone said from behind us. Laura stiffened in my arms, and we turned.

"I won't deny it, dear. I didn't think you'd be able to go through with it." The devil took in our tear-stained faces and grinned. "I should have brought a box of Kleenex."

Chapter 22

"I am not happy that Betsy had to go through that terrible ordeal just to get you to show up," the Antichrist began. "And she went through that for *me*! I can never thank her enough. So don't you be mean and don't you make fun of her."

"But how will I fill my evening?" Satan smirked. "Or yours? And my dear, dumb daughter, Betsy did it so much more for herself."

"Hey!" I yelped.

"No, you're right." The devil paused. "It's not that you're dumb, Laura. It's that you only know about this singular plane of existence."

"Okay, that's b—wait, I'm still offended on both our behalves."

"But she does only know about this plane. And you did go through all that to escape your own tedious reality."

Through pure force of habit I opened my mouth to

protest, then thought it over and shrugged instead. "Yeah, well. It's true. But that doesn't make you right all the time, Lena Olin."

Laura looked at me, big blue eyes puzzled. I figured I should elaborate, but before I could, God's Problem Child stepped all over me, verbally speaking.

"In the guise of helping you, Betsy gets to run away from the train wreck of a life she's made for herself."

"Hey! Don't imply I had anything to do with any trains or any wrecks, you—"

"The dead roommates, of course. The half brother. The dead parents."

"The Ant," I forced out through teeth that wanted to gnash my molars into dust, "was not my mother."

"Her best friend is in a funk, and not just because she's recently realized her parents are my permanent guests. Jessica's love life is in, as we say, the shitter."

"Who is *we?*"

"Then there's her pathologically illogical hatred of all things Thanksgiving—"

"Hey, I'm not alone in that one! Just ask a Native American. If you can find one. See? See? My point."

"And let's not forget the vampire king—"

"Who is *let's?* Who is *we?* Who *are* these people?"

"—who has spent the last several days in a cold rage at his wife. Or perhaps at himself, for marrying her. *My* point, daughter, is that you mustn't ascribe your sister with qualities she *does not have.*"

Laura, aghast, looked at me. I opened my mouth . . . then shrugged again. "I got nothin'. She's right. My life is so shitty right now, a day trip to hell sounds like a good idea."

I had it. I'd figured it out. This, *this* is what experience meant. It meant I wasn't any more capable of keeping myself out of disastrous jams, I just knew that the car I was driving? The one with no brakes? Was also on fire. Headed for an orphanage. Which was also on fire. And chased by cop cars, which were ablaze.

"Experience sucks," I explained to my sister and her mom. "That's all it means."

Chapter 23

That was . . . hmm, what *is* the word? Ah! Pointless. A word that leaps effortlessly to mind whenever the queen of the vampires expresses an opinion."

"Well, excuse me for having a moment of self-awareness!"

"You are excused; I know full well how rare and wonderful such moments are for you. Now." The devil clapped her hands together, like a kindergarten teacher briskly bringing the rowdy ankle-biters under her command. "Since you have both agreed to come to my domain, there are a few elementary rules you must—"

"No."

The devil blinked. "Pardon?"

"*We* say. Not you. Because I know something you prob'ly wish I didn't. You need us." I paused, relishing the sweet, sweet words about to tumble from my lip-glossed mouth

(Too Faced in Drop Dead Red). "You need *me*." Ha! Reap the whirlwind, Satan!

"Yeah!" Laura echoed, but she was a shit poker player, because the doubt? It was writ large, as they say. "You need me. Uh. Her."

"I smell a list of demands," Satan said, but to my relief, she didn't seem annoyed, or even put out. "Speak, O Vampire Queen."

Bark, bark! "You want Laura to see your domain, or whatever the hell you call it."

"Was that supposed to be a pun?"

"Not on purpose. And you know Laura wouldn't come by herself. So I'm gonna get her to the Underworld for you. In return, you're gonna fix it so I can read the Book of the Dead without going nuts."

Laura made a muffled squeaking sound, sort of a gasp crossed with a sigh. "The book! Betsy, I don't think that's a good idea."

"I'm sick to death of the damn thing being in my house and always being right, while at the same time nobody can read the stupid thing."

"But, Betsy . . . it's bad. You know it is. Anybody who looks at it for more than a second and a half can feel how bad it is. How can being able to read it be any sort of improvement? Think of what it might cost."

"Worth it. Can you imagine all the shit we could have avoided over the last three years if we could *read* the fucking thing?

"I'm tired of guessing and wondering. I want to *know*. I need to know. Your mom's probably the only one who can—uh." Probably said too much. "Anyway," I finished with a forced cough, "that's my price for bringing your kid back for Old Home Week."

"Agreed," she said at once. And the way Satan said it—the word out so quickly it almost stepped on the end of my sentence—it was a tone I'd never heard from the devil. She had the air of a person who knew she was getting off lightly.

"But what's in this for you?" As if she'd tell us. But I'd at least ask. I'd at least know, when this whole thing went screaming off the rails, that I'd asked. That I'd tried. "What do you care if Laura ever sees hell? Maternal obligation isn't exactly the phrase that springs to mind when we're talking about you."

"I want her to see my home because not seeing it will eventually drive her mad."

There was a painful silence as Laura and I digested this. Then I forced another cough (which sounded more like a croak) and said, "You mean *make* her mad. Really piss her off. Like how people get when they get dragged to their high school reunion. Right? That's what you don't want to risk. Right?"

"You think the dreams are bad now? You think the pains are bad now?" Satan asked her kid. The fallen angel looked as concerned as I'd ever seen her. The devil was a caring mom; who knew? "You have no idea, Laura. And I mean for things to stay just that way. I mean for you to never have an idea. For you never to know how bad it could have gotten. I'm not here for her. I'm not even here for me. I'm here for you."

"You mean . . . you didn't do that? You didn't make that happen to get me to come?"

"By my father, *no*! I could never hurt you—and even if I could, I *would* never. You coming into harm—serious, permanent harm—how does that help me?"

That was logical enough to be true.

"Laura, you look human. You sound human, you talk like a human. You smell and speak and excrete like a human. You menstruate and—"

"TMI!"

Satan ignored me. "But you aren't. You're only partly human. And all that is me, within you, that part of you calls to my home, and will always call to you. The part of you that isn't human yearns toward the dimension where my will shapes reality."

"I don't get it," I admitted.

"Laura is an Arabian horse," Satan explained, "who was raised on a pig farm and thinks she's a pig."

"Your analogies are hideous." Did that make me queen of the pigs? Or just queen of the pigs who were already dead? "Almost as hideous as—" I eyed her up and down. "As hideous as—wait."

"I prefer not to wait for your tedious mental grinding to bring you up to speed. Now, when we go to my dimension, you'll need—"

"Wait!"

I'd been so caught up in figuring out who was going to do what, and who was going to get what, and who wasn't going to go crazy, I'd barely glanced at Satan's ensemble. But now . . .

Now, there was no shutting it out.

"Your feet."

"—pay close attention to—"

"Your. Feet."

"—for the sake of your immortal—"

"Your feeeeeet!" I shrieked, and launched myself at my sister's evil evil evil evil *evil* mother! Who was wearing a sleeveless gray and black checked shift with a gathered waist and a round neckline, a dress subtle and pretty and which was the perfect outfit to wear . . .

. . . with . . .

. . . my sacrificed Valentino black-lace pumps!

I figure Satan wasn't used to bitchy vampires jumping her, because she went over as though she were made of feathers. I even got in a right cross to her demonic jaw before a thousand firecrackers went off behind my eyes and the bricks above the fireplace jumped forward and slammed me in the back.

The good news was it didn't hurt a bit . . .

Chapter 24

I see I can gloss over the hell-is-another-dimension-and-not-easily-visited portion of my lecture."

"I hate you," I said without opening my eyes. There didn't seem to be any point to getting an eyeful of where I was and what was going on. "So, so much."

"If I were human," Satan bitched, "I would have an unsightly black eye. This is how you treat a guest you invited into your home?"

"Invited is a strong word," I replied.

"Are you okay? How many fingers am I holding up?"

"Child, she hasn't opened her eyes."

"That's true, Laura. I haven't."

"Does it feel like anything's broken?"

It was nice; Laura sounded superconcerned. "Only my sense of reason, purpose, and childlike wonder." I opened my eyes. And blinked. Lots. "Where the hell are we?"

"Yes," Laura and the devil said in unison. Followed by the devil adding, "I'm astonished you got it right the first time. I had allotted twenty minutes for you to eventually guess right, and then need everything explained at least twice. Starting two minutes ago. And now, see? My entire evening just opened up."

"Yes, well, let that be a lesson to you." I sat up, wincing, then lurched to my feet. My back ached from neck to butt, and I had a whopper of a headache, probably from the devil tossing me ass over teakettle into the bricks above the fireplace. Luckily I'd fed recently, and thank you again, would-be rapists.

Dead or not, I could still be hurt. I could still die (again). Tough to kill didn't mean invulnerable. It *did* mean tough to kill. So I bounced back pretty quickly, and never was I happier about that than when I woke up in hell.

Which was really, really good, since I was betting she'd fractured my skull and possibly, for funsies, shattered my spine. In hell for—what? Seventy seconds, and already hideously crippled.

"And I left my overnight bag in the stupid parlor next to the stupid Book of the Dead!" Great. Already this field trip sucked. "No lip gloss." (I dunno if all vampires were prone to dry lips, or just me, and there was no way to tell, because I had *lived* on Chapstick since I was six.) "And no change of underwear!"

"Tsk. I can't tell you how much—" Satan cut herself off and got a peculiar look on her face. She looked as though she were listening to voices. Which she most likely was. Unlike the average citizen of the damned, the voices in her head were probably real. "Well, that's just terrific. Sorry, ladies; I must fly. Something has come up."

"But—" Laura began, already sounding panicked. In hell for a minute and a half and ditched by the devil? *Muy* uncool.

"My assistant can answer your questions and give you a tour. Just go through that door."

We looked; we were standing in a room of nothing.

Okay, I'll elaborate: we were in a nondescript room with high ceilings and cheap carpeting. Everything was blah gray. No windows, no doors. No sound. No light source. It was almost like we were standing in a fog bank that had walls. It was a room of nothing.

"But Baal—" Laura began.

"I'm good, darling, but even *I* can't be in two places at once. As I said—my assistant will take over until I return. She's through that, there. No worries; no one here will bother you. Unless I tell them to." Satan grinned, and blinked out of sight.

"Well, this is off to a suck-o start. What's amazing is that I hear myself, and I actually sound surprised."

"She might not care if you die," Laura said, clearly trying to be reassuring, which would have gone over better if she didn't look terrified, "but she seems to care if I do. So if you stick by me, Betsy, I think we'll be safe."

"And I think I'm weirded out." I gestured. "That's a door."

"Uh . . . yes. It *is* a door. See? I'm not scared. You shouldn't be, either."

"Laura, you sound like an episode of *Sesame Street*. There wasn't a door three seconds ago. There wasn't anything three seconds ago."

"Should we—?"

I looked at her, then back at the door. The doorknob

gleamed innocently. I was pretty sure. "I guess we'd better," I said.

I stepped forward and gingerly gripped the knob. I was expecting it to be hot. You know . . . hellish. But it just turned when I turned it.

So we went in.

Chapter 25

Hell was a waiting room with fading fluorescent lighting and out-of-date *Good Housekeeping* and *Redbook* magazines. Also: hell smelled like a doctor's office, that sharp, sting-y smell that promised you were gonna get hurt, one way or another, before the visit was over.

"Uh." Laura was looking around, as wide-eyed as I was. "This is unexpected."

"To put it mildly." I glanced down at a *Redbook* from April 1979. Those bell-bottoms! Those how-to-satisfy-your-man self-help articles! When the urge to vomit became too much, I knew exactly what I was going to aim for.

The room was furnished with dinged-up, knocked-around cheap furniture; no one was sitting at the check-in desk. The carpet was a perfect mixture of snot green and eye-booger gray. And there were doors, doors about two inches apart along every wall except where the desk was.

"Subtle," I observed, nervously eyeing one of the doors. "I guess you're supposed to get around hell with these things."

"Doors in a waiting room?"

"That's all this is." I glanced up at the ceiling as another ailing fluorescent started to flicker. "People wait. In one of the yuckiest spots ever. You can tell just by standing in this room that unpleasant things are right around the corner. Like an audit you think is done, until they pull out more paperwork." I shuddered. "It's brilliantly evil."

"Thank you," my dead stepmother said.

Of course. Of course the Ant was here. Of course she was the devil's right hand. With the possible exception of Eva Braun, no one could be more suited to the job.

"Well, *great*," I said, eyeing her. "The good news is, being dead hasn't made any sort of imprint on your eclectic personal style. *Eclectic* being another word for *hideous*."

"Says the vampire!" my dead stepmother cried, her overly be-ringed hands flying up to pat her shiny blonde hair. Her hair was as it had always been: the same shade, consistency, and shape of a ripe pineapple. "Only *you* could have been more a pain in your poor father's ass *after* you died."

"Uh, whoa," Laura said, glancing from the Ant to me and back again. "At least this isn't stressful. Or weird."

"So, the devil's handmaiden is really . . . the devil's handmaiden! Ha! Color me the opposite of surprised. Ugh, what are you wearing? You can't tell me all the clothing designers went to heaven. Can't you dig up . . . I dunno . . . Yves Saint Laurent? No. Wait. He was just a coke hound who liked to drink. That's not really the sort of thing people burn in hell for. Too bad he didn't kill someone and cover it up. Cavalli? I'm pretty sure he was blasphemous when he wasn't cranking out panties . . . aw, nuts. He's not dead."

"Maybe we're getting off track," Laura began.

"Oooh, Donna Karan! Right? The whole fur thing? Dammit, I think she's still alive, too. Uh . . ."

The Ant puffed out a harassed breath, apparently never having noticed her hair never, ever moved. (It was interesting to me that people kept habits like breathing and sighing when they didn't need them anymore.) "It's nice to see you again, Laura."

"Thank you, Mrs. T—"

"No, no, no. Please, my name is—"

"Mud," I suggested. "Mud Barfbag Taylor. Call her Asshat for short."

"—Antonia."

Laura stretched an arm over the Ant's desk (hell didn't supply Post-Its, I noticed) and they shook. "I just wanted you to know, Mud Bar—um, Antonia, that though I understand Baal is my mother, you carried me for nine months and—"

"Then dragged my dad to the altar, had sex with him, then bit off his head and devoured his still-twitching body."

"Oh, Betsy, really!" Laura frowned at me. "Grow up."

"See? You're already turning evil. This place is gonna be a bad influence on you; I can already tell. I sense it, as I sense the Ant needs a makeover."

"When I heard you would be visiting us," the Ant was yakking, "of course I asked the Morningstar if I could help. I just didn't think I'd be able to so soon. I hope you understand you are foremost in her thoughts—"

"Vomit," I said to the ceiling. Interesting that there now was one. And it looked like every waiting room ceiling I'd ever seen: a yawn-inducing popcorn ceiling, pitted with little holes from where people tossed pencils at it. "And again, I say vomit."

"—even though she was called away. But I'll look after you." I felt a narrow-eyed glance. "Both of you. I guess. Hmpf. Meanwhile, if I can answer any questions, please just come right out and ask."

"Excellent. Because I've got lots of questions. When you decided to whore yourself in order to break up my mother's marriage, did you do it because you were an amoral slut, or because you didn't get enough of Daddy's attention when you were a little girl? Or some weird pervy combo of both? And when you'd do it with my mother's husband, did you talk to him about all the bad clothes and bad hair treatments you wanted him to buy, or just grunt like animals?"

"Betsy!" mother and daughter shrieked in unison.

"Yeah, that's what I thought." I yawned. "So are we getting a tour or what?"

Chapter 26

We followed my stepmother as she gave us a tour of hell. Laura was staring around, wide-eyed and fascinated, but I was mostly annoyed. I knew hell was going to be awful, but nobody warned me it'd be chockful of clichés.

There were pits of boiling oil, complete with screaming souls trying to do the breaststroke. There was the whole rolling-a-boulder-uphill-only-to-have-it-squash-you-when-it-rolls-all-the-way-back-down thing. (I guess this was also hell for dead ancient Greeks.)

There were people getting whipped, burned, and shaved. There were people who fell, again and again, into pits filled with snakes, lizards, mice, gummy bears.

There were people running, only to be run over by chariots, horses, tanks, RVs.

There were people drowning and people being buried.

There were people being attacked by wild dogs, bears, eagles, ferrets, whippets. Oh, and—gross!

"Otters?" I asked, not expecting an answer. "Were those otters?"

I expected to feel a lot of things in hell, but I never expected boredom. (Although the otter thing was sort of unusual.)

It scared me, to be truthful about the whole thing. Seeing suffering and finding it anticlimactic. I hadn't been a vampire long, but I was beginning to see how the old ones, the ones even older than my husband . . . they were bored by everything; screams and pain and despair and horror left them pretty unmoved. They ended up causing tons of trouble because at least that was something different.

I wasn't scared to be in hell. I was scared that I wasn't scared to be in hell.

But I was here, and I vowed to pay attention and learn what I could. Then I could go back home and spend the next fifty years repressing this entire week.

I pondered, then decided that was as good a plan as any. Pay attention, learn, get what needed to be done *done*, have the devil pay up what she promised, then get the hell, no pun intended, back home.

That was my plan, and I was sticking to it.

Yes, of course I didn't think it'd be that simple. I'd never been a Mensa member, but that didn't mean I needed to read the directions on a box of cereal to make my breakfast.

Chapter 27

Tell you what: hell was like a big evil torture-laden hive. If you stood back from it, you could see there were all sorts of chambers, going down and down and back and back, too many even to count, with something yuck-o or boring or stupid or terrifying or weird going on in each individual cell. As you got closer, you could make out faces and the like. If you pulled back, you couldn't see anything specific but had the sense that lots and lots of stuff was going on all around you.

Hell: nature's *other* beehive.

I could hear the Ant and Laura having a quiet conversation; I'd been so busy musing and looking around I'd dropped about twenty feet back. They must have thought if they kept their voices low enough, I couldn't hear them over the screams and moans and bitching and tantrums of the damned.

"Of course I jumped at the chance," the Ant was saying. Laura's head was bent attentively toward her birth mother;

she had about five inches on the Ant. Laura looked almost protective as she walked beside her. "I had a chip, you know. The you-possessed-me-to-have-a-child chip, and in all this time I never played it. I never wanted to. But then I heard you were coming. That you were alive, I mean, and coming, and Lucifer said I could help show you around."

"Is she nice to you? Relatively speaking?"

"Sure. It's all hype, you know."

"I don't, Antonia. Could you explain?"

"Lucifer doesn't spend all her time thinking up ways to torture the souls who come to her. Hell is—it's almost a business. One she's been running for tens of thousands of years, with no sick time or vacation days. Or holidays. Or even maternity leave." And then she—did she? She did! She actually elbowed my sister, a sort of yuk-yuk elbow dig.

I rolled my eyes. Boo-hoo. Poor Satan. All work and no dental benefits; sounded terrible.

"Can you imagine?" the Ant exclaimed in what sounded like genuine sympathy. I couldn't be sure, though. Since I'd never actually heard that tone from her, you'll understand my confusion. "I thought the customs line at O'Hare was dreadful. That's part of the reason you're here, you know."

"What? What do you mean?"

The Ant shut up, in the way she alone shut up: she kept talking. "I, um, probably shouldn't have—it's not appropriate for me to be talking to you about this."

"But—"

"Oh, look, there's Ted Bundy being raped and strangled again today."

"Aaaiiggh!" Laura clapped her hands over her eyes. "Antonia, I don't want to look at that! Please don't call my attention to things like that. And now please finish your thought."

What thought? I snickered but managed not to say it aloud.

"I really need to finish this tour," the Ant said, sounding rattled and nervous.

"I don't want you to get into trouble, so I'll leave off it for now. But . . . is that part of the reason you're helping her? Is Baal . . . this will sound so silly, but is Baal overworked?"

"Not so much overworked as I think she's lonely," the Ant said after a long pause. Mother and daughter had lowered their voices more, and I ruthlessly decided not to mention I could still hear them. "She's the only one of her kind, you know. And she's been doing this for a long, long time. Ever since the terrible fight with you-know-who."

The building super? Her mechanic?

"Yes," the Ant concluded. "I'd say she was lonesome."

Laura stopped short and glanced back at me. "Oh, look," I said, pretending I hadn't been eavesdropping. "Kenneth Lay is being buried alive in Krugerrands. Gah, that must hurt— look at the welts! They're doing that to him naked? Oh, ew, did you see where some of those Krugerrands *went*? Hey!" I yelled. "How 'bout in your next life, you come back as some-one who *doesn't* screw people out of billions?"

"Don't taunt the damned, Betsy," the Antichrist chided. "Isn't it bad enough they're stuck here?"

"It's bad enough *we're* stuck here."

"*Stuck* isn't really the right word," the Ant said. "No one is here against their will."

"What?" I gave up all pretense of pretending I couldn't hear. "Not even him?" I gestured to Henry VIII, who was on his knees begging Anne Boleyn not to let a French swords-man cut off his head for witchcraft. Old Anne wasn't looking very forgiving. "Because I don't see an egotistical pig of that size—and that's not a fat joke, although there must be Stair-masters in hell—signing up for hell of his own free will."

"But he did. We all did."

"But why?" Laura asked, and I admit, I was interested in the answer myself.

"This isn't a place," the Ant began. She was speaking slowly, but I didn't have the sense she was lying. Just trying to explain so we'd get it. Proof I was in hell: the Ant knew lots of things I didn't, and had to break them down for my understanding. "Not a place like Africa or the Mall of America. You can't get in your car and find it.

"Hell is a zone, a plane, where spirits can visit. Any spirits. At any time. You two are special because you still have your bodies. We"—she gestured vaguely—"don't anymore. In hell you're only limited by your imagination . . . just like heaven."

"I don't get it," I admitted, and boy, did that one hurt.

To my astonishment, the Ant didn't seize the opportunity to try and squash my ego or cripple my will to live. "No, I don't think either of you can—not right now. It's really, really hard to explain."

"Nevertheless," Satan said, popping in from wherever, "I shall try. Thank you, Antonia, that's all for now."

"Ma'am," the Ant said, and blinked out of sight.

"Wait! Shit."

"Have no fear nor fret, Betsy, you'll see her again."

"Don't you threaten me, Satan. I just had stuff I wanted to ask." Why did she haunt me right after she and my dad died? Why did she quit? Why did she play tour guide? Where was my father? Why did she choose to have awful hair in hell? These were the questions beating against my brain for answers.

"Is it true, Mother?"

"Which, darling?"

"Is my birth mother right? Are you lonely?"

"Of course." No denials. No sarcasm. Just a simple statement. I won't try to deny it; I was impressed. Why couldn't Satan be like this all the time? "I've lived long and long. It's why I had you."

"What?" I asked, because Laura suddenly seemed afraid to say anything.

"I want you to take over the family business," Satan said to her, as if Laura had asked the question. "I'd like to retire."

Chapter 28

"Retire where?" I asked, because I couldn't help picturing the devil buying a condo in Boca Raton. She could then go from angel to fallen angel to mistress of hell to retiree to snowbird to, inevitably, crazed nursing home resident.

"I don't know. But that's the beauty of retirement." Satan actually looked wistful. "Choices. You have choices."

"Mother, I had no idea." Laura was looking at the devil with sympathy writ large all over her pimple-free, wrinkle-free complexion. "You must be . . . I didn't know."

"You're not gonna be one of those stage mothers, are you? You know—they didn't win Miss Teeny Miss Whatever, so they raise their daughter to be Miss Teeny—"

"I wouldn't force Laura," Satan interrupted. "But I would ask. A mother can ask."

Now Laura's big enormous anime eyes were filling with tears. "You poor thing!" she cried. "You poor, poor—"

I interrupted again. Laura feeling sorry for Satan was not the plan. Laura taking over hell was soooo not the plan. I didn't know what the plan was, but I was sure it wasn't either of those. "But if you've been doing this for tens of thousands of years, how can—oh."

"What?" Laura asked.

"That odd look on her face?" Satan asked. "She isn't constipated. She's realizing something for the first time."

"Shows what you know. I haven't taken a dump since I died, so by definition I'm constipated all the time."

Laura frowned. "Uh, I'm not sure—"

"How long do you expect Laura to live?" I asked, working to keep my voice level and nonshrieky. Because none of this had occurred to me before. "Will she be like you? Are you immortal?"

"By my father, *no*." Satan actually shivered. The thought of what could give the Lady of Lies the shakes was giving *me* the shakes. "Just long-lived, like all my race."

"Angels?" Laura asked.

"Yes, for lack of a better word. We can be killed, certainly. But we never get sick and we age slowly."

"I'll say. You don't look a century over eight thousand." Of course, her *stolen shoes* helped keep her looking young, the hateful . . .

"When Father created us, he knew he would need helpers who had long life spans. A child can grow up in a decade and be dead not even ten decades after that." Satan snapped her fingers. "Like *that*! Poof. The light goes out."

"Yeah, the fruit flies of humanity," I said. "That's us. But why do you need to live long in the first place? Especially when the average life span these days is—uh—" Seventy-five? That sounded low. Ninety? Too high. Where was Marc when I needed him?

"Seventy-five for men," the devil supplied. "Eighty for women. Quite an improvement over, say, the Neolithic era, which was twenty. Can you imagine being considered a doddering elder before you could legally drink?"

"Stop it!"

Satan blinked. "Pardon?"

"Stop being so helpful. It's freaking me out." A thought struck me, and for a moment I thought I was going to fall down. "Retire—so Laura—how . . ." I tried again. "How long do you expect Laura to live? You yourself, you've lived for—"

Laura seemed to pale before my eyes. "M-mother? Will I—will I be as long-lived as you?"

Now, some people might be psyched to find out they could live for thousands of years. But Laura, who was occasionally a complete mystery to me, looked horrified. I could almost feel her counting up all the loved ones dying of old age, her parents, her friends, her future husband and children, and their children, and theirs, while she went on . . . and on . . . and on . . .

"I don't know," Satan replied, no screwing around, no smirky, mean grin. "I don't know how long you'll live, Laura. Nobody knows that, except maybe our father." A ghost of a smile. "And he's quite famous for hiding his cards."

Things were starting to make sense, but instead of liking it, I was becoming more uneasy. The devil might have a perfectly legitimate gripe and reason for getting me to bring Laura to hell.

And she might not.

Or it might be both. Either way, we were probably in huge trouble. If this was some big-budget movie, I, the intrepid heroine, would do something fabulous and heroic. But it wasn't a movie and I wasn't an intrepid heroine. I didn't even know what *intrepid* meant.

I turned to Laura. "Okay, so, we've had the tour and the devil wants to retire and it's possible you've got the life span of Japan, the U.S., and France combined. Let's retire back to earth and ponder. For years."

"Ah." Satan cocked her head. "One moment, please, ladies." Then she blinked out.

"Great," I fumed. "Stranded in hell. Too bad I didn't see this coming. Oh, wait, I did."

"She wouldn't strand us here," Laura said, sounding pretty reasonable for a half-angel psycho with a murderous temper and a loathing for lemon bars. "If nothing else, she needs me, right? She wants me to take over. Is it true?"

"Which part?"

"Will I live for a long time? Tens of thousands of years?"

"I don't know. But I'm thinking about the Book of the Dead."

"Which predicts you'll rule for five thousand years."

"That's the one."

We stared at each other, surrounded by the damned, sisters who had no control over events or even, sometimes, themselves.

"She needs me," Laura ventured after a long moment. "So she has to be nice. To both of us."

"That's true," I conceded. And it was probably why the Lady of Lies was being just sooo helpful today. "An awful lot has happened in a very short time."

"Par for the course, right?" Laura had a peculiar expression on her face . . . she was trying to eavesdrop into the hell cells without the people in the cells knowing what she was up to. "I can't thank you enough for agreeing to come."

"Chalk it up to brain damage. Ongoing brain damage, because I think I'm definitely in shock."

"Do you need to lie down? I guess I could ask one of the damned for a cot. Or maybe a quilt? Um, excuse me? Excuse me—sir? No, not you, sir, the one in the cell next to you having what looks like involuntary dental surgery . . ."

"Something's fucked up severe," I announced.

Laura came close to me, her hands fluttering ineffectually. "Do you feel faint?"

"Yep. Definitely in shock. Because I'm having trouble taking all of this in."

"It's okay, Betsy." The Antichrist patted my forearm. "It's hard for both of us, I think."

"For example, Laura, you have sprouted enormous wings. I think I probably should have picked up on that earlier. Yep, definitely."

"What?"

"Yeah. I'm pretty sure I should have. Weird. This is a very weird day."

Chapter 29

$\mathcal{I}$'ve got *what?*"

"Wings." Laura hadn't noticed, either. I felt less dumb.

"Where?" Laura twisted from side to side, which had the effect of someone wearing a backpack trying to *see* their backpack . . . every twist and turn just angled the item away. Which is how I ended up . . .

"Phhhfft!"

. . . getting a faceful of feathers.

I waved her away from me, spitting flight feathers. (Who knew that report I did on migratory snow and blue geese in eighth grade would have a practical application in hell?)

"Are they there? I can't believe it! What do they look like? I didn't feel a thing!" *Whack. Whack!*

I tried to wave her away. "Stop it, stop it, I can't see a thing except for primary and secondary feathers!"

"You know about birds?"

"Eighth grade. Never mind." I was reminded of the best Christmas movie with dead people ever, *Scrooged*, when Carol Kane's awesome Ghost of Christmas Present is twisting and jumping around and keeps whacking Bill Murray in the face with her wings. This was exactly like that, except it wasn't December, it was November. November in hell. "You want to see them? Pop them out. You know—extend 'em."

This was pretty dumb, because I was standing in exactly the wrong spot. So at about the same half second I realized Laura had a near seven-foot wingspan, her extending left wing crashed into me.

Those suckers were *strong*. Picture a sparrow, lean and tough from being busy all day. And also with long blonde hair, and jeans.

"Oh my God! Betsy!"

"Could you help me up, please?" I groaned from the floor. Hell carpet. Bowels of the pit. Whatever.

She hurried over to me and hauled me to my feet. Her wings weren't the stereotypical snow white you see in old paintings of angels. They really were like gigantic sparrow feathers—a plain but cute mix of mottled browns, powerful and practical.

"Sorry to disappear on you like that; I admit to being something of a micromanager. Oh, good, you've been doing some exploring."

"Mother! I have wings here. Wings!"

"Of course you do," Satan said, gazing upon Laura with maternal pride. "Your mother is an angel."

"It's so creepy when you refer to yourself in the third person."

"Shush. Satan doesn't wish to hear from the vampire queen at this time."

"Creepy!" I shouted.

But the devil wasn't paying any attention to me; she only had eyes for Laura, who, annoyingly, was even more striking with gorgeous yet practical wings sprouting from her back. "As I was saying before what's-her-name spouted off—"

"You're being a pill!" I said, keeping a wary eye on my sister's wingspan.

"—you're half angel. My lineage didn't change when I left heaven."

"Got kicked out, you mean."

I was very surprised to find my feet were a foot off the floor, as Satan had closed the five-foot distance in half a blink and hoisted me up by the front of my shirt. "I. Was not. Kicked out. I left. On my own."

"Touch-*y*! D'you mind? I've only worn this shirt twice; also, it's from Eddie Bauer, which means it's practically indestructible." So, a fine choice for a jaunt through Demon Town. Oh, Eddie Bauer, only you understand my vacation clothing needs.

"Let her go!"

Super. *Two* winged freaks battling over heaven, hell, and my turtleneck. "Laura, I'm fine." I tried a smile to show the Antichrist that being hoisted into the air and strangled by the devil wasn't such a big deal. Shit, I've been on dates that were less pleasant. "It's not like I need to breathe. Or mind dangling a foot off the ground. But if I have to grow my larynx back, you're gonna be sorry!"

"Worth it," Satan muttered, and let go.

Instantly I bent over and checked out my footgear. "You are sooo lucky I didn't get a scuff mark, you big, jerky fallen angel!"

"I tremble as I consider that close call," Satan said with a yawn.

"Will they work? I mean, can I fly?"

"What? Back on the wings again? After I had to suck up yet another felony assault from your mother? My Eddie Bauer shirt is *fine*; thanks for asking."

Satan's wings appeared out of nowhere just as suddenly as Laura's had. The malicious cow waited until I was out of Laura's line of fire, and into hers, before she showed us her damned (literally) wingspan.

"I have had enough"—I cut myself off and spat feathers again—"of facefuls of wings! Which is not a sentence I thought I'd ever, *ever* have to say! Hell just sucks, and that's all there is to it."

"Yours are all black, like raven's wings," Laura said, awed. She put out a tentative hand and stroked her mother's wing.

"Or really dirty ones. Like you spent a lot of time lurking in chimneys. Or the Koch refinery smokestacks."

The pseudo-angels ignored me. Getting to be a common theme around here, I was sorry to note.

"Of course they work," Satan was explaining. "But like anything, you will need practice. But you're mistaken in your assumption that they've only now 'appeared.' They have always been a part of you, just like your Hellfire weapons. But they can only be seen by all eyes in this dimension."

"So when I'm home—St. Paul, I mean—they're there, but no one can see them."

"Yes. It's too much for the human eye to take in. I'm not sure I'll be able to break this down for you, but I'll try. Our wings sort of shift between realities. Your Hellfire sword and crossbow are always with you but can be seen only under the right circumstance—for example, on earth, they can be seen when you are stressed, when you are vengeful. You call on them and they appear to all. But they were always there. You aren't making them appear, you're simply making use of them. Your wings are much the same."

"Like how Jessica can't always get a taxi. If she's somewhere late and deserted, cabbies don't always see her. They don't even think they're being bigots about it; they'd pass a lie detector test that they never even saw her." They both looked at me. "What? I'm trying to contribute to the weirdest conversation ever."

"Well, all right. And I will say you've come up with a parallel that isn't completely stupid or terrible," the devil admitted.

"Aw. I'm getting all choked up and everything."

"Choked, at the very least," the devil muttered. My! Satan was Ms. Crabby Pants today.

Chapter 30

It's time to get down to it," Satan said, and I managed not to shout, *It's about time, you angelic devilish psycho!* "I can talk—"

"And talk. And talk," I added. "And still: talk. Talk, talk, talk."

"—but experience is the best teacher."

"So! Much! Talking!"

The devil made a sound that was a cross between a sneeze and a snarl. "You've spent two decades on earth learning what it is to be human. Now you need to explore being an angel, for lack of a better word. You need to master moving from your father's lands to mine and back again. In this place, in my domain—hopefully someday to be your domain—you can get a more accurate idea of your potential, your abilities. I'm sure you've noticed I come and go as I please, and I imagine you're wondering how I can do that."

"Not really, no."

"Quiet, Vampire Queen. I was talking to the smart sister. From hell, Laura, you can travel anywhere on earth, and to any time. But accuracy and control require experience. To put it another way, you could read a dozen books on how to ride a bike but still not know how to do it when the bike is actually before you. So I want you to start traveling."

I didn't like the sound of this at all. "Travel where?"

"Wherever her abilities take her."

"Hold up, Lady of Lies. I agreed to bring her here. I didn't sign up for time-traveling field trips."

"Why do you think you're still in this conversation? So, dear one, are you game? Will you try?"

"No," I said at the exact moment Laura said yes. I turned to her. "Oh, come on! Do you really not see where this is going? You know how we end up accidentally neck deep in Fiends or killers or zombies or babies or werewolves? And then we're all, 'I shoulda seen this coming.' Well, we can! We can *absolutely* see this coming and you know it. In my opinion—"

"Which no one asked for," the devil snarked.

"It's a perfect time to run away like a craven dog. I am pro-craven dog. Let's be dogs together."

Laura was shaking her head with real regret, and with a sinking feeling I realized I was about to have two choices: ask the devil to put me back in my own time in my own house, or tag along with the Antichrist. Which was no choice at all; I had no intention of abandoning Laura while she was trying to learn new skills. The learning was essential to her sanity.

Besides, she was formidable but she didn't look it. God knew the kind of desperate characters she might run into (literally . . . God knew; I didn't). They'd eat her alive, prob'ly. Like I wanted that on my conscience this month of all months. Or any time, really. Two roomies dead in my service were plenty.

And Satan, that deceitful wretched bitch, knew it. She even smirked at me when Laura wasn't looking. Real mature. And I was self-aware enough to realize that if *I* thought someone was being immature, it was time for them to reexamine their life.

"Betsy, I have to learn. I can't—the dreams are so—I have to do this. But you don't have to come. In fact, I think you should—"

"Shut the hell up. Of course I'll come. Don't be a stupid bitch." Okay. Sharper than I'd intended, sure. But I was pissed. And scared. And *pissed*. "I hope *you're* happy."

"But I am, Betsy. I absolutely am. And unsurprised. I've been tempting people for an age; how could my own daughter resist?"

"That sounds a little creepy," Laura admitted.

"A *little*! Ugh. Satan, you're terrifying. And not in a good way. But don't get cocky."

"I defined cocky, you idiot. And how typical for you to underestimate me."

And how typical of you to be unable to resist telling me how smart you are. That's it, Satan . . . open wide . . .

"I can tempt anyone, Betsy. I was *this close* to talking Jesus into changing sides."

"You tempted Jesus?" I didn't bother to hide my shock . . . and I hoped I was hiding the admiration.

"Of course. And he gave it serious consideration. He didn't want to die, you know." For a moment, the devil looked pensive and a little sad. "He knew it was coming and he knew it would be awful. I offered to change all that."

I realized we were smack dab in the middle of hell as opposed to being on the periphery—all new tortures and degradations were going on around us. But I couldn't look away from the devil.

Her face. The look on her face.

"I told him he could be ruler of all earth, subservient only to me, if he renounced his control-freak father. Who is, if you recall your Sunday school lessons, also my control-freak father. I even threw in invulnerability to physical harm. *That* was the only one that truly tempted him. Nobody likes the idea of a bad death."

"But he said no?" Dumb question. Of course he'd said no.

She smiled, a wintry grin with no warmth. "Yes indeed. He told me he'd pray for me. He quoted Scripture to me; how dull. He told me to ask for his father's forgiveness. And I told *him* he would die with the smell of his own shit in his nostrils. And I was right."

"Mother!" Laura sounded shocked.

"You just don't like to lose." *Jeez. Poor Jesus!* Weird to think of the Savior as a flesh-and-blood teenager who was afraid to die, and more afraid to die badly. "That's why you got all pissy with him at the end. You set the standard for being a sore loser."

"Darling, I have never truly lost. Not when it was important. Not when it was something I very much wanted."

Umm, I thought but didn't say, *we're supposed to believe you wanted to be asked to leave heaven?* I arranged my face into a polite I'm-listening-go-on expression.

"The boy would have been amusing company, but his betrayal and death did nothing to inconvenience me, so it all worked out in the end."

I decided to pretend that didn't send cold chills down my

back. "So what you're saying is, Jesus was the one who got away?"

Satan snorted through her delicate nostrils. "I'm one of humanity's three enemies, along with sin and death."

"Don't forget taxes."

"Ha! Even I'm not that relentlessly greedy and evil."

"Point," I conceded.

"I'm simply a giver of knowledge."

"Actually, you're a giver of crap. A giver of headaches and menstrual cramps."

The devil ignored me, clearly much more interested in reaching Laura than sparring with *moi*. "Knowledge is like a hammer, you know. It's neither good nor evil. What matters is how you apply it. My father disagreed."

"God, you mean?"

"Of course, you twit."

"No one told me," I commented, "that there'd be so much name-calling in hell."

"We had a rather large falling out over that difference of opinion, in fact." Satan paused, examining the toe of her pretty, pretty shoe. "In retrospect, I could have handled it better."

"Ya think?" In retrospect, the Bubonic Plague sounded uncomplicated and pleasant compared to a war in heaven. Satan: the master of understatement. It reminded me of David Carradine's character in *Kill Bill*: "I may have over-reacted." Shyeah!

"My point, Laura, is that what you learn on your travels isn't good or bad. It just is. And you're probably the only person in several planes of existence who can learn any of this. My children," she added dryly, "don't precisely grow on trees. Laura is a ruby."

"Uh-huh, and I'm a Capricorn. So help me out here. Laura was born of the Ant—and thank you sooo much for arranging that little reunion, you awful, awful harpy—so that makes Laura her daughter, not yours."

"It doesn't, actually. I have no physical body. I've never had one; no angel has. We take the form best suited to please our father . . . or not. That's how I can possess mortals. So whomever I'm driving at the time—that person *is* me, with all my thoughts and griefs and abilities. In this way, I am your mother, Laura . . . as I was, for a time, Betsy's stepmother."

"Now you're just being mean."

"What is all this about any time as well as any place?" Laura asked, momentarily distracted as the three of us walked past Lincoln shooting John Wilkes Booth in the head. "Do you really mean that? You can time travel and maybe I can, too?"

"There is no maybe about it, Laura. Why do you think I've lived so long? Why do you think you will likely live well into your thousands?"

"I don't get it," I confessed, flinching as Lincoln popped another cap in John-boy's head.

"I am unsurprised."

"You don't have to be such a bitch about it. It's not my fault I partied too hard in college and got kicked out before I could—oh. Wait. That's completely my fault. Okay, bad example. But you're still a bitch."

Satan rubbed her forehead with her perfectly manicured fingertips, as if fighting a migraine, or a tax audit. "I'm not talking down to you, Betsy, though I'm certainly prepared to do so at any given moment. You truly—your human brain, you can't grasp it. Einstein couldn't grasp it."

"Oh, like Einstein is sooo great." I made a herculean effort not to sulk.

She sighed. "All right. Pay attention. Time does not move. We move. And some of us can move backward as well as forward. If the average sack of meat and blood and pus could manage the trick, could stand still long enough, they would eventually catch up to their childhood, even their birth."

"Wait. What? Oh, and that sack-of-pus thing? Gross."

"You're saying if you live long enough, you could reenter your own past?" Laura asked.

"Yes. Which is why no ordinary human could ever do this job. The human life span—" She snapped her fingers. "Like that."

"Yeah, well. That's how quick we're gonna be neck deep in shit." I snapped mine. "Like that."

Chapter 31

I must warn you . . . although theoretically you can travel to any time or any place, you'll be drawn toward those events that had a significant impact on you—or her." Satan pointed at—dammit!—me. "Because Betsy is part of your learning as well. And I will understand your dismay. Bad enough she's part of your blood, yes?"

"Don't talk about her like that," Laura said, but she had a peculiar expression on her face. Like she was somewhat concerned, but not all there. I think, in her head, Laura was *already* traveling to other zones and other times. "It's not nice."

"I only wanted to give you a last warning. As you mature, you won't necessarily be at Betsy's whims. But that could take time."

"Luckily, this all didn't sound awful and scary enough," I said. "I'm glad you've saved the worst for last." *We're stuck together because my sister and I are two of the few people on the planet with the potential to live for five thousand years. Ye gods.*

Take time? Like what? How much are we talking exactly? A baseball season? A school year? A decade? A century? Why do I have the feeling that spending a few centuries as sidekick to the Antichrist might have a detrimental effect on my sanity? Not to mention my wardrobe.

I shook my head but kept those thoughts to myself. "And again, thank you so much."

The devil shrugged. "It wasn't a coincidence that I shot-putted you into the parlor room wall so you could wake up here. I needed to show you a demonstration. The fact that your hollow, empty head sustained a concussion was just a bonus.

"You see, Laura is only *part* angel, something that has always held her back but which I could work around. Unfortunately, since I am complete in myself—"

"Complete in yourself?" I started to laugh.

"—my blood, my abilities, aren't diluted by a human strain. But Laura's are. I can move from here to there to there and back to here simply by the force of my will. Laura can't . . . at least, not yet. To move from place to place, or time to time, she needs to have strong physical contact with a blood relative. Her father is dead."

"No shell," I guessed. "Only his spirit. So no chance of physical contact with him." Satan raised her eyebrows. "What? I pay attention sometimes."

"Mmmm. So that leaves me. Or you. Which actually means you, Betsy, because she won't learn if she simply taxis along with me for the ride."

"What does strong physical contact mean?" I asked. "A face full of pillow? Should we cha-cha? Thumb wrestle? What?"

"It means strong physical contact. I shall now give you a few moments to deduce what I mean."

"Shows what you know. I won't need a few—hey. Uh. What? Hey! Dammit!"

"You may now curse me for twenty seconds."

"You tricky, treacherous, shoe-stealing cow! You *bitch*! This is so *bogus*! *What is wrong with you?* Why do you have to be so sneaky . . . and creepy! Aw, fuck a duck." I took an unnecessary breath and yowled, "I hate everything!"

"And . . . time."

"Especially you, Satan! Especially you!"

"Mmmm." Satan closed her eyes, a dreamy look on her face. "Those words are meat and drink to me."

Chapter 32

We were back in the tacky office-waiting-room section of hell. The devil wasn't kidding about how her will shaped reality here. Not that she was much of a kidder anyway. Although it seemed like we'd been walking and talking for hours, she turned us around and took something like three whole steps and *boom!* There was the waiting room again.

"As Betsy surmised, this room is symbolic of your ability to travel. As I said, your brains simply can't—"

"Since you said it, a few times, I think, why are you saying it again? Let's get this abortion over with."

"Watch your mouth," Laura said, looking irritated.

"Sorry. I guess being in *hell* where my sister has to *smack* me to teleport through *space* and *time* to avoid going *insane* has made me a little *grumpy*."

"That's enough, drama queen," Satan said, nicely enough.

"It's vampire queen. And I'll be the judge of what's enough

if you don't mind. And even if you do." I brightened. "Especially if you do."

"To leave, open a door and step through." Satan pointed.

I walked over and inspected the closest door. Pretty standard. It even had a red neon EXIT sign above it and an old-fashioned handle. There were at least half a dozen in the room, each spaced about two feet apart.

"To come back, Laura, you'll use your Hellfire sword to cut a doorway for you to return through."

Laura nodded. "All right, Mother. I'm not very good with it . . ."

"Yet," Satan said.

"I try not to use it."

"I trust that will change." Satan was unsmiling, even a little tense. "Your life will depend on it."

"Gosh, Satan. I've never seen this sentimental side of you. And I won't deny this; I feel cheered up. It doesn't sound like one single thing could go wrong with any of that. Sure, I was nervous at the start of the tour. But now all my worries have been thoroughly laid to rest."

"It may take several tries for you to make it all the way back," Satan cautioned, "but you know what they say about practice guaranteeing perfection."

"Nope," I said. "Nothing at all will go wrong. How could it? It's all so simple. So easy. So free of potential disasters."

"My hope," Satan continued, ignoring me, "is that eventually you will move all about the universe simply by thinking it. That you will need no props"—a vague gesture at me—"and no weapons."

"Speaking *as* the prop," I said, "aren't you going to give us a panic button or something? What if we're stranded somewhere dangerous?"

"Oh, I expect you will be," Satan said, terrifying me. "But you won't learn if I rescue you."

"But we could—" Wait. That wasn't the way to her black, black heart. "But *Laura* could get seriously maimed. Or killed. Or kidnapped by nuns and forced to marry Jesus. Or exposed to . . . uh . . . horny Boy Scouts."

"I know. It's a risk I'm willing to take."

The scary part? She was not kidding. At all. She'd really given it some thought and weighed Laura's possible demise against what her daughter could learn, and judged it worth the risk.

And I thought the Ant's maternal instincts were poisonous.

Chapter 33

"All right," I said, tapping one of the doors. "You wanna make with the teleporting, or should we find out how awful the restaurants are in hell?"

"I guess we'd better. The first one, I mean." Laura looked and sounded doubtful. And who could blame her? Never had an office waiting room looked so sinister to me, and that included the time I had to go to the DMV two days in a row to pass my driver's test. "So . . . I'll just . . ." She stretched out a hand and turned the knob. Which didn't move.

I tried it myself, which was as dumb as hitting the elevator button when I'd just seen someone else do it. It's like we all think *our* magic fingers will do the trick.

"So. Make with the strong physical contact."

Laura reached toward me with tented fingers. She rested them on my chest and sort of eeeeeased me back, then tried the door again. No luck.

"*Strong* physical contact," the devil reminded us.

"You're supposed to let her figure this out for herself, so back off. C'mon, Laura. You can do it." But I wasn't sure I wanted her to. If she couldn't pull this off, if she was *too* human, we could go home! Before more death and weirdness! I'd be able to give Tina a good laugh by describing hell.

For that matter, if I could have gone back to the mansion and grabbed someone to bring with us (assuming Satan would have obligingly played interdimensional taxi cab), it'd *be* Tina. She was supersmart and she didn't rattle, two qualities I didn't have, and thus admired.

"Um . . ." Laura gave me a friendly chuck on the shoulder. No joy.

"I think I'm going to leave," the devil said, sighing. "If I have to watch any more of this, I may vomit. Or kill one of you."

"Quiet back there. Laura, have I mentioned those nightmares you've been suffering have wreaked havoc on your complexion? You have *serious* bags under your eyes."

"Oh, I believe it. That's one of the reasons we're here. I can't thank you enough for being here with me."

Well, *great*. "And your clothes don't match. And your shoes are dead to me."

"Really? I know you don't think I should buy shoes at Target, but they're very pretty and inexpensive. What's wrong with my clothes, though?"

She glanced down at herself: conservative long-sleeved navy T-shirt, faded blue jeans. A wide, beat-up man's leather belt, I assumed one of her dad's (her adopted dad, I meant), made her waist seem even smaller than it was.

I would have looked like Owen Wilson if I'd tried to pull that off. But the masculine touch at Laura's waist just made her seem more beautiful and feminine. I pinched my nose and shook my head. Some days, it really didn't pay to get out of bed. Maybe Laura could master time travel really quick and take us to two days ago, and then I wouldn't be in hell trying to goad the Antichrist into socking me in the eye.

"I admit the jeans are a little big, but then Dad said I could borrow—"

"There's nothing wrong with them," I sighed. "You look beautiful." Damn the luck. "But . . . your midwestern accent! You sound like a cross between Frances McDormand in *Fargo* and Ed Rooney's secretary in *Ferris Bueller's Day Off.*"

"Wasn't she terrific in *Fargo*? So earnest and nice, but really smart, too. She's *soooo* talented. Did you see her in *North Country*?"

"Hells yeah! Can you believe that was based on a true— dammit! Let's try to focus."

"Okay."

"You have bad breath. And . . . your hair . . . is stupid."

She looked shocked and covered her mouth with her long, tapering fingers. This was getting us nowhere. I'd known my sister was good-natured bordering on comatose, but this was just stupid. Which was how I felt right now.

"Do you think I should switch toothpastes?"

"Fuck it," I said, and hauled off and slapped her face. The sharp *crack* seemed to fill the room. There was an even louder *crack* as her fist crashed into my nose.

I think I just got my second concussion of the night, I thought, observing that the room was getting wavy and . . . was that right? Yes. The room was going away.

Good-bye, weird office lobby in hell, good-bye . . .

Satan's laughter was the last thing I heard before the hell fell away from us.

Chapter 34

"top me if you've heard this before," I said, too scared to open my eyes, "but I hate everything."

"I'm so sorry! You surprised me. And it really stung! But you're not bleeding. If that, um, makes you feel better."

I cracked an eye open. Laura was bending over me, possibly starting a future crow's foot, she was frowning so hard. Oh, who was I kidding? She'd never have a wrinkle. "Don't do that. Your face'll freeze that way. Where are we?"

I sat up.

And instantly wished she'd hit me harder, so I could have enjoyed an hour or two of unconsciousness.

We were in the past, all right. Her first jump ever and she'd pulled off time travel. If the big, ancient-looking church wasn't a tip-off, ditto the eighty zillion horses and horse-drawn wagons, what I didn't see or hear would have given me the answer.

It was too quiet. No cars. No background hum . . . no horns, telephones, no ring tones. No streetlights. No motor-cycles or mopeds. No ten-speeds.

I could smell the ocean, but, more surprising, nothing really stank. I won't deny surprise; in addition to no motor-cycles, there was no deodorant, hairspray, or strawberry body scrub from the Body Shop. But the salty air was surprisingly clean and refreshing. And the town looked tidy and sweet. These old-timers were serious about keeping the place tidy.

I wondered if everywhere in America smelled like this right now. Smelled *real*, before we forgot what even dogs know and started shitting where we ate.

There weren't many forest sounds, though there were enormous trees just past the main street or path or road or whatever it was. An occasional bird call, but that was it.

Mostly what came to my ears were raised voices. Angry voices and frightened voices. Shouts and threats. Begging. Crying. Hectoring.

And it was all coming from the church, which appeared to be the focus of the town . . . it wasn't off to the side or tucked away. It was smack in the middle of everything, and it sounded like most of the townies were inside. Which made sense, since there were a number of horses hitched just out-side the big white building. Lots of wagons "parked." And nobody but us time travelers on the street. No, the action was inside the church, which was a huge break for us.

"Okay, so . . . should we go?" I let Laura haul me to my feet. "Do you know where we are?"

"Sure. We're in Salem, Massachusetts," she said.

"I'm not *that* ignorant." Well, I would have guessed a state that started with M for sure, though my first guess might have been Michigan. "Is that one of your supersecret devil powers? You always know where we end up?"

"No." Laura pointed over my left shoulder. I looked.

Plastered on what would be a bulletin board if it had been made of cork was the front page of the *Salem News*.

17 WITCHES HANGED; 58 MORE ARRESTED
TRIAL TODAY
June 10, 1692

"Ohhhh, shit."

Laura nodded. "Uh-huh."

"This is not a good place for two gorgeous and unhanged chicks like us to be."

"Betsy, I'm with you a zillion percent."

"Excellent! So. We know you can time travel. Good job, by the way. Remind me to mention your name to the Nobel committee. Now cut a door with your evil sword from hell and bring us back to your mom's house. In hell."

"Okay." Laura sucked in a breath and nodded. "I've never done this before. But now would be a good time to learn, I think."

"Please! It is not true! *Please!*"

"A very good time," she added. And all at once, her sword was in her right hand. It was like watching a bunny leap from a magician's hat. An evil, horrible bunny from a hat of purest evil. And as always, her sword glowed so fiercely, I could hardly peek at it. It was dazzling and dangerous. Rather like my kid sister.

"I am no witch! I am innocent! I know nothing about it!"

I glanced at the closed church doors.

"I do not hurt the children. I scorn it!"

Laura's lips were moving. "What?" I asked, most of my concentration elsewhere.

Again that same voice, the high pitch of a woman with her back to the corner and nothing but hyenas in front. "If I must tell, I will tell. It was no spell, it was a Psalm."

"Okay, Betsy. Here goes."

"Great, good, that's fine, whenever you're ready."

"It is all false. I am clear!" Whoever was speaking was still afraid but now beginning to be angry as well. Which I thought was kind of cool.

"I never afflicted a child. Never in my life. And all here know this!"

Laura was waving her sword around and talking. Probably to me. I was pretty sure to me. She was prob'ly ready to take us back to hell, or maybe she wanted to steal a horse.

"You do not know my heart. But I know yours. A sad thing, your vengeance. A pitiful thing."

She had some balls, this ancient woman from a zillion years ago.

"The only devil I ever saw was you, William Putnam. And you only saw the devil in me when I would not sell you our farm."

"What?" Ye gods! I knew the Salem witch thing was a bunch of uptight, sex-starved, religiously obsessed idiots killing dozens of innocent men, women, and children, but I hadn't known some people got killed—got hanged!— because other townspeople coveted their property.

"If I am guilty, God will discover me. So hang me, coward. Kill me, butcher. Send me to God, thief. But never will I admit to a sin I did not commit."

"Awesome!" Then, to Laura, "Stop waving that thing around. We're staying for a few more minutes."

My sister lowered her weapon at once. "What are you talking about?"

"Can't you hear that?"

"Hear *what*?"

"Then for the horrible crime of witchcraft, which you practiced and committed on several persons, it is the ruling of this court that you shall be hanged by the neck until you are dead."

That's what you think, fuck-o.

Chapter 35

Betsy, no! You can't!" Laura started to scurry after me. "Nobody's seen us and we can get out of here safely, and even if we couldn't, we can't interfere. Are you *nuts*?"

"All sorts of men and women and kids, *kids*, Laura! Hung for no reason at all. No. Worse than that. Hung because nobody could be bothered to stand up and say, 'Cut the shit, you Puritan fucks.' Well, I'm gonna."

I'd gone up exactly one step to the church doors when Laura tackled me from behind.

"Ow! Laura, if I get tetanus from splinters, I'm gonna have to walk for a long time to find an appropriately stocked ER." I tried to stand—I'd fallen right against the steps—but she was hanging on to my calves like grim death.

"We can't interfere!"

I stifled the urge to stomp on her knuckles. "Why not?"

Laura opened her mouth, but nothing came out. Unfortunately, that had no effect on her grip. For a cutie in jeans and her dad's belt, she had the grip of a crack-addled anaconda. "Come on, have you never seen a movie or read a book about time travel? Things always get worse when people meddle."

"Meddle?" I squatted and started gently prying her fingers off me. "You sound like you're channeling a villain from *Scooby Doo.* 'And I would've gotten away with it, if it wasn't for you meddling kids and your stupid talking Great Dane.' "

"You could make things worse!"

"Worse than this?" I gestured at the church, supposedly a symbol of light and love, but right now nothing more than a prison run by asshats.

"You could really screw things up. What if you accidentally kill—um—Benjamin Franklin's grandfather?"

"Jeez, Laura, I'm not going to kill anybody." Probably. "I'm just gonna give that awesome witch a helping hand. Not that she's a real witch." Probably.

"Please don't make this worse!"

"Oh *that's* nice! Do you recall me spending most of our field trip to hell explaining to you, multiple times, that we should not time travel, we should not teleport, you should not grow wings, and we should not go to hell in the first place? Huh? Because I remember it all very vividly, Laura. So don't get in my way now unless you're running for hypocrite of the year."

I bent down to loosen her grip again, but, stricken, she let go. Her big eyes were shining—she wasn't crying, but only just, and I instantly felt seriously shitty. "I didn't think of it like that. You're right. It's pretty mean for me not to support you when you've been doing so much to help me."

Well, nuts. That took the wind out of my sails. Call me a dumbass, but I almost didn't like it when people sincerely apologized while I was still mad. I'd be all puffed up and pissed, when, *whooooosh*. And you can't keep bitching after you get the apology. That is not cool at all.

"It's all right," I said, because it also wasn't cool to not acknowledge the apology I didn't want at that time. "Just, you know. Watch it. Or something."

"But I'm not going in there with you." Which would have been more of a threat if she weren't telling me this while following me up the stairs. "I'll just sort of hang back."

"Good idea. This won't take long. Then we can shuffle off to hell again."

Chapter 36

_I_ raised my foot, had a split second to admire my navy blue loafer (Misty Moccasin, Beverly Feldman, $265, because sandals didn't seem a sensible choice for hell) before my leg pistoned out and the church doors flew open, slamming back against the walls with a satisfying double crash.

"Don't even," I said as Laura cowered behind me, groaned, and covered her eyes. "This _is_ me being subtle, so don't even say it. Hey! Asshats!" I stomped down the aisle, ready to kick some uptight bigoted Pilgrim ass. "You guys. All you old white guys. And also your uptight wives. And why are there _kids_ in here? You want your children to watch you lie and get hysterical and trump up charges and scare and hang innocent people? Let me guess: there's gonna be a potluck supper afterward."

The woman on trial—it had to be her, she was standing in front—looked at me with eyes gone huge. And the first thing I noticed was how gorgeous she was.

Don't get me wrong, it's not like I surround myself with the deformed. If anything, I usually found myself hanging out with men and women who were obscenely good-looking (I had yet to meet the fugly vampire). Hell, Tina alone could have won Miss America blindfolded with two black eyes and a runny nose. And pimples! Okay, maybe not with pimples.

The would-be witch was quite small—the top of her head was way, way below my chin. But then, I was tall for an undead heathen.

Her hair, a gorgeous rippling brownish red, was piled on top of her teeny head. She had so much of it, it seemed as though the weight of all those tresses would yank her head back if she let them down.

Her skin was pale, except for two hectic flares of color on her cheeks—*not* blush. (I was pretty sure Revlon hadn't been incorporated yet.) It was the hectic color of anger or fright or excitement . . . or all three. And her eyes seemed almost to take up half of her face, enormous and so deep a brown they were nearly black, with dark slashing eyebrows and long lashes.

Her outfit was right out of a museum exhibit: a big fat dress—fat because of the hoopskirt thing. Big-time modest, too; she wasn't exposing so much as an elbow dimple. The gown, too, seemed to emphasize her tiny frame and delicate features; she looked like a kid playing dress-up.

Her dress was pale blue; her neckerchief thing was transparent white lace. Long sleeves, long skirt—I could barely make out the toes of her shoes when I glanced down.

She smelled terrific, like clean cotton and sunshine. If I could have bottled that scent and brought it back to the twenty-first century, Sinclair *and* Jessica could have thrown their zillions away.

She had only one piece of jewelry I could see: there was a

black ribbon tied around her wrist, and from it hung a little painting of an older woman. It was so small I could only make out the woman's graying brown hair and teeny-weeny face.

Taking in the would-be witch's museum-exhibit clothing had only cost me a couple of seconds, which was good because it meant people were still astonished, and no one was sneaking up behind me to brain me with a hymnal.

I pointed to the gorgeously wronged Massachusetts resident who stared at the tip of my finger and backed up a step. "You think this is a witch? This is not a witch, jerk-offs."

"Be gone from here, wretch, and cover yourself!"

"Okay, um, *no*. And is that any way to introduce yourself?"

"To be fair," Laura called from the back of the church, "by their standards you're wearing the Puritan equivalent of a garter belt and peekaboo bra."

"Oh yeah?" I looked at the other person standing, the guy, I figured, who was after the lady's farm. He, too, looked like he'd stepped right out of a colonial America clothing exhibit ("Gift shop on your left, and yes, we validate parking"), with a white linen shirt, black culottes (or whatever men's suit pants that only came to the knee were called), and a matching black coat with dazzling gold buttons.

He was clutching a cane so hard his knuckles were white. So was his face, but from fear or rage I hadn't yet figured. I was smelling lots of fear, sure, but it was coming from the pretty brunette, not to mention the thirty people sitting in pews behind us.

"Tell me, do my awesome leggings and Eddie Bauer shirt make you bitches nervous? Hmmm?" I wriggled my shoulders back and forth, shaking my tits at the head asshat, whose face went redder. Cool. If I flashed him, I could probably give him a stroke. Ah, good times. "Or is it just female sexuality in general that freaks you out?"

The congregation was too startled to so much as murmur, and they were shaking their wriggling fingers at me. At first I thought I was observing the invention of American Sign Language. Then I realized they were all forking the sign of the evil eye at me. Ha! If that didn't work for my old babysitter, it sure wasn't going to help them.

"This is what you do? Because TV and the Internet haven't been invented? You make up lies and then hang your neighbors? Or rack them? Or crush them to death under big rocks? Pathetic, with a capital *P*."

Dead silence. Nobody was even shifting their weight.

"Wow, really? Nothing to say? Because I heard plenty from outside. Cat got your tongue? Or maybe the devil?

"You want a witch? You think torturing people will save your moldy black souls? Do you *really* think when you show up at the Pearly Gates, God's not gonna have *serious* questions for you? And especially you, fuck-nuts."

The man in the black suit was, I just now noticed, clutching a Bible, which made me laugh.

"You think lugging that around means God's not gonna want to give you the old one-two punch and send your ass to hell? How will you ever justify telling him that you lied and sentenced an innocent to death . . . so you. Could get. A farm. A farm! When there are, like, a hundred people in the whole country right now and zillions of acres up for grabs! When you're living in a time when there is more than enough land and resources for every single person on the planet, you *piece* of *shit*!"

I was seriously considering placing a private bet on when

he'd pass out. He stood straighter and straighter, and got whiter and whiter. "You will not speak so, witch!"

"Oooh, that hurt my feelings." I yawned.

He brandished the Bible. In fact, he'd been clutching it so tightly, his fingers had left marks in the leather. I was willing to bet Mr. Big Shot hadn't been talked to like this by anyone, never mind a saucy wench dressed in what he assumed was her whorish underwear.

(I had whorish underwear, of course. But *he* was never going to see it. That was strictly Sinclair's domain. Mmm. Better not think about him, or I'd start worrying about that weird stupid fight.)

"—to the bowels of hell!"

"What? Sorry, I zoned out for a few seconds. I assume you predicted I'd go to hell? You think that scares me, the day I've had?"

I turned to the woman. "And you. Are you okay? They didn't start with the torture before I got here, right?"

"That—that is correct, ma'am."

"Actually, you can call me B—" Laura made frantic hand slashing motions . . . hmm, good point. "Beverly," I finished. "Beverly Feldman, yeah, that's me." *If only.*

I turned back to the congregation, who were frozen in shock or fear or anger or maybe all three. "That wasn't rhetorical, by the way," I said, addressing them as well as the head jerk-off. "I really do want to know how you can reconcile deep, honest religious faith with *this*." I pointed at the tiny brunette. "What's she supposed to have done, anyway? Do you even know?"

Nobody said a word, and then I got another surprise. *She* spoke up. "They claim I . . ." Her voice shook, and she made a visible effort to steady it. I could see her throat working as she swallowed and tried again. "They say I witched their cheese and their milk."

"Witched it?"

"It spoiled. It went bad. They—they say I did it a'purpose."

I gaped, then whirled. "You decided she's a witch because no one's invented *refrigeration*? Dairy products go bad because you're storing them in warm cupboards but that's *witchcraft*?"

"It seems flimsy to me," Laura called from the back.

I was so furious I was actually dizzy with it. There were so many bitchy, sarcastic observations to make, I was having a sarcasm stroke. "My God! You people! You're—you're so stupid you're making my eyeballs throb. They're throbbing, dammit!"

Their duly elected witch started to laugh, which she then choked off by clapping both hands over her mouth.

"No, no," I said. "Don't be nervous. Laughing? Just now? Is totally the correct response. If you can't get to a gun, I mean. What else?"

"I would not marry."

"Uh-huh. Let me guess. Jackass McGee here, right?" I jerked a thumb toward Black Suit.

"He is called Will—"

"Silence yourself, witch!" he roared, and finally his face was getting some color.

"William. Putnam," she said, and her voice wasn't shaking at all now, nope. From the look she leveled at him, I half expected Putnam to burst into flames. That would have been a cool way to end our trip. "He funded the building of this church. He thinks it is his church and his town and that we are all his, and he does not like that I am not."

"Mmm, wow, there's nothing more attractive than a sore loser who's also a bully. The ladies must love you, Putnam."

"It's true," Laura called. "That's just terrible, Mr. Putnam. Little kids know better."

"Yeah, well, maybe not in this time and place. That explains why you're up here, cutie."

I was walking back and forth, almost pacing, while I voiced my thoughts. "But how about the other ones? The ones you guys killed? The ones you arrested and *will* kill? You got them stashed somewhere? Jail, I'm guessing? And for what? So you can get your name in the paper as the big bad witch hunters? Well, why?"

I took another look at Black Suit. Yes, he looked quite tidy and prosperous. In fact, he was the nicest dressed guy in the room. Built the church. Liked getting his way. "Let me guess. Political aspirations?"

The congregation seemed to sigh all at once.

"Aw. That's just charming." I glanced at Laura, who was making time-to-go motions. And she was right, we'd certainly pushed our luck more than long enough. But I wasn't satisfied. I didn't want to leave just now. This will sound weird, but I was hoping the jerk-off would try something really stupid so I could—

He took three quick steps (more like stomps, actually) forward and brandished his cane. "Witch! Filth! Devil's whore!"

"Well, which one is it?" I asked.

"Be gone from this place! Cover your nakedness, cover your lewd flesh, lest you tempt honest men from God's path!"

"Oh, thank you," I cried, jerking back so he couldn't brain me—the brass tip of his stick was easily two inches across, and he swung it like it had some heft. I heard the soft *whshhh* as it passed about three centimeters from my nose. "You've made me so happy."

Chapter 37

I caught the stick. Yanked it from his grasp and heard a teeny *crack*, like a skinny breadstick being snapped in half. Putnam yelped like a pup, and I realize I'd snatched it so hard and so quickly I'd broken one of his fingers.

Awww.

I snapped the stick in half with my hands alone (no breaking over the knee for *this* vampire chick). Tossed the pieces over my left shoulder, where they hit the floorboards with a clatter that probably sounded louder than it actually was.

Then I seized Putnam by his lapels and yanked him forward.

There it was. I could smell it now. The thing I had been looking for. The thing I needed from Putnam before I could walk away.

Fear.

"Here's the thing, Billy-boy." We were eyeball to eyeball

and again, I have to hand it to the Neanderthals . . . I could smell more of cotton and linen and wood than anything else. I'd assumed everything prior to, say, 1930 or so would smell like mud and shit. "None of the people you killed were witches. And none of the ones you had arrested are witches. And the young lady here—"

"Caroline Hutchinson," the would-be witch offered.

"Yeah, her. Also not a witch. See, Putnam, you couldn't tell a witch if she offered to strip and sit on your face."

"Gross!" Laura said.

"Hard times call for hard talk," I said, which was total bullshit; I just wanted to rattle Putnam's cage. He was like a big fat worm I wanted to poke and poke. And then set on fire.

"You know how I know these things, Buttmunch?" I'd started shaking him like a maraca. "Because I'm a vampire. And the pretty blonde in the back? She's the daughter of the devil."

"You have a lovely church," the Antichrist called.

"And the thing is? Even though I'm a vampire? Check it." I let go of him with one hand to snatch away his Bible and held it up over my head. "Please note that I'm standing in a church and the only reason I feel sick is because you're stupid. Please note how the Bible isn't giving me a sunburn. That's because I believe in God and I love him. Although sometimes we go awhile without speaking because the good Lord *will* insist on always getting his way. My sister back there? She believes, too. And she wouldn't burn an innocent woman to death if you stuck a gun in her ear."

"That's so nice, Beverly!" The Antichrist was beaming.

"So what does that tell you, Putnam? Huh? For those of us not keeping up, I'll lay it out: it tells you that you're gonna have *lots* and *lots* to answer for when you die. Which will hopefully be in the next half hour."

"Do your worst, pit spawn!"

"Don't be stupid. I promised the Antichrist I wouldn't kill you. Heck, who knows how long you could stick around?" Wikipedia, maybe, if he'd been a big shot. There were probably entire lists of all the parties involved in the whole let's-pretend-our-neighbors-are-witches campaign.

"I'm glad you remembered your promise," Laura said.

"You could hang on for a couple of decades. But sooner or later, there's gonna be a reckoning. You, and these sheep—" I jerked him toward the pews, then yanked him back until we were face-to-face again. "See, I'm not threatening, I'm warning. Nobody lives forever. So you guys might all want to get your stories straight."

Then I dropped him. He hit the floor ass first and stared up at me like a man who'd gotten the shock of his life. Which I guess he had.

I handed him his Bible, and he held it up as if to ward me off. Or hide behind.

"Cut the shit," I suggested. "Let the others go. Stop lying to increase your land ownings. Trust me: you don't want us to come back. Ever."

"It's true," the Antichrist said. "Beverly Feldman will probably be even less polite next time." She added in a mutter, "If that's possible."

"I heard that," I snapped. "So, to sum up, everyone, behave or, you know, face our wrath and stuff." I grabbed Caroline's arm. "Come outside with us for a second."

I took a last look around at the good people of Salem, shook my head in disgust, and followed Laura out the door and down the steps, hauling Caroline along for the ride.

Chapter 38

Okay, listen." The three of us were back on the quiet, deserted street. I could hear excited and urgent murmurings inside, but nobody had gotten up to follow us. "We have to go now, Cathy—"

"Caroline."

"Yeah. But the thing is, I can't let this ruin your life."

Caroline blinked big, pretty eyes at me. "You have saved my life. I do believe you are witches. Though my thought is that there can be good witches in a world as strange as ours."

Honey, you don't know from strange. Still, I admired her guts. I could only assume most people in her shoes would be drooling like drunk chimps by now.

"Right, strange world, yep, good witches, okay. I just wanted to tell you that the deck won't always be stacked like this."

"Deck? As on a ship?"

I glanced at Laura, who shrugged. I took an unnecessary breath. "Okay, this is going to take a really long time and it can't. All I'm saying is, women aren't always going to be on the bottom of the dung heap of life. So you can't let a day like this make you think there's no point in following the rules if all it's going to get you is burned alive.

"There'll be a time when you can vote. You can be doctors, you can be mayors and governors and you can run for president. I mean, you won't see it, and your kids won't, but trust me when I say, better times are on the way.

"You don't have to get married and have kids if you don't want. You can decide for yourself if you want to join the army or stay home and make babies or run off and join the circus. You just—you just kinda gotta hang in there, you know?"

Caroline nodded once, cautiously. "Is it your wish to tell me there is no call to despair?"

"Yeah! Exactly. No call for it. At all. So just—you know. Keep being brave and gorgeous and things will work out."

"You are kind to lie, but a lie told in friendship is still untrue: I am not brave."

I laughed, but nicely. And Laura smiled at her. "Uh, sure, hon. You were *so* not brave, in fact, you called the richest guy in town a thief to his face and dared him to kill you. If that's not brave in your book, I can't wait to see what is."

"That was my woman's vanity, my pride," Caroline practically mumbled, clearly embarrassed or ashamed. "I did not speak for being fearless; I was angry."

"I know. Most people in your shoes would have been pissing themselves. Caroline Henderson, you're one in a million."

"Hutchinson," she said. "And I thank you, good lady, for your efforts on my behalf and your great kindness."

"Well, if we ever meet up again, you can buy me a Frappuccino and we'll call it even."

I took her tentatively proffered hand and shook it gently, and let go. The teeny portrait around her wrist banged against my hand, so she put both her hands behind her back, as if afraid I'd been offended.

"Maybe you should leave town, Caroline," Laura suggested. "We aren't saying you were wrong, but they might take it in their heads to punish you for what we did."

We, that was classy. Since it wasn't we at all; it was me.

"I had already given your wise advice to myself," she said wryly. "And i'truth I would not stay here if they all fell to their knees and swore upon their souls to be kind. I have money saved away. I shall go west."

"Really?"

"My heart has been there long and long," she said, but didn't elaborate. And why should she? Her business was her business.

"Okay. Well. Good luck with the west and all."

"Good luck with the Lord's work."

"Uh. What?"

"Is that not what you are doing, you and your kin? You are saving the wrongly condemned; you are doing his work."

"Not exactly," I replied, even as Laura was fighting a grin. "But we appreciate the sentiment. Don't we, little sister?"

"Yes indeed, Beverly." Laura also shook Caroline's hand. "Go well with God, Miss Hutchinson."

"And you," she replied, and spread her skirts and dropped a perfect curtsy, so pretty it was like a dance.

That was Salem, Massachusetts.

Chapter 39

I can't believe this worked out so great."

"It's something, all right."

"And the blue ribbon goes to the Antichrist," I said, making no secret of my relief and admiration. "Time and space travel accomplished simply by the force of your will, in about seventy seconds."

"It was no big deal."

"I agree! The movies have lied to us, Laura. Time travel's a piece of cake, and you just proved it. I'm not denying it: I am *im*-pressed. And also a tiny bit scared."

"Betsy . . ." Laura began with a rebuke.

"But that's normal, right? When big sisters find out their little sisters can twist the rules of space and time like a wad of damp paper towels? It would be weird if I *wasn't* freaked out. In a supportive way," I added, holding my hands up in a calming gesture. "Freaked out in a loving and respectful way.

Gently freaked out, I guess, is a better way to put it. Softly freaked out. Sweetly freaked out . . . ?"

Laura's expression relaxed into a wry smile. "Okay. I'll admit, this whole, um . . . how can I put this in a way that isn't—"

"This whole time-traveling-from-hell-and-then-back-to-hell thing. There's no way to pretty it up, Laura. There's no way to say any of that in a way that isn't startling and weird."

"It went better than I thought."

"Way better."

"In a way, you could describe the last thirty-five minutes as—"

"Awe inspiring."

"Anticlimactic."

"No!" we both cried at the same time. I shouted down Satan's stepchild with, "Awe inspiring in the sense that *all* our adventures should be like this. We should *aspire* for more days where there's lots of fretting but no real damage of any kind. We should feel *awe* that we haven't realized before now that these weird things that keep happening do not have to have a body count!"

"Don't misunderstand; I'm glad no one was hurt. I don't want people to get hurt. Most people," she added in a mutter I found a tad terrifying. "But this seems wrong, somehow. Like we forgot to do something. If this was an action movie, we'd only be into the second hour."

"But it's not. So we aren't. And what, are we standing here all day or what now? C'mon. Let's go find your mom and tell her we accidentally left Salem a smoking crater. Then, while she's still screaming, we tell her she can't plan on retiring for at least eight thousand more years. Oooh, the look on her face! Let's make it ten thousand."

"What do you mean?"

"Eight thousand just doesn't sound bitchy enough."

Laura shook her head. "Not that. What did you mean about standing here all day?"

I stared at my sister. We'd been having this entire conversation, patting each other on the back the whole time, in hell's waiting room. Did she need a puppet show? Signs?

Once we'd gotten out of sight, once the church was beyond the hill and Catherine or Carol or whoever couldn't see, Laura had hauled out her Hellfire sword—*bink!*—sliced a big half circle through the air, we clasped hands, she stepped, I stepped, we both stepped through, and here we were in the waiting area.

Ta-da!

"I've been standing here talking to you because I assumed you had something to say, eventually, and when you were finished, finally, we could then walk out the door and into hell proper."

"Okay, well, we're gonna talk about that snotty little eventually-finally thing you just did there, but we'll do that later. What are you saying?"

"There *is* no door."

"What? There's tons."

"Yes, those. But there's no exit anymore. Look around."

There was no denying the sinking feeling . . . which was interesting, given that my blood barely moved and my heart barely beat, but stress and adrenaline still felt like sinking, swooping dismay.

But yeah. Laura was right.

There was no door.

Chapter 40

O kay, don't panic!"

"Betsy."

"We just need to calm the hell down!"

"All right."

I had my sister by the shoulders and shook her briskly. "Just don't go all hysterical on me, Laura! Stay calm! Stay focused."

"It's hard for me to see when you do that," the Antichrist pointed out politely, and I could see what she meant. What with all the shaking, her hair was flying around like blonde cotton candy.

"Sorry! I'm a little freaked out!" I let go of her and tottered around the room, fighting the urge to rend my clothes or tear my hair out. "Okay, let's see. Let's just calm down and see."

Except there wasn't much *to* see. It was the same old waiting room. But there was no way to leave the room. So it was the nasty carpet and the flickering fluorescents and the beat-up receptionist's desk. And doors, of course. Lots of closed doors. Lots of locked doors.

"I think," Laura said, studying the room, "our celebration was a little premature."

"No shit."

"And I think we're supposed to pick another door."

"My! We're really clever today, aren't we?"

"Better clever than bitchy."

"Hey!" She looked at me and waited, eyebrows arched, but I shrugged. "Yeah, I got nothin'. I *was* being bitchy. It's my superpower."

Laura seemed to lighten up a little. "So we can run around this stinking little room and yell and have hysterics. Or, we can get back to work."

"I s'pose doing both isn't an option."

"It is, but it seemed so dumb and bitchy, it was hardly worth mentioning."

"You're enjoying yourself."

She shrugged and smiled. "Not . . . entirely."

"Ugh. Fine, fine. You know what? My own stupid fault for being dumb enough to think we could go to hell and travel through time and things *wouldn't* suck." I threw up my hands again. "Pick a random door, which will throw us into a random corner of hell. Or earth. Or earth's past. Good thing we've got a guarantee that nothing will go wrong. Oh, wait! We *don't*."

Laura grasped a handle. Shook it briskly—no joy, locked firm. Then her eyes widened and she pointed. "What happened to your shoe?"

Terror the likes of which I rarely felt unless someone was on fire rose in me, and even before I looked I had a shriek ready. But it was weird, because I couldn't see my shoe at all.

All I could see was . . .

. . . was . . .

How come I could only see Laura's fist and why was it coming at me in slow motion and wow my head hurts a lot but at least I'm a fast fast fast fast

A fast healer! That was it! That's what I was.

Yup. Definitely.

Right?

Chapter 41

This time, I just stayed where I was. I didn't even open my eyes. "Hey, Laura?"

"Yes?"

"There wasn't anything on my shoe, right?"

"Right."

"Thank God. Nice fake-out."

"I'm very sorry." But . . . was that a muffled giggle I heard? She might think she was sorry, but deep down where she really lived, she probably wasn't. So was this good for me, or bad for me?

And where were we now?

I opened my eyes—and yelled. "Aggh! I'm blind! That rotten bitch-cat mother of yours arranged for me to be—"

"Betsy."

"—cruelly blinded because she's jealous—"

"Oh, Betsy, jeepers!"

"—of my awesomeness in general and also my shoe collection, which will—"

"For heaven's sake."

"—never be hers, never, I tell you! I'll set every pair on fire myself if I have to. Oh God, my poor babies. I'll burn 'em and then give 'em all an acid bath—"

"Will you shut up and just look?"

"—which is the least of what I'm gonna do to that rotten—oh, hey, I'm not blind anymore."

I sat up, blinking. Laura had crossed the floor and yanked at what looked like shutters for the inside. There was a clatter, dusty light fell onto the floor, and I realized we were on the first floor of a barn. An old barn—it was cow and cat free. It smelled like ancient shit, dust, dirt, and corn.

"It's late afternoon outside," Laura was explaining as I hopped to my feet and crossed the room to look out the grime-streaked window. "I dragged you in here . . . I wasn't sure if you'd wake up or not."

"Dragged—" I glanced over my shoulder and groaned. Yep, dirt from my shoulders to my calves. Where was I going to find a pair of leggings in my size, in a color that didn't make me think of dried puke, and long enough to fit my freakishly long frame? "Aw, shit. I foresee problems ahead, kiddo. For starters, depending on where we are, it's possible the inventor of leggings hasn't been born. Or has, but hasn't been to high school."

Laura shrugged. "Sorry. It was all I could think to do."

"And it was perfect." I looked out the window again. Another small town. And no streetlights. No telephone poles or lines that I could see. And no electric lights—not that I could see, anyway. "I know, you're used to me squawking for longer, but time is precious, my little time-traveling tadpole.

Dragging my big butt in here was sensible and quick. We need not speak about the damage to my leggings at this time."

"Oh. Well." Laura ducked her head, and I could see, even in the dim light of the barn, she was blushing. She could be so adorable when she wasn't lying about shoes and giving her only beloved sister her second bloody nose of the day. "Thanks. I—you know, I feel stupid, but it never occurred to me. I know you won't burn in sunlight, but . . ."

"But what else will we have to worry about, right?"

"No offense," she added hastily.

"Yeah, I know I'm a vampire, Laura. You don't have to worry about pointing stuff like that out. Well, I used to be out cold from sunrise to sunset. Then . . ." I had started brushing dust and dirt off my clothes, and swallowed two sneezes in half a second.

"Then you read the book."

"Yeah. Big mistake—bit Jessica, raped my husband—"

"What?"

"And started waking up a couple of hours before sunset. Not exactly a trade I was looking for, but . . ." I shrugged.

"Okay, well." Laura sneezed, and like everything she did, it was cute and delicate. Like how bunnies sneeze. "I'd like to circle back to the raping Sinclair thing."

"Perv."

She laughed. "I deny nothing!"

"It's always the virgins. Those are the ones you gotta watch." I usually made a concerted effort not to think about the Antichrist's love life, but one of these days, my not-even-drinking-age sister was going to lose her virginity, and it'd be great if nothing too world-ending was happening that same week.

And why was I thinking about Laura's sexual inevitability when we were time traveling and I had dirt down my shirt?

Because, I answered myself, *it's something to worry about that doesn't include time travel, or hell.*

Yeah. My brain was like everyone else's—when I got stressed, I couldn't help thinking about stuff that was so *not* important to current events.

"But maybe," Laura was saying, "I can worry about my poor brother-in-law's rape—"

"It wasn't a rape exactly. I mean, he was all for it. But he didn't notice I was evil."

Laura nodded politely, then resumed where she'd left off. ". . . at a time when we're in our own century."

"Yeah, you noticed the lack of traffic, smog, electricity, and iPods, too, huh?"

"Yes. Also the lack of an ocean."

"So not Salem again."

"Most likely not."

"D'you think this is like episodes of *Knight Rider?*"

"I don't know wh—"

"Never mind. I hate being reminded of how young and dumb you are."

"Don't you mean young and gorgeous?" Laura grinned at me.

I started to grin back, always ready for some friendly-like joshin', when I stopped. There was something I didn't like about that smile. And since when did Laura actually own her gorgeousness?

Time traveling—or maybe just hanging out in hell— was giving her all sorts of confidence. I was remembering other incidents—hell, *this* time around she'd knocked me on my ass before I'd barely realized we were headed out of hell.

A far cry from her earlier, tentative efforts . . . the devil had been so scornful of those she'd threatened to leave.

So, yeah. I was uneasy and getting more so. Trouble was, was I threatened by that because she was young and hot and smart? Or was I threatened because—ha, ha!—she was supposed to take over the world one of these days?

"I guess my point was, d'you think we're supposed to do little jobs whenever we jump through time's door, so to speak? Or is it enough to just be here, before we try to go home?"

Laura shrugged. "I don't know."

And she didn't seem particularly worried, either way.

What's to worry? my inner bitch whispered. *She's the one who can move from world to world, and time to time. You're the one who's riding her like a taxi. So what happens when Laura realizes you're so much dead weight?*

Hell if I knew.

Maybe literally.

Chapter 42

So, what? Should we go outside?"

"To do what?"

I gestured, but I'm not sure why. Frustration, maybe. Anyway, I was waving my arms in a darkened dirty barn, leaving a cloud of dust wherever I paced. "Look for someone to help, maybe?"

"You're assuming we helped Caroline," Laura pointed out. "We might have messed up the time stream. She might have been fated to die and will instead live to be the great-great-grandmother of another Hitler."

"Yeah, and if my grandma had balls, she'd be my grandpa. But she doesn't. And she isn't. Look: we can do the coulda-shoulda-woulda dance until our knees lock and it won't help. So, we either stay here in McBarn Town and try to get back, or we go out, take a tour, save someone (or not), and then try."

"Well, okay, but you're assuming—"

"Kids? Kids! You put that wagon in the barn, then c'mon and help your mother finish packing!"

I must have flinched pretty good, because Laura seemed startled. "What? Is someone coming?"

"A couple of someones," I said just as the double doors at the other end of the building opened. "But I don't think we're in the soup just yet."

The couple of someones were short. And young. And cuter than bugs' ears. They were lugging a wooden wagon—the homemade version of the Little Red Wagon, I figured—and stopped short when they saw us.

"Oh, hello," the boy said. He was exactly the same height as his sister, and they were portraits of extreme cuteness.

They both had dark hair, carefully trimmed so they had matching bangs. The girl's was longer, and braided; her braid was long enough to touch her own butt.

Other than that, and the fact that the girl was wearing a checked yellow dress (with filthy bare feet—a sensible precaution in a family that probably saved their shoes for church), they were portraits of identical cuteness.

Twins! Like anyone who wasn't a twin, I thought they were fascinating yet creepy. These two hadn't fled screaming, which I couldn't help admiring.

"Hi, kids," I said.

Laura followed with, "We're not dangerous," which I thought was a rather large lie.

"What happened to your clothes?" the girl asked, seeming more surprised than frightened.

"Where to begin?" I answered. To Laura: "I thought we were in a town, not on somebody's—"

"Our farm's on the edge of the Grove," the boy explained.

He was wearing a dirt-streaked linen shirt in dark blue, and black trousers. And little suspenders! Also bare, dirty feet. His eyes were so dark I couldn't pick out the iris from the—the other thing in the eye that wasn't the white part. (It wasn't the first time I'd come to regret getting a C– in Biology.) "Past our place is just country. Town's the other way."

"What town?" Laura asked.

The boy opened his mouth to answer just as a piercing shout made all four of us jump. Laura didn't have any trouble hearing *that* one; none of us did.

"Erin! Eric! You two get in here and get these puppies out of my kitchen!"

"Oh God." I groaned. I'd forgotten all about this potential disaster. "Puppies." I looked at my sister. "We so don't want to hang out if they get a whiff of me."

Laura nodded but couldn't keep the grin off her face. She knew one of the more annoying consequences of my being undead was the fact that dogs drooled and slobbered helplessly when they saw or smelled me. That would have given the Salem thing the final, surreal touch: freeing witches, fighting with town elders, then being chased from the church by packs of baying, slobbering canines. Ugh.

"Sorry to bother you," Laura said to the girl. "We'll get out of your way."

"But your clothes," the girl—Erin?—was persisting. "Why are you wearing such funny underwear? Don't you have proper—"

"*Erin and Eric Sinclair!* You two get your butts in this house right *now*! These dogs aren't gonna let themselves out!"

"Oops," Erin Sinclair said, not looking too freaked. "Mama's getting mad."

"We're s'posed to start to move to Minnesota tomorrow," my future husband told the Antichrist. "We're not done packing. But we almost are."

"She's not mad about the packing," Erin Sinclair explained to the freakish strangers in her barn. "She just doesn't want t'move to Minnesota. Aunt Tina's making her."

"It's *private* business," her twin said, managing to look intrigued and scandalized at the same time. "Not supposed to tell *strangers*."

Laura didn't reply. I contributed to the nothing by saying . . . nothing. Shock had my vocal cords in a vapor lock.

"Well . . . 'bye," my soon-to-be-dead sister-in-law said, giving me a small wave.

As for the boy? He smiled at me, a shy grin, then trotted after his twin. He looked back, once. "You're goin' now?"

I managed a nod. Got another cute smile for my trouble, and then the wooden doors slammed shut.

Which was good, since I was going to fall down pretty much any second.

Chapter 43

Okay," I managed after what felt like ninety minutes. "Okay. That's . . . okay?"

"We're on your husband's farm!" Laura had grabbed my arm, and her sensibly short nails were doing a dandy job of sinking into my tender vampire skin. "Your husband's family's farm!"

"Not for long. Argh, quit it!" I removed her claws from my flesh. "They're moving, remember?"

"So Sinclair's parents were farmers?" Laura goggled at me. "*Farmers?* I thought he was—I don't know—a trust-fund baby. Or something."

"Yeah. It seemed weird to me, too. When we met, I mean." I shook my head. Fucking time travel; it made polite conversation impossible. "In the future, I mean. It was weird. Here's this big rich classy scary vampire guy, and he got his start farming. I always thought that was kind of funny. I mean, I'm not wrong—Sinclair dresses like a city boy."

Laura nodded. "He sure does. And didn't you tell me his whole family . . . ?"

"Yeah. Died. In fact, Tina found him in the cemetery the day of his parents' funeral. I think—"

Shit. What did Tina tell me that night? It had been a couple of years, and I'd barely paid attention at the time. In my defense, I'd been thrown into a pit and was a little more worried about getting out than listening to the babbling of my new friend.

"Okay. She told me she turned him that night. I remember being surprised, because the Sinclair I knew wasn't a guy who inspired sympathy, you know?

"And . . . I always thought that's how they met, that Tina met him the night she gave him the old one-two chomp. But the kids—the little twins—were talking about *Aunt* Tina." We looked at each other. "She knew them before. She was a friend of the family. Before."

Laura had paled, from fright or stress or both. "Then what happened?"

"Then . . . nothing. I mean, that's all the story I got. She saw him, she turned him, they've been friends ever since."

A small lie. In fact, that was all the story I ever bothered with. I lost all interest in The History of Eric Sinclair once I found out I was supposed to spend five thousand years ruling vampires with him. Soooo not on the career aptitude test I took when I was a senior at Burnsville High School.

In my defense, the Sinclair I met had been conniving, sneaky, sexy, slick, underhanded, horny, sexy, scheming, sexy, and duplicitous. He'd tricked me! I'd had sex with him under false pretenses. And all those orgasms were under false pretenses, too!

"Let's get the hell out of here," I said, but Laura was way

ahead of me. Her sword was already out, was already cutting a circle through the dusty barn air.

Just like last time, getting back to the waiting room was the easy part: we clasped hands and took a big step together, and the barn and the twins and the dust fell away from us. Cake.

"Thank goodness," I said, "we're back in hell."

Not a sentence I thought I'd ever say.

Chapter 44

We both looked for the door that led back out into hell proper, and neither was exactly astonished when it didn't show up. The devil wasn't done teaching us Time Travel 101.

"Now what?"

"Now it's the same decision we were looking at the last time we were in this room that isn't a room. We either stay here and hope my mother takes pity on us—"

"Yeah, *that's* likely."

"Or pick another door. And find whatever it is we're supposed to find."

"Yeah. No choice at all, then. But listen—wait, wait!" I backed up. Laura was getting really quick with her fists, and if I hadn't been undead I'd be at two shiners and counting. Or two nosebleeds and . . . eh, fuck it. Nobody cared but me. "Can we at least try to get clean clothes while we're here?"

"Or maybe period-appropriate clothing! Oh, Betsy, I never, *ever* would have thought of that!"

I won't lie; that cheered me up. Laura seemed so independent and cool these days, like she didn't need me so much.

Which was a weird way for me to feel . . . I'd never known she existed before a couple of years ago. So why would I want to be needed? That wasn't just pathetic, that was Ant-level pathetic. Level-one pathetic! Ye gods.

"I'm so glad you brought that up. I could use something more appropriate than jeans. One of these time jumps *we* could be the ones accused of witchcraft. Let's—" She glanced around. "Uh . . . I'm not sure how we would do that."

"I'm not sure, either. What if you waved your sword through, I dunno, my dirty leggings?"

"No! I could hurt you. Even kill you." She shook her head, a hard series of snaps: left, right, left. "Killing you wasn't part of the time-travel-in-ten-easy-lessons plan."

"Yeah, you're right . . . killing me would really put the stink on our shitty week. Look, your sword only disrupts paranormal energy, right? So if a werewolf jumped on you, you could slice him—"

"And he'd turn back to human, yes. But our clothes are real. They're not paranormal energy. There's nothing for my sword to disrupt."

"Well, nuts." And me without my overnight bag! I knew I'd been right to pack one. And not just because it was a spot to stash my letter from Sinclair.

I bent, brushed as much dust and dirt off my legs as I could, then straightened. I thought about l'il Sinclair, and couldn't hold back a smile. That open-faced cherub had been long gone—long *dead*—by the time I'd met up with his grown-up self. But it still was kind of a kick to meet my heart's own love as a child. A brother. A *twin*.

"Okay, so, let's get to it."

"Are you sure you're ready?"

I beckoned Laura with my fingers, a come-on-and-hit-me gesture I might make to a fighter. If this were a martial arts movie. And I was trapped in it. "Don't mind me, I'm just going to cringe and flinch and cry like a bitch until I wake up in Stillwater, circa 1961—ow!"

Chapter 45

"If this is somebody's idea of a joke," I said, gently rubbing my throbbing lower lip, "it stopped being funny about a hundred years ago."

"It was never funny," my sister lied loyally. "I think you're being an awfully good sport."

"And *I* think I'm being slowly driven insane. So this is . . . whatever this is." I was looking around and I suppose I should have been all excited and interested and, I dunno, eager to assimilate. If it were a movie, my character prob'ly would have been all these things and more. Instead I was all, "So, what indignity awaits me in *this* hellish time stream?"

I never said I wasn't a sore loser.

This was the first time I'd been conscious (mostly) and outside. At the same time, I mean. It looked like another small town, but there weren't a zillion horses. There also weren't any cows. Or Volkswagens. So it could have been the Roaring Twenties. Or the Depression. Or both! Or neither.

Actually, I thought, taking a closer look at the buildings, it looked like we'd been plunked, once again, into a downtown area. But the place looked familiar. Maybe because all these dinky little towns looked the same after a while. Or maybe they kept using the same movie set for all the old Westerns I'd seen. That would explain a few things.

"D'you have any idea where—"

"Hastings. Minnesota," the Antichrist added, as if I wouldn't recognize the name of a town less than twenty-five miles from where we lived. A town my mother lived in! "I think it's the early twentieth century."

"How do you—"

She pointed. I turned around, picturing all sorts of horrors. A hangman's noose. A firing squad. The opening of the first-ever Wal-Mart. Wait, that wasn't likely, was it?

That's when I noticed the Spiral Bridge, one of those old-timey things we'd long outgrown but Minnesota was weirdly proud of. And because I'd grown up and gone to school in the area, I knew two things your average time traveler from hell wouldn't.

It went up in 1895.

And didn't come down until 1951.

Chapter 46

You girls! If you're going swimming, you should be ashamed of yourselves! And if not, go home and cover yourselves!"

"Oh, yeah? Well, fu—" *Fuck you and the horse you are literally riding in on* had been where I was going with that. But the Antichrist had the reflexes of a rabid mongoose released in a reptile hut, so she did that arm-wrap-around-the-neck thing you usually see big brothers doing to little brothers, clapped her fingers over my mouth, and cheerily called, "Yes, sir! We sure will!"

"I'm going to drool like a beast on your fingers, you hateful cow. I'm gonna start slobbering any second now. Just as soon as I work up some saliva. Then you'll be sorry. Then you'll wish you were time traveling with someone else."

"Too late on that last, Betsy. If they mistook modern clothes for bathing costumes—"

"They deserve to be set on fire," I finished. "Why is our

swimming or not any of their damned business in the first place? Ashamed of ourselves? Who appointed that jackass general of the Morals National Guard? I get that it's ancient America and all, but it *is* still America."

"Yes, and we're women in ancient America. Black guys had the vote before we did, remember, and once upon a time, they thought those poor guys were *property*. Property got the vote before we did. That's like the Levee Café getting to vote before we did. So look demure, darn it."

"I have no idea what expression I should arrange my face into. Demure? That's not even a real word, is it?"

"Sedate," the Antichrist suggested.

"Not in a million zillion years. Hey, do we even know what the year *is*? I still don't see any cars. When the hell did the Ford family take over the country?"

"Not 'til the late 1800s," Laura explained. "Not the Fords. When cars were invented. Nobody has a hard-and-fast date, but in the late part of the century is what people figure. They started showing up around then."

"Wow. And here I was afraid this time travel thing would be hideously dangerous and boring. But it's only hideously dangerous. How d'you know when cars started to show up?"

"My minor is midwestern American history."

"You have a minor?" It was probably rude to ask my own sister what her major was. That was something a big sister would know, right? Wait. I think I knew this one. Let's see . . . if I was a virginal Antichrist and had a partial scholarship to the University of Minnesota, what would my major be?

Food business management? Animal science? Not evil enough. Applied economics? Plenty evil, but not virginal enough. Civil engineering? Environmental design? None of these seemed quite right . . .

"And that was in New Jersey, I think."

"What was?"

"That first *car*, please pay attention. But, see, they wouldn't have gotten to a small town in Minnesota for years and years. So I'm guessing we're somewhere in the 1920s."

"Where's a bulletin board right out on the street, with the day's newspaper helpfully plastered on it?" I squinted into the afternoon sun and reminded myself to count my blessings. I was the only vampire who *could* be outside, squinting into the sun, and it was best to keep those things in mind. "I miss Salem."

Laura sniggered. "Bite your tongue."

"I'd like to bite somebody's. I hate to add a problem when we've got a saddlebag full, but I'm getting kind of hungry. And did you notice how I slipped a 1920-ish colloquialism into my conversation? That's right, baby! Never let it be said that the queen of the undead can't blend."

Kind of was a sizeable lie. (So was *blend*.) Because the truth was I was always hungry. Okay, thirsty. Whenever I opened my eyes. And whenever I closed them. And often for long periods in between.

Most of the time I could just grit my fangs and bear it. But I did occasionally have to give in to my unholy craving for human blood. The rapists had held me for a while, but . . .

"Uh . . ." Laura's hand had gone to the collar of her shirt, where she was absently fiddling with it. I doubt she was even aware of it. So I decided not to call her attention to it. "That could be a problem."

"For the greatest time-traveling team since Lewis and Clark? No chance, baby." Ignoring Laura's snort of laughter, I continued outlining my sinister plan. "Ideally, we'll catch some bigoted wife beater in the middle of committing a felony. Or in the middle of a coma. I usually try to limit my chomping to rapists, thieves, murderers, and DVD bootleggers. And the occasional student loan officer. So keep your eyes peeled for a felony. Or a stupidly high rate of interest."

"I think—"

"Enh, who am I kidding? Beggars can't be choosers. Watch for misdemeanors, too."

"I think we might have lucked out again," Laura said, sounding guardedly optimistic. "The town seems almost deserted. In fact, I haven't even seen anyone on the street since that man yelled . . . at . . . us . . ."

She'd trailed off because she'd seen what I'd heard a few minutes ago—the jingling of many horses.

Three teams of two, in fact. Dressed in black—well, whatever you dressed horses up in (reins? leashes?), in 1920s (probably) Hastings, Minnesota. And the horses were pulling three big black wagons.

Each one toting a coffin.

Dozens and dozens of townspeople were now streaming into town; it was obvious nearly everyone had been at the wake and had walked into town afterward. I was even able to catch snatches of conversations over the jingling and clip-clopping and wheel-squeaking.

Laura sucked in breath, then let it out in a slow gasp. "Oh my G—"

"Shut up."

She shut. I was sorry to have had to snap at her, but I needed my concentration to listen.

"—poor things—"

"—after losing the daughter—"

"—poor boy, all alone now—"

"—catch them?"

"—naw, long gone by now—"

"—sheriff couldn't even—"

There were more murmurings, but I'd gotten the jist of it. And the jist sucked. "Aw, dammit."

Laura was already shaking her head. "No."

"This is bad."

"No."

"It's—"

"No!" Laura had actually clapped her hands over her ears. "I can't hear you!"

"Yeah. You can. And there's no point in telling you, since you already figured it out."

She lowered her hands and her face—it was so stricken. She felt as badly as I did. "It's them, isn't it? It's Eric's parents."

"And his twin, Erin." I watched the horse-drawn hearses pull past us. We were standing under one of those old-fashioned hangy-porch things, a perfect view to watch the procession. To watch practically the whole town go by. "A triple funeral for the Sinclair family. They're taking the coffins up the hill to the cemetery."

"No wonder that man yelled at us."

"Yeah. I'd have done the same thing if I saw a couple of doorknobs in bathing suits ready to hop in the Mississippi the day of a triple funeral."

"Okay." Laura cleared her throat. "This is bad, but we can work around it. I—I don't mean that the way it came out."

"I know you didn't."

"Okay. Once they're all past, we should be able to find—hey!"

I'd seized her hand and headed for the street. "We're going."

"Back to hell?"

"Worse." I waved at a lone man driving an empty wagon. "We're going to the funeral."

Chapter 47

Have you lost your damned mind?" Laura hissed. "You led that poor man on and—and seduced him! With your evil! So we can crash the funeral of your dead in-laws!"

"Anything sounds bad when you say it like that. Eyes front, Mikey."

"Okay." Our driver, Michael something-or-other (it was Smith or Thompson or Freidricksson . . . something catchy but forgettable) obediently looked ahead, clucked his tongue at the horses, and our wagon jolted ever forward. We were last in the procession, which was just the way I wanted it.

Also? My kingdom for some shock absorbers. No wonder someone got fed up and invented the car.

"You are very, very, very pretty."

"It's my conditioner," I assured him. "I don't think it's been invented yet. That's why you're attracted to me. Sexually, I mean. Also, I'm a vampire and I've bewitched you into giving us a ride to the funeral of, as the Antichrist put it, my dead in-laws."

"Anything sounds bad when you say it like that," Laura snarked. Her arms were folded across her chest and she was in full-on brat mode.

"You don't really think all this stuff is a coincidence, do you? Your mother said so herself—you need my blood, and then there was something about how I'd draw you. No, that wasn't it. How you'd be drawn toward stuff in my life that was stupid or weird."

"I don't—"

"Can't say she didn't warn us, but she definitely down-played this whole thing. She could've just said, 'For a while, it will seem like you're trapped in a really bad episode of *Lost*,' and I would have understood perfectly. But yeah, you're sup-posed to be drawn toward weird dumb stuff from my life."

"I don't think that's a precise quote." But Laura was nod-ding; I could see that, in fact, she *had* thought a lot of this was coincidence but was rapidly revising her opinion. "I see your meaning. We've seen your husband, and now we've seen his poor family. And if Tina is supposed to turn him—"

"Then she's here, too! She's in town right now, and this is too good an opp to let go by. Look!" I pointed and Michael obediently turned the horses in that direction. Unfortunately, the largest river in the country was also in that direction. "Ack, quit it! Drive us to the cemetery, the *boneyard*, duh!"

"Sorry, miss."

"And keep us out of the Mississippi River, if it's not too much to ask."

"Yes, miss."

"And even if it is."

Laura was shaking her head. We were huddled on either

side of Michael, trying to keep warm. Stupid open wagons with no heaters. "If this all means something, what was that business in Salem?"

"What, you're asking *me*? You forget, I'm just as piss ignorant as you are. Salem was practice, maybe, or maybe your mom lost a bet, who knows? The important thing is, we're here now. I bet we're supposed to do something. Or fix something. Or find something. Or kill something."

"But this isn't a TV show. This is just me, getting practice so I can one day run hell if I want. All this extra stuff—" She gestured vaguely toward Michael, who had (once again) stopped watching the road and was instead watching me. I could see no way to avoid ending up in a ditch this evening, or a river, really I couldn't.

"Eyes front, Michael!"

"Okay."

"No," Laura said, still working on her train of thought. "It's practice for sure, but we're getting bogged down with the day-to-day human stuff."

"Bogged down?" Didn't care for *that* phrasing one little bit.

"Well, if I wasn't half human, my mother would have come up with some other way for me to learn this stuff. But I am. So she needed you. And because I need you in order to learn, I'm getting bogged down in things like your in-laws' murder and such."

"Maybe you didn't catch my shrill bitchy tone, so I'll try again: *bogged down?*"

She flapped a hand to show what she thought of my bitchy tone. "You know what I mean. Don't make it into a thing."

"I'll make it into anything I—Michael, will you *please* drive these *fucking* horses *straight* before I *kill* one of them to drown you in their *blood?*"

"You're really, really pretty."

"No, I'm not! I'm filthy, I'm not wearing any makeup, I haven't seen a hairbrush in well over a hundred years, I'm covered with ancient dust from my dead in-laws' farm, and somebody thought I looked so ghastly they figured I was going swimming earlier today. I am the polar opposite from really, really pretty and it hurts, Michael, it *hurts*. An entire frontier town full of people," I groaned, burying my face in my hands, "and I had to get the one they invented the short buses for."

"Actually, frontier town is a misnomer, since——"

"Oh, enough, history girl. You do understand that if I committed felony assault all over your skull, there wouldn't be a jury in the world that would convict me. You get that, ri—well, finally!" I could see glimpses of headstones sort of peeking out from all the trees . . . I'd have been able to spot them sooner if someone had gotten off their lazy butts *and invented flashlights*. And headlights for wagons. And brake lights for wagons. "And check this—almost dark!"

"That's odd. They normally had funerals during the day. It's not like they can haul out a bunch of klieg lights and turn them on in another hour."

"Maybe they're in a hurry to get the Sinclairs into the ground."

"Yes," the Antichrist said. "Maybe they are." Then she shivered. "Brrr! I gave myself the chills with that one. Do we know how they were murdered?"

I squirmed. "No," I admitted. "I just know they were murdered the same week his sister was. It might even have been the same day. But I don't know the circumstances or anything. Hey, Michael, do you know what happened to Erin Sinclair, and Mr. and Mrs. Sinclair?"

"Yup."

We waited for a long moment, but Michael had started humming under his breath. A simple creature, our driver, not overtaxed with many of life's burdens.

"Well?" we asked.

"Oh. Yup, ah, Erin, she took it in her head that she wanted to go to college. An' the Sinclairs, y'know, Henry and Bobbi, they always did like to spoil her—she's the youngest, y'know, by near four minutes. So they took her up there to sit for them exams. And I guess she wasn't even the first woman to sit for 'em! Haw!"

"Haw," we dutifully echoed.

"But there was this fella there, he didn't work for the college but he said he did, and he tried to lay with Erin but she wasn't having none of that, so he hit her, and they figure she fell, 'cuz her neck got broke."

Laura looked ill. I probably did, too, but I was more pissed than sick. "Then what?"

"She just shoulda stayed home. We all warned her."

"Oh, you mean stay on the farm and squeeze out a few babies and never try to learn anything new or visit anything new or see anything new?"

"She's not seein' nothing new now."

"Touché, Mikey. Let's go find Susan B. Anthony," I suggested to Laura, "and kiss her on the mouth." Thank you, thank you, Susie B., for getting the idea in your head that women were worth more than the theoretical children they might have. I knew we were in olden times and all, but cripes, that kind of talk made me *nuts*.

And if Erin was only half as independent as her twin, and half as stubborn . . . well. No effing wonder she'd wanted to go to college. I thought it was pretty cool that Mr. and Mrs. Sinclair gave her a ride, come to think of it.

"Then what, Fred Flintstone?"

"Well, you know Henry."

"Yes, we know Henry," Laura said, encouraging him to go on by *not* throttling him. "Whatta kidder, that Henry. Yes indeed."

"Yeah, well, he 'bout lost his mind when he found Erin all smashed up and suchlike, and he went charging up the stairs to get that fella, and nobody's really sure what happened next, but he an' Bobbi both turned up dead. Smashed." He gestured to his own head. "The bones in their heads were all smashed up."

"Excuse me, did you say *smashed*?"

"Do they know who did it?" Laura interrupted before Michael could elaborate on smashed.

"We know who sez he did it . . . this fella claimed he was on the board what founded the university up there. 'Cept that was a lie, because the university got started back in fifty-one and this fella didn't look no older than Erin."

Laura's eyes got very big and she mouthed *vampire* at me. I nodded. "That's—that's very interesting, Michael, thanks for telling us. Laura, look, there's the crowd . . . let's just sort of hang on the outskirts, see what we can see. Michael, you can let us out here."

"But you're so pretty."

"Yes, one of my many burdens."

"But you're so—"

"Good-*bye*, Mikey."

"But you are," he wailed as we hopped off the wagon and scampered into the brush like big blonde gophers. Breaking hearts wherever I went, that was the motto of the vampire queen. Also, never leave your own time period without a lint brush and a change of clothes.

Chapter 48

We'd been lurking, and freezing, for over an hour. The minister had come and gone; the townspeople had come and gone. It was full dark, and we were both shivering.

Finally, only Eric Sinclair was left beside the graves.

I wasn't quite sure why I was hanging out here. Sure, I felt shitty for the poor guy—his entire world, wiped out in, what? Half an hour? Less? But the only thing I could do by staying was screw up the time line.

I guess it was as simple as this: I knew my love was suffering. And even if I couldn't help directly, I just wanted a look at him. To, as Stephen King put it, "refresh my heart."

What was shocking was that I'd always assumed Sinclair had been turned in his late twenties or early thirties. But Erin, according to her headstone, had been only nineteen. ("Spinster territory," Laura had told me. "Probably one of the reasons she wanted to go to college. She knew nobody was waiting around town to marry her. Or she had turned them all down, which is another mark in Mr. and Mrs. Sinclair's favor. Not to mention Erin's.")

Eric Sinclair had never looked nineteen to me, and now I knew why: the shock had aged him, had carved lines around his eyes and mouth that weren't supposed to show up for another fifteen years.

And yeah. I won't deny it. I felt guilty, too. I'd never bothered to find any of this out. I could hide behind the well-Sinclair-keeps-himself-to-himself argument, but that would have been lame even for me. He would have told me if I'd ever pulled my head out of my own ass long enough to ask.

What was weird was seeing him *alive*, you know? We weren't having to be especially stealthy; he was in a world of his own. A world where his hearing was normal and he had zero interest in drinking blood. A world where he was mortal and hurting and, as of this week, entirely alone.

Laura nudged me and I looked. Tina had appeared from nowhere, it seemed, and was watching Sinclair with her big dark eyes. He hadn't spotted her; she was several rows back and standing so still I was a little surprised Laura had managed to spot her.

And Eric not only hadn't seen her, he wouldn't, I was surprised to see. He had turned and was sort of stumbling toward the cemetery entrance.

And Tina was watching him go!

"What the fuck?" I hissed, then yelped as Laura seized my ear and hauled me facedown beside her.

"Be careful! Remember vampire hearing."

"I'd like to remember my *own* hearing—ow, ow, *ow, ow!*"

I jerked away and rubbed my now-throbbing ear. Cripes, at least it was still attached. Barely. "Since when have you been so grabby?"

"I think you must have gotten the story wrong," Laura breathed, so quietly I could barely make out the words and I was standing right next to her. "See?"

I saw, all right. Sinclair was leaving, and Tina wasn't doing shit.

"No way," I said, seizing the Antichrist's hand as I started running for Tina. "I got it *right*. She turns him. They both told me the same story at different times. And we're gonna make it right. Right now!" Hmm, that was a lot of *rights* in not very many statements.

I'd worry about evening it up later.

Chapter 49

"Where the hell do you think you're going?"

Tina looked more than startled—she looked borderline horrified.

"Well? Don't just stand there staring at my awesome-yet-smudged shirt and filthy leggings! Go turn Sinclair into a vampire!"

"I can think of at least five other ways we could have done that more efficiently. And quietly."

"Shut up, you. Tina, come on." I stepped forward, seized her arm just above the elbow, and tugged her toward Sinclair. "Bite already. Gnaw away. Chomp like you've never chomped before."

"Who *are* you?"

I opened my mouth . . . and stopped. What, exactly, should I tell her? That I was the long-prophesied vampire queen she hadn't ever heard of? That I was the wife of the teenager currently stumbling his way out of the cemetery? That I knew the killer of her friends was a vampire, and oh, by the way, I knew she was, too, so go ahead and bite that old family friend and also, don't kill me?

I really couldn't think of anything to tell her that wouldn't earn me a shot in the mouth. Or a broken neck.

"You have to help him." Hey, that sounded pretty reasonable. Which is probably why Laura thought of saying it. "He needs you."

"I failed him," Tina said, visibly upset, practically crying—not with tears, vampires don't have excess moisture just lying around for them to excrete, but you get the jist. "I failed them all. How can I ever face him?"

"How can you abandon him?"

Ohhh, good one, Laura! Thank God I'd brought her along on these dumb time-traveling trips.

"It's monstrous. I could never."

"You're just going to abandon him, then? Leave him with his grief?" I nagged. "You've seen him. He'll stick a gun in his mouth by the end of the week."

Tina flinched. Unlike Laura and me, she was appropriately dressed for the time. The big fat dresses from Salem were gone, and thank goodness. Instead, Tina was wearing an ankle-length skirt, which was pencil straight, pinching her knees together so that it was almost hobbling her. The top, a long tunic, completed the pencil look (I assume she was going for a pencil look); she looked skinny as a (pencil!) stick, but the deep cherry red of the tunic and the cherries-on-white print of the skirt made her look more substantial than she was. A big blonde hulk like me? If I'd worn a print like that, I would have been mistaken for the cherry tree. Petite women had all the luck.

Her hair was worn up, the big blonde waves carefully pinned up and away from her face. Her dark eyes were wary and full of pain. Which was sad and all, but her shoes! She had the most adorable red flapper-style shoes! Thick, chunky heels and delicate ankle straps completed the outfit, and Tina was a pretty, stylish picture indeed.

The shoes weren't much help . . . she wasn't dressed flapper-style, but was wearing those kinds of shoes. So it'd be easy to assume, okay, probably 1920s. Except this was Hastings, Minnesota. Not exactly the center for all things fashion. So it could have been as early as 1910, or as late as 1935. No way to tell.

"—have to bite him! Tell her, Betsy."

"Eh? Oh, yep. You sure do have to bite him. Bite him and bite him and then bite him some more. He's gonna want to catch the killer."

"I will catch the killer," Tina said, and for a second she didn't look cute and beautiful and sweet; for a second, I felt a very real chill, and not because I was dressed in a bathing suit (sort of). Looks were deceiving, and who'd know better than a former Miss Congeniality? Tina was a predator, a beautiful woman used to getting her shit done while surrounded by men who assumed she was stupid, incompetent, or both. Her camouflage was excellent.

That was something I should probably keep in mind at all times.

"Listen, you have to chew on him, then, when he rises, you'll become his loyal sidekick, his Gal Friday, like a super-secretary except cool, and then you'll be perfectly positioned to . . . to . . . what, Laura?"

"Will you stop babbling things you have *no way of knowing?*"

"How else am I gonna bend her to my will?"

"Wait one moment," Tina interrupted. "When he rises, since it appears clear you two understand about vampires, he'll be a mindless beast for years, driven only by hunger and need. Why would I ever become the assistant of such a beast?"

"Because hemmmpph!" I snapped at Laura's fingers like a pissed-off bulldog. "Don't grab me, and *don't* stick your fingers in my mouth. Listen, Tina, the thing is, I know this stuff because you already did it. I know—I know you—" Would I create a paradox? I was pretty sure the answer was no, but . . . it wasn't just my future I was screwing with. It was Sinclair's, too. "I definitely know . . ."

"Your full name!" Laura prompted. "You've never seen us before, right? So how does the mysterious weirdo know your whole name?"

"Oh ho?" Tina looked at me.

I turned on Laura, so pissed I could only see her through a sort of red mist. "Have you ever met me?" I hissed. "Of course I don't know her full name! I'm lucky I remember it's Tina!"

"Well," Tina replied, unimpressed.

"Try," Laura encouraged. "Think. Exercise that teeny brain."

"When this is over, I'm going to beat you to death. Let's see. We were in the pit—"

"The *what?*"

"Yeah, I know. The vampires threw me in a pit. Then Tina jumped down into it."

"That does not sound one bit like me."

"Look, I didn't question your motives at the time, so don't be questioning mine. And . . . she said—you said—it was the least she could do. And since I'd been having kind of a shitty day, I figured she was right. And . . . uh . . ."

"I suspect you might be mentally ill."

"You wouldn't talk to me like that if the Antichrist would let me tell you who I was," I whined. "You just—I do know a name!"

Tina had folded her arms across her chest and raised a polite eyebrow.

"And here I thought you might only make things worse," Laura observed, "and yet, how wrong I was."

"Nostro! How's that for a name?"

My half-assed plan worked; Tina looked shocked and her eyes opened wide, like I'd slapped her.

"That's right!" I crowed. "I made that idiot my bitch! The guy currently making your life suck rocks; I *owned* his ass. And I did it *with your help.*" I turned to my sister. "There, see? She knows stuff, but not enough to destroy her own future, probably."

"You could only know that name if you were in league with him, which," she said, looking me up and down with all the warmth of an overworked customs inspector, "I don't believe you are. Or if you were telling the truth. So I suppose I must assume you mean what you say."

"That's right!"

"So the only living child of my dear friends must be damned to a lifeless existence."

"Lifeless?" Clearly she'd never had sex with undead Sinclair. Lifeless was so *not* the word springing to mind. "You don't understand. This will change . . ." I saw Laura shake her head. "Tons," I finished. "It'll change tons. It'll change everything."

And for the first time, I owned the queen-of-the-undead

thing. Because I *had* changed everything. Not alone, of course. With the help of all the mobile people in this cemetery (*not* Michael, but I assumed he was back home by now), I'd kicked out an asshat dictator, saved the Fiends, defeated various forms of evil, while maintaining a residence where all were (sort of) welcome, marrying the love of my life, becoming a mom (sort of), forming an alliance with seventy-five thousand werewolves . . . what could I say? It had been a busy couple of years.

"Great. So you'll do it? You'll bite Sinclair?"

"Is there a reason you never refer to him by his first name? Have you forgotten it as you have forgotten mine?"

"We do *not* have time for your picky, irritating questions, Tina. Now go chomp."

"We have to find him again first," Laura observed. "Because while you were convincing Tina you were an intimate friend who didn't know her full name, your boy took a walk."

We looked. I cursed. Laura was right: Sinclair had bailed.

Chapter 50

He can't be that hard to hunt down," I opined. "How many nineteen-year-old studs in the depths of grief are wandering around 1920s Hastings, Minnesota, right this minute?"

"Too right. So you think it's 1920s Hastings, do you?"

"Don't answer that," Laura said quickly.

"Duh, Laura. Hey, look, is that Satan over there? What year is it, exactly?" I whispered to Tina when Laura actually— get this!—fell for that. Putz.

"You are an odd one," Tina observed, falling into step with us as we left the cemetery. "You and your sister."

"How did you know we were sisters?"

"The family resemblance is remarkable."

"Really?" This was thrilling as *nothing* had been on this wacky time-traveling misadventure. Laura was hot! It would be awesome to also be hot. To have people look at her and then look at me and be all "sure, I can see the hotness run-ning in their family." It made having the devil for a step-mother almost not sucky. "So, Sinclair went thataway."

"I know. His scent is distinctive. I have known it for—for some time."

"I heard—I mean, I know the kids thought of you as Aunt Tina." Not the time to mention that, a few hours ago (at least in my head), we'd seen l'il Sinclair and l'il Erin, and the only thing they had on their minds was how grumpy their mom was because it was Moving Week. "You must be a close fam-ily friend."

"I knew their mother." Long pause. "And their grand-mother."

"Yeah, I bet you were best friends with those guys. Those ladies," I amended. "So did they not ever notice you weren't aging, or did they pretend to believe you were your own daughter and granddaughter?"

"My friends . . . my friends didn't care. When my grand-mother moved to Minnesota, Eric's great-grandmother was her best friend. It seems the Sinclairs have always welcomed me; it seems I have always been in their lives." There was a long silence as the three of us walked together. Then: "They knew I was, ah, different. We never spoke of it. And they—they paid me the honor of guardianship of their children."

"So you're Sinclair's legal guardian now? No. Wait. He's an adult . . . barely."

"He is the—he is the closest thing I shall ever have to a grandchild of my own."

I could practically hear the *click* as long-unasked questions were answered: why had Tina stayed by his side so loyally all those years? Why had they never hooked up? They had way more in common than Sinclair and I did, and nobody knew that better than me. (Frankly, I'd always found Sinclair's interest in me a complete mystery.) And why did she regulate herself to the periphery of the power? Why did she never make a move for the crown herself?

Not that the crown, so to speak (there actually *wasn't* one, how was that for false advertising?), was so great. But a lot of people seemed to think it was.

"You must be so angry about what happened to your friends and Erin," Laura said.

"Angry. Yes. I am angry." She said this with all the heat of *I am wearing yellow.* "And he will pay and pay."

"From what we heard, it sounds like a vampire?"

"Yes. That's what it sounds like. But he didn't act alone. And Erin Sinclair was only a means to an end."

Hmm. Sinister, creepy Tina was something new. Of course, she and Sinclair had lots in common: both of them lost practically their whole family in a matter of hours.

"You think maybe they were after you?"

"I have had dealings with those men before," she replied evenly.

"Okay. So, turn Sinclair and he can help you. It can be all vengeance, all the time. It can be *Die Hard: The Early Years.*"

Laura snorted while Tina said, "I don't understand you. And that is the second time you've made reference to Eric being able to help me. But I think there is something you don't understand about vampires."

"Only one thing?" the Antichrist sneered. I gave her the finger when Tina wasn't looking.

"Eric will be useless to everyone, including himself, for at least five years after rising. The new undead, they are savage. They think only of the thirst. It takes years to deal with such things. And such knowledge is hard won."

"You're wrong." Because this, I *did* remember. I remember being in that nasty pit and hearing Tina explain that some vampires wake up strong. That it was very rare, but occasionally, a vampire would rise strong.

In fact, there were only two vampires I ever heard of who came back to life strong.

My husband, Eric Sinclair.

And me.

Chapter 51

"Psst."

"So how'd you become a vam—"

"Pssst!"

I sighed. "Excuse me, but my little sister can be very rude and selfish at times. She's the cross I must bear when I'm not time traveling all over and saving the world. Worlds, maybe. Maybe I should get a plaque for all this grueling world saving."

"*Pssst!*"

"Two plaques. What?" I fell back a couple of steps so Laura and I were walking abreast. "What is it?"

"I think we should go."

"How come?" I was genuinely surprised.

"You fixed it so Tina will turn him. If there was a way to utterly destroy the future—our present—you've made sure we'll return to a smoking crater where Grand Avenue used to be. It's time to go."

"But I need to make sure he gets taken care of."

"Why?"

"Why?" I gaped. Laura wasn't normally this dumb. "Because—because I have to! What are you talking about, why?"

"You're only saying that because it's *him*. Your love is clouding your usually awful long view even more than usual."

"I can't just gaily hop back to hell without knowing he's going to be . . . uh . . ." *Okay* probably wasn't the right word. *Set on his loveless track toward cold vengeance, enduring decades of isolation and loneliness until I pratfall into his life* just sounded weird. "Look, I see your point, but—"

"Shhhh!" Laura hissed, grabbing my hand and yanking me off the dusty road. I knew it, I knew it! I *was* inevitably headed for a ditch tonight. "Look!"

We were cowering off the gravel road, sort of hunched down in the shallow ditch, and I could see Tina had caught up to Sinclair.

"What's she—?"

"Shhh! And duh, clearly she's talking to him."

". . . dreadfully sorry."

"It doesn't matter now," Sinclair said, and I shivered. He sounded like a robot. An incredibly depressed robot. "They're gone. She's gone."

"Eric, I promise you, something will be done. These men won't get away with—"

Sinclair flinched. "Men? I thought—I thought she'd been raped—and there was an accident—?"

"There is—there are more things at work here than you can know."

"Explain them to me."

"Eric—"

"Right now."

I started to cheer up. *Now* he was starting to sound like the Sinclair I loved to loathe. Or loathed to love. He just needed a mission. All those *Death Wish* movies couldn't be wrong.

"Eric, there's no time. I need to get on their trail tonight. I'm only here for the funerals. But I couldn't leave without saying good-bye."

"Was it another vampire?"

Tina didn't speak for a moment, and Laura and I traded glances. I could tell she was rattled that he'd just come out with it like that. *Are you a vampire? Are the stories about monsters true? What happened to you? And what happened to my family?*

And how much of it is my fault, for never questioning anything?

"I—yes. How did you know?"

Eric, embarked upon his last night of life, started to laugh. I had never heard him laugh like that and hoped never to hear it again.

"How did I know? How did I *know?* My God, a better question would be when did Erin and I not know? Our grandmother's best friend? Who was always beautiful and clever, who never lost her wits or her looks?"

"Pretty big clue," I admitted, and Laura nodded.

"A friend who never seemed to leave her teenage years, who always seemed to relate to the elders far more easily than people her own age. People who *looked* her own age," he qualified.

"You never—"

"Our mother told us, when we started asking questions.

Before we were invested in the Sinclair family secret. She said you were an angel. A dark angel, sent to protect us and watch over us." His hands flashed, and suddenly he was gripping Tina's shoulders and shouting into her face, "An angel!"

"She lied, of course," Tina said calmly, as if she wasn't being tossed around like a cocktail shaker on a gravel road in a small town in the middle of nowhere in 1920 (probably). "She lied because she couldn't reconcile the truth with her religious upbringing. She couldn't understand how a vampire could also be a friend of the family. She couldn't understand how a creature of darkness and blood could enjoy the company of farmers, could babysit and take vacations with you. Could love you.

"And rather than question it, she created a convenient fairy tale, as her mother had done for her, and her mother before her."

"Then why couldn't you save them?" he cried, and his voice cracked like the adolescent he still was. Though I was betting nineteen years old in the (maybe) 1920s was the equivalent of thirty-five in the twenty-first century.

"Because I'm a vampire, not a goddess, and we're not infallible. The reverse, if anything. Our appetites often lead us to trouble. Even our destruction. The only guarantee our state brings is freedom from aging bodies, never-ending thirst, and great strength and speed. Those are helpful much of the time. But they aren't a promise. They are no guarantee."

"You're off, then. After the killers."

"Yes."

"Not by yourself. I won't leave ugly work like this to a woman."

Ahhh, there was the charming chauvinist I often fantasized about strangling. And not in an auto-erotic way, either.

To her credit, Tina didn't go into gales of humiliating laughter. "I appreciate your concern, my dear. But I have been involved in ugly work long, *long* before you were born."

"Exactly. That's why you're going to make me one of you." Sinclair took a deep breath. "And teach me. Everything. You'll show me everything. And they'll pay. They will pay and pay, and when I've finished with them . . . in time . . . there may be more to live for than vengeance and a living death."

Another short silence, and I could have sworn Tina glanced at us pseudo-hiding in the ditch. "Yes, that . . . that seems to be the thing to do, doesn't it? Eric, you must understand—"

"Vengeance. I understand vengeance. If I'm damned because of it, then so be it."

Again a glance in our direction. "I'm not sure damned is . . . exactly . . . the appropriate word."

"We should go," Laura whispered. "There's nothing else for us to screw up."

"Not yet."

"Why?"

I didn't know. I couldn't figure it out myself, much less explain to Laura. I couldn't shake the feeling that it would be a personal disaster to leave just now. But I didn't . . . know . . . *why*.

"Let me tell you what it will be like."

He made a curt gesture. "Irrelevant. There's nothing I wouldn't endure for vengeance. Losing my soul is the least of it."

You won't, though! I almost shouted. Soulless was so not how I'd describe Sinclair. He came off as chilly and indifferent, until you got his pants off. I mean, got to know him.

"The . . . act itself isn't unpleasant. You'll get tired. You'll sleep. And, as I plan to steal your body, you needn't worry about waking in a coffin six feet in the earth. I cannot tell you how upsetting that is," Tina muttered.

Jeez. I could imagine. I was learning more about Tina in one night than I had in three years.

"But you'll be . . . disoriented. You'll—it might take a while to . . . to learn . . . how to be strong . . ."

I leaped to my feet. Strong! That's why we were still here!

I scrambled out of the ditch. Laura lunged but, since I was in superspeedy-vamp mode, missed by a mile (almost literally). I was moving so efficiently, Sinclair was only now starting to turn toward the racket I was making. And Tina, who *could* have stopped me, seemed frozen in surprise, or maybe disbelief.

Eric didn't turn quickly enough. I nailed him from behind, rode him all the way into the gravel, and sank my canines into his neck.

Chapter 52

What are you doing?"

"Oh, Betsy! This is so inappropriate," the Antichrist scolded.

The teenaged Eric Sinclair also tried to protest, probably, but since he was facedown in the gravel I couldn't make out what he was saying.

I won't lie: his blood? His live blood, electric with the high-fat diet of the 1920s (probably)? Unbelievable. His live blood was worth the huge pain in the ass our time traveling had been. At least, I thought so. Laura probably wouldn't agree.

Make no mistake: I always liked the taste of Sinclair; we often spent days and days where we only fed off each other. But live Sinclair, yummy with electrolytes and a healthy midwestern diet?

His blood sang with meatloaf and roast duck and buttery

biscuits and lamb and chicken and radish roses and deviled eggs and potato salad and turkey and oatmeal and veal and beans and jelly and crumb cake and ham and gingerbread and beets and bread pudding and pork chops and rice pudding and oh, my, what is *this*? Teenage Sinclair was in *excellent* shape, what with all the farming and being gorgeous and suchlike.

Oofta.

Sinclair raised his head. "Uh, miss? I think you might have fallen on me by accident."

"Go to sleep," I told him, sitting up. Then I yelped and shoved my hands forward so his head didn't clunk facedown into the gravel, but rather onto my palms. Probably should have thought that one out.

"Okay," I said, looking up at Tina and Laura, who were staring down at us like they'd seen a woman in her thirties molesting a teen—oh. Huh. Ew. "Now you can bite him."

"All right," Tina said cautiously. "I'm not quite sure how to proceed. Do I take you to task for hurting a friend, a boy I think of as my grandson?"

"Could we stop with the 'boy' talk? He's a grown man. Right? I'm not gross and inappropriate. Right?"

"Or should I bite the boy—"

"Dammit!"

"—and teach him all the ways of a living death?"

"Trust me, he's not hurt. But he's sure out cold. Ooof! Laura, I'm gonna carefully put his head down and then stand up, so if you could—"

"Wait!" I heard a tiny clinking, and Laura bent and picked something up as I lurched to my feet. Sinclair's yummy rich blood was making my head swim. "This fell out of his pocket."

"Oh!" I managed not to snatch it out of her grip, just gently grasped it. "He's not gonna want to lose this; it's Erin's. I mean, it was Erin's." I held out the tiny cross on the gold chain to Tina. It would be mine, almost a hundred years from now. Sinclair would give it to me, his most treasured possession, and he wouldn't know why.

At the time, I wouldn't know why, either. Only that the jackass vampire I couldn't ever seem to ditch had given me something of great value, great *personal* value. And when he did, for the first time I was able to see him as a person instead of a pain in my ass.

Tina backed up very, very slowly. "I can't touch that. But you can." She leaned forward and seemed to peer at me. "You *are* a vampire! I couldn't tell before."

"She probably figured it out when you leaped on him and gnawed like he was your own personal Chew-eez."

"You're very unattractive when you're all sarcastic and snarky like that."

"Who *are* you?" Tina asked. She seemed as intrigued as she was startled . . . maybe even frightened. Or just really weirded out.

"No one of consequence," I said, ruthlessly stealing a line from *The Princess Bride*. "So, we're out of here."

"Oh, thank God! I've had enough of Hastings."

"What've you got against Hastings, Laura? It's a perfectly nice river town. Um, *now*. Because I don't know that it's nice in the future or anything. I don't have a clue."

"Truer words," Laura muttered.

"So, best of luck with everything. With the turning and the training and such."

"Ah . . . thank you, miss."

I knelt, tucked Erin's necklace back into Sinclair's pocket, smoothed his hair back from his dirty cheek, and kissed him. "See you in the future," I whispered, and it would have been an awesome and touching moment, except Laura grabbed my arm and hauled me off down the gravel road, so the last thing Tina heard was the vampire queen yelping like a stomped pup.

Chapter 53

"Oh, come on!" I couldn't believe it. Back in the waiting room *again*, and still no way to the front door. Or back door. Or whatever the fuck it was. "I don't recall your mother mentioning that Time Travel 101 was going to take, I dunno, the best years of my life!"

"It's true," Laura said, already standing in front of a new door to try. She didn't look terribly put out, I was annoyed to see. She seemed to be gaining confidence by the hour. By the door, as it were. "She didn't. But she keeps them close to the vest, wouldn't you say?"

"I would say."

"So, ready?"

"Ugh, no. What's next? We save Laura Ingalls from being set upon by vampires?"

"Only one way to find out."

"You know what's weird?"

She'd been reaching for a new knob but now looked at me and grinned. "I have to pick just one thing?"

I smiled back. Yes, this was dangerous. Yes, it was annoying. But I'd never had the chance to spend so much time with Laura, and I was finding the experience pretty cool.

Okay. To be fair: I'd never *made* the chance to spend so much time with her.

"Good point. What's weird is, the past doesn't stink. It sucks, make no mistake, but it's not smelly. I figured that with no running water or regular showers and such, and air freshener not having been invented, or antibacterial soap, that everyone would stink. But they didn't. Things were dusty, you know, but not filthy or gross. Wait'll I tell my mom." My mom was a college professor specializing in the Civil War. She'd hang on my every word but would be too polite to say out loud, "If only you'd been exposed to death and danger during the battle of Gettysburg!"

"She wouldn't say it, but she'd think it," I muttered.

"Fascinating. So, onward and upward, sister mine. Next stop, who knows? Watch the birdie!"

"What? Dammit!" I clutched my now-throbbing eye, the knob easily turned beneath Laura's hand, and we were off again like Magellan and Columbus. Or Abbott and Costello.

Chapter 54

Seriously? You still have to beat on me to move through time? I assume this is all because God hates me this month."

"Yes, Betsy. It's all about you."

"Sometimes it is," I whined.

"And sometimes it isn't. Anyway, smacking you around for the greater good is a sacrifice I'm willing to make."

"Yeah, real willing, don't think I haven't noticed." I caught a glimpse of my reflection in the window. Fortunately, I was still awesomely pretty. "Well, what fire do we have to . . . put . . . out . . . ?"

I'd trailed off because we'd materialized beside a house in the suburbs. A modern house in modern suburbs! With electric lights and everything! In fact—

"Isn't this your old house? The one that had termites—whoof!"

She'd gasped because I'd picked her up and twirled her around and around. "Yes, yes, *yes*! It *is* my bug-ridden abode. It's the house I lived in before Jessica and I moved to the mansion. We're back! Laura, we're back!"

"But why are we at your old house? Nothing ever happened here."

"Hardly, ignorant child." I set her down, but I could have danced her up and down the block for an hour and a half. "I was living here during the Ferragamo debut. And let's not forget the hangover of 2000; gah, I thought I was going to yark up my liver. And the pseudo date-rape of 2002, and I say *pseudo* because I kicked his balls up so high he was strangling on them by the time the cops showed up. Ahhhh . . . good times . . ."

"But why would we be here? Does this mean we're back? Maybe we should get a cab back to Summit."

"I s'pose—wait."

"We don't need a cab," Laura observed, watching the car pull into what was once my driveway. "Because here you come now. Do you think you'll give us a ride?"

"Oh . . ."

"Shit," the Antichrist agreed, and then we both dived out of sight as I got out of my car and headed up the walk to my front door.

Chapter 55

Stupid!" I fumed as we lurked behind my old house. "I saw the damned car and didn't even think of it!"

"What?" Laura was crouched beside the eight zillion chives I hadn't tried to grow . . . did you know that if you plant, like, *two* chive seeds, three years later you've got an acre full of the buggers? Me neither. "Wow, it really smells like onions back here."

"Nick Berry's in there!"

"The cop? Jessica's ex . . ." Laura trailed off, and I didn't blame her. The thing with Nick was something we all felt bad about. And that I was deeply ashamed of.

"Yeah. Jessica's ex, who I bit, and when that fucked him up, Sinclair 'fixed it' by mind-raping him. Which he never recovered from, and the more he remembered, the more nightmares he had and the more scared he got until he made Jessica choose, which he never would have done if we hadn't messed with him in the first place, and he lost and they broke up!"

"Shhhh!"

"You shhhh! He's in there right now!" I said, squashing the urge to shake her until her teeth fell out. "And stupid, newly risen, starving *me* is gonna fall on him like he was a six-foot Godiva truffle."

"Oooh, don't say that. You realize we haven't eaten in all this time?"

"But not this time, devilish sidekick. This time I'm gonna not let myself have the chance to bite the poor guy."

"I think you're *my* sidekick, actua—"

"We're gonna fix it," I said, and Laura must have seen something in my face she didn't care for (or was having cramps from hunger pains), because at once she began shaking her head.

"Okay. You need to stall me—the younger, dumber me— and while you're doing that, I'm gonna grab Nick and get him the hell out of the suburban hellhouse."

"No, Betsy, you can't!"

"Watch me," I said with a sort of steely tone, like Ellen Ripley telling an alien queen to *get away from her, you bitch,* oooh, yeah! That would—"Ow, don't pinch!" Had Ellen Ripley ever whined? I was pretty sure she hadn't . . . though if anyone had earned the right . . .

"Listen, I put up with saving that gal in Salem. And helping Tina help Sinclair. But you're messing with very serious things! Just because we haven't noticed a consequence—*yet*— doesn't mean there aren't any! You can't do this. I won't help you. I'll—I'll try to stop you." The Antichrist looked frightened but determined. "I just can't let you keep screwing with the time stream. Who knows the damage we've done? It's my fault, too, for not standing up to you. Maybe that's what my mother wanted me to learn. But not this time, Betsy."

"Laura, there's no time, and you can't stop me, but think about this while you're stalling the other me: we're already the product of a screwed time stream, and once you help me with this? I'll prove it. Now stall me, or stall the other me, but either way, keep outta the way."

She might be the Antichrist, but she was still, at the end of the day, a human, and no match for vampire strength.

I think she realized that as well, or was unwilling to get into fisticuffs with me. Because when I went to duck around the side of the house, headed for the backyard, she didn't try to stop me. In fact, she went the other way. Toward the front of the house.

Toward the other me.

Chapter 56

I raced around to the back, snatched up the dead tomato plant (other than chives and dandelions, nothing ever grew in my old yard), dug through the dirt in the pot, and found the spare key.

Not that I needed it; I was so keyed up I could have booted the door right off the hinges. But a racket, I did not need to make. If the other me didn't notice, Detective Nick sure would.

I let myself in—you ever noticed how hard it is to be in a hurry *and* be quiet? Yeah. I had an advantage in that I was much, much stronger and faster than Nick would expect, but still. A lot of shit had to go down if I was going to fix one of my worst postdeath blunders. And an awful lot could go wrong. Must be a Tuesday!

I eased into my old kitchen, and was greatly helped by my sister, who had set a pack of cheetahs on fire. At least, from the racket coming from my garage, that's what it sounded like.

"What the hell?" Detective Nick came hurrying from the bathroom, where I could hear the toilet running—nice! We had been friendly at this stage, not friends, but still . . . ever heard of a warrant, Ponch?

I remembered what he'd said when I asked him that exact thing: "I didn't need one, seeing as how you're dead."

Note to self: once you die, civil rights go right out the window.

"Well, look who it is!"

Nick flinched, went for his gun, then realized the lawful owner of the house he was in, warrantless, was home, and relaxed. "Jesus, Betsy, you scared the shit out of me."

Dude, you have no idea how much more scary this encounter could be. "Yeah? What's up?"

"What's *up*? You're dead, Betsy. Except, according to Jessica, you're walking around."

"Practical joke?" I suggested.

"Do you know how many laws you're breaking?"

"I'm a child of divorce. Have pity." I could hear Laura knocking things over in the garage; presumably Other Me was dealing with the racket. "I'm fine, go away."

"For your information," he began, ignoring my groan, "I didn't believe Jessica, but I promised her I'd check it out. And here you are! You've got a lot of nerve walking around dead."

"Tell me."

"I know things haven't been easy since your assault, but Betsy, you just can't pull this shit."

Ah, the assault. That would be the Fiends, feral vampires who leaped upon me when I was coming out of Kahn's

Mongolian Barbecue (all you can eat, $14.99). My garlic breath scared them off (I'm not kidding). But what I didn't know was that, at the time, they'd infected me with the vamp virus. So when I was run over by a Pontiac Aztek, I didn't stay dead.

I'd reported the assault like a good citizen, and Detective Nick had taken my info. We'd stayed in touch . . . friendly, as I said. Not friends.

"I don't know what happened," I lied, improvising rapidly. "I think it was some kind of practical joke by my stepmother."

"Having met her at the funeral home," he muttered, "I can believe that."

"But I'm fine, everyone's fine, go away now." I seized him by the tie and began dragging him toward my back door. "Thanks for checking on me. So, um, why don't you ask Jessica out?"

"Huh?" He seemed to be having trouble keeping up, the poor, poor man. I was all choked up thinking what a stressful week this was. For *him.* "Aw, no way."

"Why not? You're not interested in me." And never was, not until I drank his blood the night I came back. And it hadn't been me he'd wanted. But my undead mojo had fooled him good. "And she likes you."

He brightened. He was *so* cute . . . my height, with brutally short blond hair and blue eyes. A swimmer's build, and those *shoulders* . . . if I wasn't dead, or married, I'd have made a try for him. But I was. And I was!

"You think so?"

Yeah, she passed me a note in study hall. "Sure. You should definitely ask her out."

"Aw, no. She's—"

"Rich?"

"No. I mean, she is, but so am I."

"You are?" This would explain the really good suits he wore. Also the BMW. I had just assumed he was a dirty cop.

"Yeah, it's an inheritance . . . but she's dinner at the Ocean-aire followed by a night at The Grand, while I'm bowling in Burnsville followed by one a.m. breakfast at Perkins."

"Yeah, yeah." I had my hand between his shoulders and was firmly propelling him out the back door. I could hear footsteps on my front porch. This was not a place to linger, for either of us. "Go ask her. Thanks for stopping in. Every-thing's super-duper. Good-bye."

"Do you think I should bring flowers?" he asked before I put a hand on his face and shoved him out the door.

"Tulips," I hissed, and let myself out. He went right; I locked the door and went left.

Laura came around the far side of the garage, one hand clapped to the side of her neck. "I slowed you down," she panted, weaving. "But you were . . . really . . . thirsty."

I caught her as she went down.

Chapter 57

"Oh my God!"

"Didja get . . . Nick . . . away?"

I clapped a hand onto the side of Laura's neck, ignoring her muffled yelp. "Jeez, you're really bleeding!"

"Well . . . you were . . . really . . . hungry."

I could feel her blood trickling against my palm and, to my shame, felt my fangs slide out. "I'm tho thorry!"

Laura giggled. "It cracks me up when you do that. The other you did that, too!"

"Laura, I don't know what to thay." I was almost crying with remorse and mortification. I'd saved Nick . . . and arranged for my sister to get assaulted instead. Oh, *well* done, Vampire Queen! Next: Armageddon.

I hoisted Laura into my arms and carried her around the front of the garage like an undead, rumpled groom. "It's okay.

You're not out here anymore. You went inside. I think . . . to sleep."

"Good," I said shortly. It was probably a terrible idea to find myself and then beat the shit out of myself, but hoo boy, was I tempted.

I set her down and rammed my fist through the passenger-side window, popped the lock, and bundled Laura into the front seat. Then I scurried around to the front of the car, belatedly remembered I kept a spare key in a teeny magnetized box under my front left fender, and squashed the urge to smack myself on the forehead. I grabbed it, hopped in the front seat, and started the car. It was April, in Minnesota. So I cranked the heat.

"You can't steal a car," Laura said, abruptly sitting up. Then: "Ack! Why didn't you remember the spare key before you broke *my* window?"

I instantly cheered up. Even better, my fangs were going down. "You sound a lot better."

"Yeah, the whole thing was sort of . . . hypnotically weird. You really have some whammy in you, Betsy. I mean, I blinked and then I was bleeding and it was almost ten minutes later."

"I'm soooo sorry."

"I know." She patted my knee, which was an improvement over a Hellfire sword through my knee. "And it worked, right? It was worth it?"

I didn't answer. Switching the victims of my assault hadn't been the plan.

"Did stupid, greedy me see your face?"

"No. So when you meet me a year or so from now, you won't have déjà vu, I'm pretty sure." She stared out the windshield and shook her head disapprovingly. "I can't believe you stole a car."

"It's my car!"

"But what are you going to think when you get up tomorrow night and your car's gone?"

"I'll have to worry about that then. Or three years ago. Whatever."

Laura shook her head disapprovingly. "I'm keeping a list, Betsy. Grand theft auto, breaking and entering—"

"It's my car!"

"—breaking and entering into a house—"

"It's my house! And I neither broke, nor entered; I had a key."

"Assault—wait. Did what the other you did count as assault?" She flapped a hand. "Anyway, we've only been here twenty minutes and we've racked up about twenty years in Stillwater. If they incarcerated women there. And why are we driving?"

"What are you talking about? I had to get you away from there."

"Yes, but why are we driving? You did what you wanted; you saved Nick. So let's go back to hell."

I hit the brakes and thought about it. "I can't believe this is about to come out of my mouth, but going back to hell sounds like a great idea."

So we went.

Chapter 58

"Let me see your neck again."

"Cluck-cluck," the Antichrist teased. Then she smiled, and I remembered that when I didn't want to smack her, I thought she was kind of terrific. She'd sure been pretty awesome on the trip. Trips. A lot of people would be drooling in the corner, not perfecting their right cross. "Really, it's okay. Come on, stop beating yourself up."

"That's my job," we said in unison. "Ugh, don't remind me," I continued. "But is it just me, or did you not have to smack me as hard this time?" I rubbed my nose, which had stopped throbbing almost immediately.

"Oh, I'm definitely getting the hang of it," she replied cheerfully. "I wouldn't want to have to guarantee a trip if lives depended on it, but yes, I think I'm catching on."

"Terrific. Maybe your mother will let us out once she decides you've learned what you needed to learn."

"So you're assuming we're not back in our time?"

"Hell, no. Not after the last trip. I'm not believing I'm where we're supposed to be until I see a copy of the *Trib* with the right date."

Laura nodded. "November second. Unless time is passing in our time while we're running all these errands, in which case it could be the third or even the fourth."

"It wouldn't be the worst thing in the world to skip the entire month of November. I've told you how I—"

"Hate November, yes, yes, your weird prejudices are endlessly weird. Which reminds me, you said you'd prove we were already the product of a messed-up time stream."

I took a quick glance around. I wasn't quite sure where we were—another spooky damned cemetery, but the electric streetlights reassured me that we were getting ever closer to the right time. I didn't see any familiar faces—the street on both sides was deserted of people . . . though there were dozens and dozens of parked cars.

My point: it looked like we had a couple of minutes to talk, and I'd be glad to take full advantage.

"Yeah, we are. I've been thinking about this a lot, when I haven't been trying to heal sister-inflicted nosebleeds."

"You got even!" she cried, pointing to her neck.

"It wasn't *me*, you—wait. I guess it was. Listen: Tina would have left town *without* biting Sinclair if we hadn't stopped her! You saw. She. Was. Leaving! We had to talk her into it."

"*We* is a generous word," she muttered.

"Now let's think about the Tina we already knew. She's *never* questioned that I was the queen when, let's be honest, the very idea was so stupid it was almost funny. She didn't know me—*we hadn't met* when she jumped into that pit to help me."

"That's a story I haven't heard yet."

"Yeah, later. I come off sort of cringing and cowardly in it. Listen: I've always thought Tina was supernice, and loyal, but I never asked myself why. I've never asked myself lots of things."

Laura gently touched my elbow. "It's not like you lie around nibbling bonbons all day. There are things going on. You haven't really had time to—"

"That's really nice, Laura, and it's also a total crock. I never made the time. That's all there is to that. But back to Tina . . . she told me Sinclair rose strong but never explained why. Now we know why: because I bit him first. Because the long-foretold queen got to him before Tina. But he never saw my face.

"Listen: Tina's been devoted to me from the second she jumped into the Pitiful Pit. And Sinclair always knew I was the queen, always knew he'd end up with me. Why? *Because I've told them.* Because we're living in a time stream that I've already fucked with."

Laura was staring at me. "You've never been more logical."

"Well, thanks." I resisted the urge to scuff a toe through the dirt and do the aw-shucks thing.

"Or scary."

"Sorry." I shrugged. "But see? I said I'd prove it."

"Sure, and you've convinced me. But what does it all mean? Why do you think—uh-oh. I know that look."

I took her by the elbow and gently pulled her back. We stepped onto cemetery property, lurking beside an enormous marble tombstone . . . almost six feet high! We could have hidden a parade back there. Somebody dead had issues, or his family did.

"Wait." Sinclair.

"What is it?" Me. About a week after I *didn't* bite Nick, by the new time line. "I have to go; I've wasted enough time in this pit."

"It's my first meeting with Sinclair," I whispered to Laura. "He's gonna get grabby, and I'm gonna throw him through a big stone cross, then run off to save Marc from killing himself, and then Sinclair will follow me to a coffee shop where Marc will instantly get a huge crush on him."

"So, same old, same old," Laura whispered back, and snickered.

I could hear myself bitching shrilly. I suppose it was interesting to see these things from the perspective of . . . well, me, just three years older. But instead it just brought back the anxiety and fear I'd felt when I woke up in the funeral home and realized nothing would ever, ever be the same.

It brought back the sheer disbelief of realizing there were all sorts of dead people running around who wanted me dead (permanently) for no reason at all. I was used to being disliked because I'd been shrill or hadn't put out or had beat someone to the last pair of Manolos. Being disliked because people decided I was too dangerous to leave alone was something new and awful.

"I wonder," my husband's voice reached me and I shivered. I couldn't wait to get back to my own time . . . I had some tall apologizing to do. And I wanted him to tell me about Erin. About his folks. What he'd loved and what he'd disliked. The things they did that would drive him batshit. Best memories. Worst memories. Family stuff. Because what were we now, if not a family? "I wonder what you'll taste like?"

I shivered again, because it felt as if he'd whispered that right between my legs. How had I resisted the big lug for so long? Hanging on to being pissed had kept me out of his bed for quite a while. All those potential orgasms, wasted. Like dust in the wind . . .

"That'th it. For the latht time, *get off me*!"

Finally! I'd throw my temper tantrum—

There was a muffled minor explosion as Sinclair sailed back and into the big stone cross. Laura whistled, watching the scene from her knees. "Oh my *God*! You're terrifying!"

"An off night," I grumbled.

"Ohhhh! He's out cold. He is going to be *so* mad at you when he wakes up."

"Yeah, I know." I was loitering by the enormous tombstone she and I had used as our temporary headquarters. "I wish he'd wake up already. Once he's out of here, we're out of here. It's a good thing we—"

"He's up!" Laura interrupted, peeking around the stone. "Wow, you vampires recover *so* quickly! Anyone else would have a concussion. And a shattered spine. And—uh. Is that right?"

"What?" I peeked.

Sinclair was on his feet all right and stomping out of the cemetery.

But he was going the wrong way.

Chapter 59

"Don't try to stop me! Don't you see? Unless I interfere, he'll never come after me. He'll never stick around and trick me into making him king by having sex with me upside down in the deep end of a swimming pool! And if we don't do that, we'll never fall in love and never rule the undead together as good guys not assholes like Nostro! So let me go so I can tell him to be a huge pest!"

"I *know*. Well, not all of that . . . stuff . . ." I realized Laura, far from trying to stop me, was actually shoving me in the direction Sinclair had left. "So go. Go!"

"Oh." I needed a second to get my balance, physically and mentally. I'd expected her to put up more of a fight, so I was having to rethink my strategy. "Okay! Stay here. I'll come back as quick as I can."

And I scampered off in the direction Sinclair had gone.

It didn't take long to catch up with him; he'd taken the

long-cut through the cemetery and was about to do a Six-Million-Dollar-Man leap over the fence and to the street when I seized his shoulder and spun him around.

"Ah, I knew you would not be able to—eh?"

"I'm so, *so* sorry about Erin and your folks," I cried. My hands had slid down, and I was holding on to the sleeves of his dark wool winter coat while he blinked down at me in astonishment. "She seemed really nice when she was five. I think she was five."

"You are wearing different clothes. Dirty clothes," he observed. "And how did you get all the way around the cemetery?"

"I didn't! So you have to go after me. Listen. You have to follow me to the coffee shop after I stop Marc from killing himself. You have to be as annoying as you can, all the time, until you trick me into having sex with you in Nostro's swimming pool."

"But what if I've made other plans?" he asked pleasantly, still looking me up and down.

"This is no time for your weird sense of humor, Sink Lair," I snapped. "If you want to spend the next five thousand years ruling at my side, you'll listen to me now."

"It would be a pity to let such an opportunity slip through my fingers."

"That's the spirit! Be like that, be like that a *lot*. So go after me and be all dogged and irritating, and ignore all the times I'm gonna tell you to take a long walk off a short pier and call you an asshat. Oh, and shoes. You'll have to bribe me with shoes. And be a huge pain in my ass until I realize I'm in love with you." I shook his coat sleeves. "Are you paying attention to me?"

"Oh yes."

The words were right, but the tone (mildly patronizing) and expression (mildly interested) were all wrong.

"Goddammit!" I swore, and when he flinched, I remembered. Our fight. Our stupid fight. And the things I could do that he couldn't. That no other vampire could.

"Look!" I said, and ripped open my shirt.

"Really exceptional," he commented.

"Look *up*, dumbass. That's right, about three inches *above* the cleavage."

He did, and the barely interested expression left his face as if I'd slapped it away. Which in a way, I had. Because I was, of course, wearing Erin Sinclair's gold cross. It meant everything to me; I only ever took it off when we made love.

"My sister's—but you're a—"

"He sees the light! Hallelujah!"

"How—" He *stared* at me. "It's . . . all true, then. Everything you babbled in a piercing whine while you were smudging my coat."

"Babbled! You asshole. I mean, right! So you need to beat feet out of this cemetery and go find me in the coffee shop. I've probably saved Marc by now," I mused aloud, "and he and I are headed for a snack."

"This is your usual practice after saving a life? Coffee and pie?"

"I hate coffee, and why shouldn't I treat myself to an ice-choked Coke after I talk a jumper down from a roof the week I came back from the dead? Plus, almost but not quite killing himself gave Marc an appetite. For a muffin, I think. It might have been a bagel; I wasn't really paying attention. So there's time for you to find me. Just."

"But what if I do not wish to be your king?"

"Please." I rolled my eyes. "One, you love power. Two, you

love me. Or you will. Because although I might need a shower, even dirty leggings can't disguise my essential hotness."

"Touché, my dear." He laughed, which was jarring in a dark, creepy cemetery, but kind of nice, too. "You seem to know me quite well. And it's good to have assurances about your essential hotness."

"Yeah, lucky you. And lucky me. So go already." I made shooing motions. "Run along. Go seduce me. You know, eventually."

"This is the oddest conversation I have ever had," he commented.

"I wish I could say the same."

"I take it you wish for me to do these things because you enjoy being with me?"

"I love being with you, idiot! I love *you*. Idiot. Even though you're arrogant. And slow to take direction. And you *have* to have your way, like, *all* the time. And you own more farms than any man could ever need. And you have extremely weird ideas about spouses in the workplace. Also, you hang all your clothes on wooden hangers. It's like living with Joan Crawford. 'No wire hangers, ever!' And you have another weird thing about buying fruit out of season."

"You simply can't," he said, appalled. "The taste . . . dreadful!"

"My point, Farmer Brown. What I'm saying is, you're a huge pain in my ass and we're in love and dying was worth it because otherwise I never would have met you, so go find me and seduce me already!"

"Not yet married but already nagged," he commented. His long fingers were at my shirt buttons; he was solicitously buttoning me up. I guess he was afraid I'd get a chill. You can take the polite midwestern farm boy off the farm, but you couldn't take the farm out of the boy, or however the old saying went. "Still, the joys of matrimony will likely make up for your shrill sweet nothings."

Then he kissed me. Which is when I, never a candidate for Mensa on my best day, realized he'd been buttoning me up to cover up the cross so he could mack on me without getting a third-degree burn.

I s'pose I should have tried to knee him in his undead gonads, a sort of I'm-not-that-kind-of-vampire message, but who was I kidding? I was horny and I was missing my husband and I was in love and we were married. Sort of. In other words: I *was* that kind of vampire. Also, of all the things about Sinclair that were right, his kissing was probably the rightest.

So I clung instead of kicked, and kissed him back instead of delivering a stern lecture on, I dunno, abstinence?

His mouth was slanting over mine, his arms were around me, I needed a shampoo in the worst way, and who cared?

Then it occurred to me: I was helping my husband cheat on me . . . with me!

I extricated myself with difficulty—it would have been easier to wrestle free of a vat of Laffy Taffy. Fortunately Sinclair seemed inclined to let me go, or it would have taken much longer.

"So. Off you go." I flapped my hands at him. "Make with the seduction so we fall in love. Shoo!"

"Yes, that seems sensible," he said, sounding dazed. "I shall get right on that. You know, there's something about you. Maybe it's the strawberry body wash." Damn. He could smell that under all my layers of grime? What a stud!

Then he wandered off . . . in the right direction, this time.

Chapter 60

$\mathcal{I}$ scampered back toward my sister's hiding place. "It worked! He's gonna go make my life a living hell until I fall in love with him!"

"I know. It was disgusting."

"You were peeking? Perv."

"I needed to make sure you had everything under control," she grumped. "What if he'd gone foaming, barking mad and tried to kill you?"

"I would have kicked his ass."

"Ha!"

"Until he decided to fight back, at which point you would have rescued me."

"There we go."

"D'you know what this means?"

"You're going to be more arrogant than usual?"

"Hell yeah! We've done everything! Your next jump will be the one that brings us home! Dammit."

"What?"

"I'd finally gotten the theme from *Quantum Leap* out of my head. And why are we still cowering back here? Come on."

I took her by the wrist and pulled her out from behind the big shiny tombstone. "So make with the Hellfire sword and cut us a door back home."

"You're certain you're finished? You don't want to tamper with your own past some more? When my mother said I'd be drawn to your history, I didn't realize it meant you'd take the chance to pull a do-over on everything."

"Yeah, I never thought I'd say this, but I owe Satan a favor. I've set things up so they'll happen the way they're supposed to. And I undid biting Nick and ruining his love life. But Laura, I didn't know it'd get switched over on you. I wouldn't have wanted you to get chomped."

"That's okay. I needed to know what it was like."

Okay, that was odd. "Why the hell would you need to know that?"

She shrugged, reached for her waist . . . and was holding her sword. "Know thy enemy and suchlike." Then she winked. "Not that you're my enemy."

"No, of course not."

I didn't like that wink.

Not at all.

"If we undid Nick getting chomped, maybe we can undo Antonia and Garrett dying!"

"No."

"Yeah, it'll be—what?"

We'd gone back behind the tombstone; Laura probably

didn't want to risk anyone seeing us when she hacked a door-way out of nothing.

"No, Betsy. That one you can't undo, and you shouldn't try. And if you did try, *I'd* try to stop you."

I almost laughed, then remembered that my religious-prude half sis was, what was the phrase? Oh, yeah. *Demon spawn.* Probably an exceptionally bad idea to laugh. Ever.

"But why? C'mon, Laura, you're one of the biggest soft-ies I've ever met when you aren't hacking your way through vampires and serial killers."

She colored. "Thanks."

"I figured you'd be the first one on board with saving lives."

"Then you haven't been paying attention. It's not that I'm against saving lives, Betsy, you know that. But undoing bad things won't necessarily guarantee good things."

"But—"

"I know you feel guilty. I know you wish it hadn't hap-pened. But if you undo their deaths, you'll never meet with the werewolves. You'll never make nice with the Wyndhams. You *won't* be aligned with seventy-five thousand werewolves. If Antonia and Garrett don't die, vampires won't be aligned with werewolves. That's too important to undo. No matter how crummy you feel."

I stared at her, appalled. That she could be so cold about it, so logical, was yuck-o enough. That she was right was even worse.

"Why don't you shut up and get us home already?"

"Don't get bitchy because you know I'm right."

"I'm not bitchy. I just need a shower, dammit! And to stop traveling all over my past!"

"Bitchy," the Antichrist mumbled, and obligingly sliced a door out of nothing.

About time, too. I'd had more than enough of this. It was good that we were done. Good that we were heading back. Laura was either learning the wrong things or learning too much. Or both.

Either way: it would be better than good to be back.

Chapter 61

No, no, no, no, no, no, *no, no, no*!"

"Okay, wait. It's not as bad as you think."

I started kicking and beating on the door closest to me. Because we were, of course, still stuck in hell's waiting room. "I hate everything! Satan, you bitch, let us out! Your daughter can't take over the family business if I strangle her with my disgusting leggings! Which I'm going to do! If you don't let us out!"

"Betsy, stop screaming and look."

"Why?" My fists were getting numb. They had good craftsmanship in hell. "Look at what?"

Laura pointed. I looked. "There's only one door left. All the other ones are gone."

I stopped in mid-pummel.

She was right. When we'd started this series of time-hoppin' hijinks, the entire room had been wall-to-wall doors, each about two feet apart. The others were gone; there was just the one left.

"This better mean what I hope it means."

"Sure it does. Otherwise, what would be the point?"

"Yeah. Why would *the devil* want to fuck with people just for the sake of—"

"Okay, okay, you made your point. Really loudly, as usual. Come here so I can hit you in the face so we can time travel some more."

"I just wish that was as cool as it sounded." I straightened and faced her. "Sock it to me. Literally, I guess."

"Nah, watch!" She gave me a gentle shove . . . and the knob turned! "See?"

"You *are* getting the hang of this!" I wouldn't deny it; I was happy for her and delighted for me. "Damn, Laura! Niiiiice!"

"Yeah, I figured it out after we came back from rescuing Nick."

"Well, that's—wait. What?"

"I just wasn't completely sure I didn't have to smack you . . ."

"Nice try. Remind me to accidentally kick you in the shins for a couple of hours." The door swung open, and we stared into the abyss. "Onward and upward."

Chapter 62

"Okay. This is . . . anticlimactic."

Laura had never spoken truer words. We were in a small cement-lined room, maybe twenty by twenty. No windows. Sizeable double doors . . . metal doors, on either end of the room. There was nothing in this big, boring room except the two of us. No table, no chairs, no carpet. Not even a shoe bench.

We looked at each other. Laura shrugged, and I stepped forward to try the doors closest to us. They opened with identical pneumatic hisses, efficient and chilly, like the back-to-school sale at Kohl's.

We could see a corridor lined with doors and, at the end of the corridor, another set of doors, these made of some sort of dark wood. Cherry, maybe, or mahogany.

Laura and I looked at each other again, and this time, we both shrugged. I extended an arm to open the wooden door, but that opened on its own, too. The place was crawling with electric eyes.

We stepped into a gorgeous office, and the first thing I saw was the enormous dark wood desk. It took up half the plush office, practically.

The second thing I noticed was the woman sitting behind the desk.

I was sitting behind the desk.

Chapter 63

"Oh, you're here. Finally," the other me said with a disapproving tone.

"Uh," I said, because as God (or Laura's mom) was my witness, I had no idea what to say. At all.

"I thought I remembered us arriving a day earlier." The other me sighed. "But you're here now. I guess."

Laura was looking at me, and then at me. And I was looking at me, too. I looked the same—same blonde hair, same red lowlights. Same thirty-year-old face. I was wearing a steel gray sheath dress with a sharp, square neckline. No jewelry . . . not Erin's necklace, nothing.

No engagement ring, no wedding ring.

"You look . . . nice."

"And you stink," Other Me said, opening a drawer and rummaging through it. "Ye gods. I can't believe I didn't take five minutes in one of those time streams to hose off. The

Mississippi River was *right there* in one of them, and I didn't take so much as a quick dip."

"Don't be so hard on yourself," I snapped back, and Laura's hand flew up to pinch her lips. But her shaking shoulders told the story and restored some of my equilibrium. "So, where are we?"

"Don't you mean when?"

"Are you going to tell us, or do we have more of your stand-up to listen to?" Yep, I was a real bitch. Times two.

"You're in Minnesota, of course. I'm entirely too attached to this part of the world," Other Me muttered. "Though I did try to like Hawaii before things got chilly." She had taken a sort of computer thingie out of her drawer—it was flat, like a pad, and only about eight inches tall and five inches wide, like a Kindle, but complex. No plugs and no buttons. Now she was sliding her fingers across it, talking to us without looking up. *So* rude. "It's July third and if memory serves, you're here to observe, panic, raise a ruckus, be irritating, ask many unnecessary questions, start a couple of fights, judge our way of life without suggesting how we might improve, then depart vowing to save the world. As you can see," Other Me said, laying her weird electric-pad computer thing aside, "you failed. Because I remember being here, talking to me. I remember you." She pointed at Laura and finally showed an expression that resembled warmth: she smiled. "I remember being dismayed at what I found here, and I remember swearing to find a way to fix it. As you can see, I didn't."

Neither Laura nor I could think of a thing to say.

"Since you now know you can't fix anything," Other Me said hopefully, "maybe you can skip all the nonsense and just return to hell. Which reminds me." Another warm smile for Laura. "Say hello to your mother for me when you get back."

"Okay," she replied, wide-eyed.

"I'm kind of in the middle of things right now," Other Me said, running distracted fingers through her fabulous highlights. "But I've arranged for a tour. And for your many pointless annoying questions to be answered."

"Well, gee whiz, I didn't get you anything."

"Yes, very funny."

The big wooden door opened and a gorgeous guy poked his head in. "Hi, you rang? Oh!"

"Yes, they're here, finally, could you . . . ?" Other Me was back at work, not looking up from her thing-that-wasn't-a-Kindle.

"Sure," Gorgeous Guy replied, and grinned at us. "Come on, I'll give you the fifty-dollar tour."

"My mom always called it the nickel tour."

"Mine, too!" Laura said, brightening. "My adopted mom, I mean."

"Well, inflation," he said, and ushered Laura and me back out into the hallway.

Chapter 64

Okay! So, what can I tell you guys?"

"How about your name?" Laura asked. "I'm Laura, and this is my sis—"

Gorgeous Guy burst out laughing. "Oh, jeez, I know who *you* guys are. Or maybe you didn't notice that she looks *exactly* like the busy lady in the office."

"It hadn't escaped me," Laura admitted.

He was looking from her to me and me to her, and his grin was so open and sunny I had a terrible time not smiling back. But most of me was still stumbling around in shock, mentally speaking. There was a lot of info to take in, and there hadn't been much time to do it.

Our tour guide was taller than both of us, a good two inches more than Laura (yeah, my sis: prettier, smarter, thinner, taller . . . bitch!), and slender, with broad shoulders and a narrow waist. He was wearing khaki pants and a blue T-shirt, practical clothing that didn't disguise his flat stomach and (I assumed, and would check out the first chance I had) awesome butt.

He was pale—not sickly or unhealthy, but the guy hadn't been getting a lot of sun, which made his shock of black hair seem darker and his blue eyes bluer. His jaw bloomed with dark stubble, but despite the slight beard, he gave off an air of youth and exuberance and—it was hard to explain—good times.

Some people, they just seem cheerful all the time, and when you're around someone like that, it's hard to stay worried or grumpy.

"Come on," he teased. "You guys can't figure out who I am? You both know me, back in your when."

So he knew us (obviously) and knew we were time traveling. (Also obviously, since Other Me had clearly prepped him.) But who could we know who was around now—whenever *now* was—but who also—also—

"Holy God!" I cried. It was the hair, really. That shock of black hair, startling on someone so fair-skinned. It was the first thing I'd noticed about him.

About my brother.

"BabyJon!"

"Aw, man." Gorgeous, grown-up BabyJon covered his face, then dropped his hands and shook his head. "I outgrew that nickname a while ago, Mom."

"Mom?" I nearly yelled.

"Okay, technically you're my big sister—like you're Aunt Laura's big sister—"

"Aunt L—"

"—but I grew up calling you Mom. But if that's freaking you out, since I'm still shitting in my crib where you come from—"

"That's a weird way to put it," Laura said.

"Look, I'll try to master the whole toilet thing as quickly as I can, but bottom line, right now in your *when*, I'm suffering the heartbreak of fecal and urinary incontinence." He threw up his hands. "I'm owning it, okay? Don't judge."

It was too much. I burst out laughing. And BabyJon—Jon, I s'pose—joined me. It was kind of nice. I remembered it for a long time, because it was about the only nice moment we had the ninety minutes we were there.

Chapter 65

So what year is it? It's got to be at least twenty years past our present," I said, eyeing my brother/ward/guide. "You're grown, and you're not a vampire."

"I don't have that sickly, pale, irritated look, huh?"

"Bingo. So maybe . . . 2030? More?"

"Uh . . . well, that's a logical assumption to make, but—"

"Oh, God. You're aging horribly and it's only been ten years, right? I'm sorry. You look terrific. Not creaky or elderly at all. Do you have a vitamin deficiency?"

"There's no way to ease you into this—"

"You *do* have a vitamin deficiency! Why isn't Other Me doing something about it?" I looked at Laura. "Maybe we should bring him back with us. That heartless cow is letting her son and brother walk around with a vitamin deficiency!"

"—except to just say it. It's 3010."

"Thirty-ten what?"

"The year," Laura said, appalled. "He means it's the year 3010."

"No it isn't. Come on!" I laughed and pointed at my tall, handsome son. "He's not a vampire! So he can't be a thousand and—"

"—seven," Jon added helpfully.

"Exactly! So . . . aw, shit. You aren't yanking our chains, are you?"

"Sorry."

"But how—jeez." Other Me looked the same. Other Me looked *exactly the same*. It was all true. I was going to rule for five thousand years. In this *when*, I was a fifth of the way through it already. No wonder I was distant and severe and dressed in gray and superbusy! (It didn't explain the lack of wedding jewelry, though.) "But Jon, how are you even alive?"

"I can't tell you, Mom. I'm sorry. Other Mom was pretty clear about that. It'll mess up the time stream and/or bring about ultimate Armageddon. And also, she'll get really, really pissed if I blab."

"Is it because of your power? How you can't be hurt by anything paranormal?"

He shrugged and sounded apologetic. "Sorry, Aunt Laura. Other Mom made me promise. You remember the really, really pissed part, right?"

"Oh, come on," I protested. "You're a grown man! Very grown, I guess. So you don't have to—"

"Um, I know you aren't talking your son into disobeying one of you when we don't know anything about him or his powers or her or what she's up to," Laura said in all one breath.

"Damn your common sense, Antichrist," I swore.

"It does get *kind* of annoying," Jon said apologetically. He smiled again. "Look at it this way: you'll be able to look forward to at least one surprise, right?"

"Is that why there aren't any windows? And why everything's steel or cement except for Other Betsy's office? Was there a nuclear war?"

"Oh, no," Jon said hastily. "Nothing like that."

"Then what?"

"I guess I should just show you."

"Oh, argh. I've seen this movie," I said, trailing after Laura and Jon. "It'll be a blasted landscape crawling with radiated mutants, and the only thing to eat will be Twinkies. And Sno-Balls," I added, remembering the second-awesomest zombie movie ever, after *Shaun of the Dead.*

"*Zombieland* reference," Jon said, nodding.

"How do you know *that*? That's a thousand-year-old reference!" I looked at Laura. "I can't think of a single movie from a thousand years ago."

"Uh . . . Betsy . . ."

"Don't say it." You know how you don't know how stupid something is until you hear yourself say it? That happened to me a lot.

Jon had stopped at the other end of the hallway, the big empty boring room Laura and I had appeared in first. He went to the other set of metal doors and waved his palm in front of what I thought was another cement block but obviously wasn't (in the place in time I came from, cement blocks didn't beep and flash tiny lights).

The doors opened, and Laura and I threw our arms over our faces. Not because of the radiation or to dodge mutants.

It was so bright. It was unbelievably bright. The sun was

shining on an endless expanse of snow. We looked, and I could see Laura's eyes were actually streaming from the brightness. There was only snow. No buildings that we could see. No light poles, no telephone lines. No trees. No cars, no houses. Just snow, snow everywhere.

July 3, 3010.

Chapter 66

"What the hell happened?"

Laura was beyond speech; she just pointed at me and nodded vigorously. The message was clear: *what she said!*

"Sorry." Jon ducked his head and shut the outer doors. We'd found out there was an enormous glass wall between us and all the snow—apparently it was forty below outside. So enormous it was a floor-to-ceiling window. So clean and clear, neither of us realized we were standing behind eight inches of glass. Glass from the future (duh), because I didn't think we had glass like that where I came from—or rather, *when* I came from.

Apparently hardly anyone ventured outside, what with the three-figure windchill, but they still liked to look. I wondered if Tina and Sinclair could enjoy the view or had to be content with looking out that big thick window at night.

Most of the complex we were in was underground. Other

Me was the boss and ran the whole show. I figured Sinclair and Tina had to be around here somewhere, too, plotting to open a nationwide chain of tanning beds.

"Sorry," Jon said. "I can't go into it. Mom made me promise."

"But don't you want us to try to fix it? Jon, we could go back and fix it! You won't have to live underground like a big, gorgeous vole!"

Jon looked at me, and I don't think I'd ever seen a more sympathetic look on a face. "I'm sorry, Mom. There's—I don't mean to talk down to you. It's just that there's a lot going on here that you're not going to understand. And a lot I can't tell you even if you could understand." Then: "Vole?"

"Okay, great, thanks for the tour. Are you allowed to tell us how long we'll be here?"

Jon looked a little taken aback at the abrupt mood shift. "Are you all right?"

"Sure. It was a shock, you know, eight seconds ago, but we're rapidly adjusting. Right, Laura?"

Laura gave me a maybe-you-should-lie-down look.

"So answer the question, Jon-Jon . . . how long are we here for? Do you know?"

"Uh . . . never call me that, please. And a couple of hours, I think. Not overnight or anything. Why?" Jon gave us a puzzled smile. "Is there somewhere you're supposed to be?"

"No, but you should go find out where we're supposed to sleep," Laura said. "In case we want to nap."

"Are you sure? I was gonna show you the soft-serve ice cream machine in the main kitchen. And we still make tons of smoothies," he assured me.

"Who *cares?*" I cried. Smoothies? To channel my hero, Liz

Lemon, "What the *what*?" How about instead we figure out how to *fix the world*? Just for funsies? Smoothies. Jesus.

"Oooh, it's a date!" Laura cried. I don't think I'd ever seen her look more rapturous. Man, there were all sorts of disturbing things to fear in the future. "Go on, now. Find out where we can nap. Seeing the decimation of the planet has tuckered us out. Right, Betsy?"

Well, no, in fact I was pretty sure Laura was having some sort of nervous breakdown. *It's a date?* Ew, she was his *aunt*. And his sister! Which definitely qualified for a double *ew*. But I shrugged and managed a yawn. "Yes, I'm exhausted what with all the . . . not napping lately. In fact, technically I haven't slept for at least fourteen hundred years." Or showered! Gah, what was happening to me?

Jon dashed off to do Laura's bidding.

"What was all that? Unless you really are tired. Is it awful if I care more about a shower than the eternal frozen wasteland in our future?"

"Betsy, what if we do it?"

"Do what?" I stopped trailing after her, and she stopped and turned around.

"What if we cause this? Caused, I mean, past tense. In their past, not ours. You heard Other You. She remembers this. And she remembers going back and trying to fix it. *But she didn't.*"

I blinked, thinking it over. "Maybe that's why nobody's telling us anything."

"Yeah, maybe. But who can't resist you, ever?"

"What, is that a riddle? Because there's the shoe buyer for Macy's. And there's Detective Nick, postchomp. And Jon Davidson of the Blade Warriors. And—"

"In *this* time line, idiot!"

"Oh, *that's* nice, demon spawn! I—" I shut up for a second. Then, hopefully, "Sinclair?"

"Right! So let's go find him. I'm sure you can bash through his defenses with a dazzling display of your utter lack of wit, then do something inappropriately sexual and bend him to your will."

I would have liked to hotly deny what she'd just said, the demon-spawned jerk, but it'd be (a) a waste of time and (b) undeniable. "But he's got Other Me for that stuff."

"Yeah, and what *about* her?" Laura looked annoyed. "Chilly and distracted and sort of distant. She never even said Jon's name, just that someone would give us a tour. She's like a CEO who doesn't know any of the secretaries' or mail guys' names. Future you is more or less the kind of executive you hated working for when you were alive."

"Everything you've said is true. Which brings me to the question, should I be mad or scared? Or just overwhelmed?"

"Figure it out later. So yeah, Sinclair's got Other You, but who's to say that's what he wanted? He's been stuck with Other You when she was *you* you. Now, young, vital, non-CEO you, I bet Sinclair hasn't seen *that* in a while." She paused. "Did that make sense? I'm not sure that made sense."

"It was genius," I assured her. "Come on. Let's get a tour and find my husband."

Call me weird, or perversely curious, but I couldn't wait to see ancient Sinclair.

"So if I've got this right, I'm about to help my husband cheat on me again, with me. Again."

Laura shrugged. "I don't make the rules."

Chapter 67

ther Me and ancient Sinclair must have a bedroom around here somewhere. Probably a whole suite. A chilly, freezing underground suite where they poke skinny computers and can't remember who makes their bed. Not that Sinclair was ever known for lurking in bedrooms during business hours. Other Me is working in her office . . . he must have one, too."

"Think Jon will take us there?"

"Sure, why wouldn't he? He's sooo sweet. And oh my God, it pains me to say anything nice about the Ant, but did she and my dad make a gorgeous kid or what? Also! He's nice because *I* raised him! Truly I astonish myself with my awesomeness. Once in a while, I mean."

"You're right about all of that, but remember: he does whatever Other You tells him. If she doesn't want you to see Sinclair . . ."

"Hmmm. She knows how I think. And she probably remembers how you think. You know what? I just realized . . . there must be an ancient you around here, too."

"I know," Laura said, looking grim. "I've been trying not to think about it."

I didn't blame her. If I'd gotten frigid and boring in a thousand years, what had happened to Laura? My mind shied away from even trying to picture it, and I let it. "So you keep Jon busy. I'll try to dig up my husband. Get it? Dig up?"

"Ugh."

"But first we'll—"

"Oh my goodness, the rumors were true!"

I knew that voice, and sheer force of habit had me turning with a big smile. A smile that fell off my face like an anvil off a cliff.

Marc.

Marc was a vampire.

He rushed up to us with near-blinding speed, and Laura flinched back, hard. He gave me a spine-crushing squeeze and a cold kiss on both cheeks. I had to clench my fists to keep from rubbing his mark off my face. Both his marks.

"And you don't look a day older than thirty. No matter what century it is!"

He sounded all right. He even looked all right. But he felt all wrong. He felt *bad*. A stupid and simple word, but one that fit. I knew, just by looking at him, that he was bad. Maybe it was a queen thing.

No. It wasn't. Laura looked as horrified as I felt.

He grinned, showing fangs. Which I happened to know he didn't need to do. They only came out when we smelled blood or were feeding. He was doing it to creep us out.

"What the hell happened to you?" I snapped, in no mood to feign happiness to see him. Laura went, if possible, even whiter. I wasn't sure why. I didn't care that this *thing* was my friend a thousand years ago. I didn't even care that I'd saved him from a high dive off a roof a thousand years ago. Whatever he was now, he wasn't my friend. If he fucked with me or Laura in any way, I'd play Hacky Sack with his balls.

"Don't you mean *who* happened to me, honey?" His grin widened, but it didn't reach his eyes. Nothing reached his eyes. I glanced into them, then away.

Nobody home.

"So, what are you saying, Marky Mark and the Psycho Bunch? Are you saying I did that to you? Or Tina or Sinclair? Don't be coy, shit stain. Cough up."

"Tina or Sinclair! That's *awesome*!" The Marc-Thing threw back his head (he'd died with a buzz cut, and it was so annoying that he was still terrific looking) and laughed, as my dead grandmother would have said, "fit to split." "Tina or Sinclair, that *is* the question, isn't it? In fact, that's my *favorite* question. Because—"

"Marc."

The Marc-Thing choked off his laugh as though somebody'd slammed an axe through his teeth. Which, believe me, was tempting.

We looked. Other Me was standing at the other end of the hallway, temporarily free of her office. I noticed she had matching steel gray stockings and sensible black flats. I was too far away to see the designer. Since it was all winter all the time, I supposed I should have been grateful the future me didn't clomp around in mukluks.

Were there any designers in the world anymore? I wasn't

sure I wanted to live in a world if there weren't. Eternal winter I could have tolerated, especially if my family was with me, but . . . no designers? That was too much to ask of anyone.

"Don't you have somewhere to be, Marc?" Ancient Me asked.

"Not really," he admitted, but he turned and walked rapidly away before Ancient Me could say anything else.

"Good dog," I called. "Woof, woof."

His shoulders stiffened. But he didn't slow or look back.

Chapter 68

I watched Infantile Me but, as I had expected and planned for, Infantile Me was so overwhelmed by all she had seen, she was reacting, not thinking.

Excellent.

Young Laura, now, *she* was thinking. She had a look on her face I knew well. Again, nothing I had not expected. Nothing I had not planned for.

Marc, though. He'd gotten so unstable over the centuries he was an utter wild card. For the thousandth time, I told myself to kill him.

I still had some residual humanity. Residual weakness. That weakness was the only reason Marc still walked and talked. I knew I should tend to that unpleasant business and be done with it, as I knew to do so would be to pound the final nail in my coffin.

Sinclair would never—

I put the thought away. Locked it away in the corner of my brain where I hid all remaining weakness.

I won't deny being intrigued at seeing my younger self, and Laura's younger self. But seeing the fool I had been was daunting. And depressing. I had been waiting for the idiot me for long years, and now that she was here, stumbling around like a puppy, I only wished for her to be gone.

I could never have made her understand anyway. She would have to become me to understand.

She needed to see what awaited her. She needed to go back determined to change her future.

She needed to fail, and become me.

She needed to learn to be ruthless for the greater good. And she needed to learn that she had only herself to rely on in the beginning. And would have only herself at the end.

Meanwhile, I had a nation to run. Over half a million vampires were crawling like ants beneath North America and needed direction. At all times, they needed direction. The world, I had long discovered, would not run itself.

"Carry on with your business, ladies," I said, and went back to my office.

Chapter 69

Decrepit Me had vanished back into her wood-lined cage, and good riddance. Also, gray was too severe a color for our complexion.

Even better, the Marc Thing had scuttled off like a rat. Better riddance.

Wait. Better riddance? Great riddance? Awesome riddance?

"Damn," Laura muttered, a rare swear. "Elderly You said jump, and he leaped, didn't he?"

"Just tell me I wasn't the one who did that to him."

"What, you'd feel better if it had been Tina or Sinclair?"

"No, but I'd like to ask them anyway."

Laura stopped walking again. What with all the stopping and starting and the mini-tour and the Marc-Thing, we'd only managed to get about eleven feet. Good thing we weren't planning on taking over the place.

"There's no point in looking for Sinclair," Laura said, hands on her hips.

"Okay, that's weird, because about two hundred seconds ago, you came up with this really great plan, remember? You said—"

"Of course I remember, Betsy, it was three minutes ago."

"Are you sure? Because it seems kind of like you don't."

"We won't find Sinclair. He either isn't here, or he won't see you."

"But—"

"*She* knows, Betsy! She knows what you're thinking, and she knows what I said. And she'll have planned for that. Remember: she knew we were coming. There are no surprises for Ancient You."

"Maybe that's her big problem," I said. "I don't deny she gives me the creeps, but I feel a little sorry for her." A very little.

"I don't," Laura said bluntly. "She scares the hell out of me. All your powers as queen in you is bad enough. All your power in *her* . . . guided by intellect. By the logic of an accountant! It's wrong, Betsy, and it's frightening."

"Well, calm down, I don't plan on turning into her in the next half hour. Let's use this chance! We'll find out what we can, and then we'll be able to—

Laura was already shaking her head. "The sooner we get out of here, the better. That's why we don't stay here long. We realize that. And we leave."

"To be fair, we haven't stayed in any time period long."

"Right, but *she'll* know we won't need to stay. Remember: she's already come to this dance. She knows all the steps."

"And that's how we're gonna get her." *Get?* Was I plotting my own downfall? *I hated time travel!* If nothing else, I never knew what tense to use. And why, exactly, was I trying to change things? Ancient Me was a chilly workaholic, but that didn't make her evil beyond compare. Right? "Because Decrepit Me has forgotten what it's like to just pull plans straight out of her butt without thinking."

"That might work," Laura admitted. "She's used to plotting. And she's had the advantage of knowing what would happen. Maybe instead of trying to stop whatever-it-was, she planned for it."

"So maybe we try to get info out of her so we *don't* just lie back and let it happen. Maybe she figured whatever-it-was couldn't be stopped. So she made sure the vampires would be taken care of. If it's July now, think what it's like here in the winter! Vampires can't freeze to death, so who better to take over when global warming bitch-slapped the planet?"

"Makes sense. So what do we—"

I held up a hand. "Uh-uh. I can't tell you. That way, in the future, you can't tell shriveled, withered Other Me. Go try to—"

"Don't *you* tell *me*."

"Right. So after we don't tell each other what we'll do, we'll meet—or not—sometime afterward. Probably."

"Well, good luck, I think."

"And to you, probably."

We embraced, then dashed off in different directions.

Chapter 70

I looked up as Infantile Me booted her way through my mahogany doors. Mahogany! The idiot child had no comprehension what such things cost these days.

"Ah, yes, you're off. No, I'm not going to tell you where Jessica and Tina are. And as I'm sure Marc told you, Sinclair isn't available to you at this time."

"Marc didn't tell me shit. He was too busy channeling Ted Bundy, George W. Bush, and the guys from *Queer Eye*. He's pretty stylin' for a sociopath."

Ah, that was unfortunate. Marc was a tool these days and nothing more. But the chisel can turn in the sculptor's hand. He'd gone off the reservation, mentally, before he could impart the information I needed Juvenile Me to have.

"He's having an off century," I said, feigning disinterest. "Thank you for stopping in. So sorry you can't stay, good-bye—grrkk!"

I'd said *grrkk* because Insane Me had darted across my carpet, lunged across my desk (*my* desk!), and hauled me to my feet by the throat. I didn't mind that nearly as much as I worried for my boucle dress. Such things were difficult to come by these days, and it didn't matter what year it was: once wool was stretched, it never went back. "Stop that!" I gurgled, kicking. I felt one of my flailing feet smash over a filing cabinet and reminded myself those files were more priceless than firewood.

"What did you do?" Toddler Me shouted. "Or what didn't you do! Tell me!"

"This—is not—correct!" How could she be doing this? *I didn't remember doing this!* "You're not—sticking—to the script."

"Sucks to be you, then, I guess," Preschool Me said with a noted lack of sympathy.

The most maddening thing? I didn't dare fight back. I couldn't risk causing a fatal injury. I had so much experience, centuries worth of knowledge, not to mention being the most powerful vampire in the history of the undead. It would be too easy to kill her. And as I had learned over the years, it was difficult to raise the undead.

Raising the dead.

Yes. I knew how to handle this. And it would give the stupid child something to ponder when she was back in the twenty-first century, struggling with a sudoku puzzle.

I took my hands from her wrists, wrenched us sideways, and managed to stab the button on the left side of my electronic blotter. The rear door to my office slid open, and as always, the zombie was preceded by her smell.

Betsy dropped me and backed off at once, as I'd anticipated. "Oh my *God*!" she shrieked, hands clapped over her mouth. "What the hell is that?"

"One of the shambling undead, naturally." I straightened the neckline of my dress. "You're fortunate you didn't smudge me. And still, it hasn't occurred to you to take a shower? Be shamed, slob."

"I'm shamed? *I'm shamed?* Why do you have a *zombie* lurking in a secret compartment behind your office that opens when you push a button on your big, ugly desk?"

I handed the zombie a subdrive (the size of a dime, the knowledge of worlds) and said, "Take this to Ops."

One of her fingers fell off, and, when she clutched the subdrive, we could hear her remaining fingers squirting and squashing. I smiled to hear Betsy's horrified groan. My zombie—the wife of one of our heating engineers, and how silly was it that in all this time, there was still no cure for cancer?—shuffled past Betsy and out the main double doors.

"What, I should just leave the dead in the ground? When they can't freeze to death? When they take orders so beautifully, don't feel pain, and don't call in sick? You want me to waste a human on chores like this?"

"Waste a human? Do you hear yourse—wait. Where do they come from?"

"Sorry," I said, which was a pure lie. "Privileges of rank. You'll figure it out eventually. *The Queene shall noe the dead, all the dead, and neither shall they hide from her nor keep secrets from her.*"

The smile fell off my face when she snapped, "Yeah, and *noe the dead and keep the dead.* That's how you interpreted that awful book? You figured out how to raise zombies? Stop me if you haven't heard this in the last few hundred years, but what is *wrong* with you?"

"Run along," I said coldly. "I could never make you understand."

"Yeah? Well, I understand that I can kick the shit out of you pretty much at will, and you don't dare hurt me back."

"I will dare. Dare and more," I muttered. "There are ways to keep you off me that won't kill you."

"Then bring it, cow."

I tried to recall the last time someone had dared insult me to my face. Or even behind my back (among other functions, fresher zombies could repeat overheard conversations verbatim . . . they were my all-seeing eyes, the rotten darlings).

To my annoyance, she had called my bluff. I sat behind my desk, my hand resting close to the zombie button. That, at least, wasn't a bluff. I had raised another dozen or so only last week. They wouldn't be too decayed to move for at least another three days.

"Run along, little girl."

"What'd you do to my husband, you fucking sick zombie groupie?"

"*My* husband's whereabouts are none of your concern." Had she really called me a groupie?

"Where are Tina and Jessica? And elderly Laura? And why are you letting Marc walk around like that? You might be dead inside, you might have crummy color-coordinating skills in your decrepit old age, but you have to see he's dangerous, he's unpredictable, and he'll probably be the end of you."

Good points, all. It was refreshing, seeing the occasional flash of logic Infantile Me was capable of. Certainly only a very old vampire would ever have any hope of killing me. Fortunately, Marc was too far gone to rally any troops. And one-on-one, as he had found out nine hundred years ago, he had no chance.

In retrospect, I shouldn't have kept him sealed in a coffin draped with rosaries for so long. I'd wanted him broken, but

I hadn't anticipated he would go insane. It had only been for fifty years, for God's sake. I still remember the disappointment I felt when I realized I had overestimated his resolve, grit, and discipline. I'd expected more from a physician . . .

"What do you want, Betsy?"

"What do you *think* I want, you psycho shithead?" she cried. I didn't like to admit it, but being insulted like this was almost refreshing. "I want you to not be a psycho shithead! I want you to go back in time and undo whatever the hell happened to Marc! He was your *friend*, you nasty cow! He was *devoted* to you!"

I stared at myself, my stupid, infantile, foolish self. I was red faced (a good trick for someone who's blood moves sluggishly at best). I was out of control. If I'd been able to cry, I would have been bawling.

"I don't know if you did it or Tina or Sinclair, but you should have saved him! And if you couldn't, you should have taken the head of anyone who *dared* touch a friend of the vampire queen."

"You *have* noticed Tina's absence," I said quietly, arranging the antique pens on my desk.

That shut her up. Alas, not for long. "I don't believe you. Or maybe I do. I can't do anything about it now. But you should be ashamed, not me. You let all this happen, and for what? So you could stay safe?"

"Not at all." I paused. Was I going to do this crazy thing? I had no memory of this conversation. My memories of this chaotic time were of realizing we were all living in a tampered time line. My memories were of seeing the future with horror and running back to my own time as quickly as possible. I didn't confront myself. This nasty little scene never happened. Laura and I had slunk home when we thought no one was looking. "So my son could stay safe."

She paused, then shook her head. "Don't pretend you did all those things because you were trying for Mom of the Year."

"I never pretend," I said evenly. "I lost my taste for it once the death toll reached ten million."

What was I doing? If I was going to match her recklessness, why not just tell her everything? Tina's betrayal, Sinclair's weakness. What I had allowed to happen to so many people.

Satan's last, great gift to me. A page from the Book of the Dead flashed in my mind's eye.

"The Morningstar shalt appear before her own chylde, shalt help with the taking of the Worlde, and shalt appear before the Queene in all the raiments of the dark."

She had. She certainly had. And then some.

"The Queene's sister shalt be Belov'd of the Morningstar, and shalt take the Worlde."

And let us not forget my favorite truism: *"The Queene shalt see oceans of blood, and despair."*

I had. And I had.

So what was I doing now? Why was I tolerating her interference? Thinking there was an alternative . . . it was more of that residual weakness. The last part of me that was still squirming and alive. The last part to be smashed like a snake.

The last environmental specialist had broadcast his find-ings to a shocked world. And when he'd finished, he had said something I'd never forgotten: "This is no world for cold-blooded animals."

Fool.

Chapter 71

There was a firm knock on the door, and Decrepit Me looked almost relieved. "That will be Laura, come to entice you away. Then you'll slink off like thieves."

"Come in, fellow thief!" I hollered. Laura did, looking shaken. "Watch out for the zombie bits on the carpet."

"So I *haven't* gone insane from the horror. It passed me in the hall. (We seem fated to never get out of the hallway.) I came to make sure you were all right. Because of your thing."

"A nice thought, but it originated from here, the poor gross thing. Among my other wonderful hobbies like allowing friends to be brutalized, in the future I take up zombie raising."

"Infant," Psycho Me muttered.

"And you!" I jabbed a finger at Asshat Me. "You don't fool me a bit, you crone. When I came in here and made you my bitch—"

"You did *not*—"

"Quiet, you ancient bitch. Younger, Cooler, Awesomer You has the floor. You were surprised when I did that. You were *freaked out*. Things might not be as cut and dried as you tried to pretend."

There was a long silence, broken by Shriveled, Elderly Me calmly saying, "Perhaps. Why not remain awhile, and discuss it? There are things—"

"You know what? I don't give a shit. We're out of here."

Laura glanced at me, troubled. "Betsy, maybe Dinosaur You has a point. We could—"

"Still not giving a shit. Take us back to hell. Right now."

"But we—"

"Laura, this is not a good time to make me repeat myself. Sword! Mystical doorway! Hell's waiting room! Now!"

Her sword was in her hand while I was still spitting out *mystical*. That was more like it.

"Ta-ta," Prehistoric Me said.

"Fuck off."

"Fuck off twice," the Antichrist added.

Laura sliced. We stepped.

Good-bye, future. Hope to see you never.

Chapter 72

ever thought I'd be glad to see this place."

"Amen."

"Ah! Back so soon." The Ant was at the receptionist's desk, still dead, and still with awful hair. "How was it?"

I pointed. After facing Jerk-off Me, I was in no mood for her idea of banter. "Get Laura's other mother. Right now."

To my surprise, the Ant popped out of sight. She was maybe doing my bidding and maybe searching for a few thousand boa constrictors to fill the waiting room with. Either way, she was out of our hair for a few minutes.

"I think it's fixable."

Laura nodded. "It's worth trying, if nothing else. You said she was freaked?"

"Completely. And she said things—things she hadn't meant to say. She seemed surprised. And—not hopeful, not really, but maybe less . . . resigned?"

Laura was still nodding. "Okay. It's better than nothing. We were able to prove to her—and more important, to us—that the future isn't set."

"There's no fate but that which we make for ourselves."

"That's from *The Terminator*."

"Yeah, which will now be known as Time Travel 101."

"I think—I think one of the things I have to do is what my mother wants. Take over hell; take her job. But not the way she thinks. Not the way Future You thought. I'll take hell, but it'll be on my terms, not Satan's."

I was nodding, too, reluctantly. I hated the thought of Laura stuck in that awful job, but if we were going to save the world from me, we'd need some big-time power. I didn't see the devil lifting a finger. So it would be up to Laura to lift the fingers, so to speak.

Besides, she looked human but really wasn't. No more than I was. She couldn't hide from her destiny in the suburbs the way I had tried to.

"Maybe that's what the book meant. Maybe instead of taking over our world, you'll take over hell."

"We're on exactly the same page," she agreed.

"I have to say, not worrying about you taking over this world will be a load off my mind."

"Um . . . Betsy? Is it just me, or . . . ?" Laura gestured.

She'd noticed what I had seen the minute I realized we were back in the waiting room. All the locked doors were gone; there was just the door *out*. The one back into hell proper, for lack of a better word.

"Of course," the devil said, materializing behind the desk.

"Of course *what*?" I wouldn't deny it: all the time traveling had made me grumpy. "I hate when you're cryptic."

"Sorry," Satan yawned.

"Why now?" Laura asked. "We tried and tried to get out before."

"The exit appeared because you needed it to appear. Before, you only wanted it to appear."

"Oh, not Zen-in-hell bullshit," I groaned.

"Sorry," Satan said. "I don't make the rules." Then she laughed cheerfully. "That's not true! I do make the rules!"

"It's so creepy when you laugh," I observed.

"Almost as creepy as when I don't. So, questions? Comments? Ah . . ." She trailed off at my eager expression. "Perhaps not comments. Maybe you should just go home."

"Maybe I will," I agreed.

So, with Laura's help, I did.

Chapter 73

It ended where it began for me: in the library where we kept the Book of the Dead. What was funny was, now that I knew what was going to happen, now that I had a brand-new mission, I didn't *need* to read the stupid thing.

Still, knowing I could made living in the same house with it slightly more bearable.

And a shower! I could shower! I could be clean! I could *not* revolt myself! Or others!

I spied my red bag beside one of the coffee tables, and lunged for it. A change of clothes! Clean underwear! Oh I loved, loved, loved the present!

I heard the front door slam, heard the bellow of a cheerful baritone, and didn't give a shit. I righted the coffee table (it must have fallen over when Satan tossed me like a tiddly-wink), snatched up my bag, and—

Saw Detective Nick Berry standing in the parlor doorway.

"I *said*, Rainbow had a sale on raspberries. So I bought about ten pints. What Sinclair doesn't know won't hurt him, right?"

I dropped my bag and stared. This, this smiling, friendly, relaxed Nick, *this* was the Nick I had known before I'd died.

"I—I can't believe it," I stammered.

"What? You think I'd leave my favorite vampire berryless? Get it? Berryless? I got a million of 'em. Did you know you've got dirt on your nose?"

"I'm your favorite vampire?"

He sighed and glanced at the ceiling. "Your vanity knows no bounds, but you make it look cute instead of irritating, so I'll indulge you: yes, of course you're my favorite vampire. Don't get me wrong, Sinclair's a handsome man, and Tina's certainly easy on the eyes, but I'll admit it: I'm a star fucker."

"Huh?"

He leaned back and glanced down the hallway. "Ah! There you are. You sure you're up for it?" He straightened and smiled at me. "Okay, so, technically I'm a fucker of the star's best friend, pardon the crudity." He leaned back out in the hall. "We can stay home if you want."

"Home?" I was having a terrible time following the conversation(s).

"Yes, home, our domicile—technically your domicile, but last I checked, even with Jessica and me staying here, there are still about thirty guest rooms left. Hiya, gorgeous."

"I'm so hungry," Jessica moaned, appearing in the doorway beside Nick. "Oh, hey, you're back. You want to come to dinner? Manny's? You can watch me eat a steak, and I can watch you drink daiquiris."

I stared.

"Betsy?"

I stared.

"Not that I care either way, but you haven't fed in a while, prob'ly . . . am I right?"

I pointed at Jessica's enormous belly. She was a stick with a ball. I always knew, when she got pregnant, she'd be a stick with a ball. "That—that—"

"What? I *said* I'd give you the ultrasound picture. And I said you could tape the birth if you promise not to go foaming barking mad when you smell all the blood. Now are you coming to dinner or not?"

"Not," I said through numb lips.

Nick patted her stomach and gestured in the direction of the front hall. "Your chariot awaits, my pregnant goddess of love."

"What, are you *trying* to make me barf? I've had six months of morning sickness and you're trying to make me barf? Cops are weird." They turned to leave; Jessica glanced back and added, "Welcome back."

"It's . . . it's nice to be back." I could feel an incredulous, stupid grin spreading across my face. "It's really, really nice to be back."

Chapter 74

Okay. I wasn't going to pretend I had any idea what had just happened. But it was all good, so I'd get the gory details later. For one thing, *she* was knocked up, and *he* was happy as a clam with a detective's badge, but neither of them wore wedding rings.

I had *tons* of gossip to catch up with, and couldn't wait. But first, my bag, my shower, and my—

"I did hear you!" Tina came in, looking adorable in a floor-length black woolen skirt and a lavender long-sleeved T-shirt. Her hair was pulled up in a ponytail. Black Christian Dior gladiator sandals (my Christmas gift to her last year) on her delicate feet completed the picture.

And the little portrait, of course. The small painting, no more than an inch long, looped over her wrist by a blue satin ribbon.

The portrait I'd seen once before. The portrait I'd never seen . . . on *Tina's* wrist.

"I'm glad you're back, Majesty. Ah, you look beautiful, but you have dirt on your nose. When you have a moment, I'd like your signature on some accounts His Majesty wants you to be able to access. I know," she added, holding up a small hand, palm out, like a traffic cop. "What's his is his, and what's yours is yours, and he doesn't own you, and he should keep his own money, yes, yes. But he wants you to have legal access to everything he owns, and now that the sale on the Brazilian pineapple plantation has come through, he has another revenue stream he'd like you to—ah. Majesty? Why are you looking at me like that?"

"I didn't know. Tina, I swear I didn't—" I took a staggering step toward her and completely lost my feet; I ended up crouching in front of her. She looked startled and embarrassed, and tried to move to help me up—she clearly didn't dig queens kneeling at her feet—but I seized her hands and squeezed, clinging as though they were the anchor line and I was the drowning dumbass and she was the anchor. "I didn't!"

"My queen—"

"I never made the connection. I couldn't understand—neither of us could understand—why we ended up in Salem where we didn't know anybody."

"Majesty—"

"I didn't mean to play God with your great-great-great-great-great-great-great—how many?—never mind, I didn't mean to wreck her life, Tina, even though I probably did. I just wanted to help, but I messed it all up. I think helping her maybe wrecked the future. But maybe not; I don't *know*, that's the awful part, but I'd never have hurt you. I mean her.

I really did want to help, and it's my screw-up and not Laura's. Laura tried to stop me. I swear it on my—on myself."

"Wreck? Oh. You—wreck?" Her eyes, her beautiful big pansy eyes went wider than ever—she was practically turning into an anime cartoon right there in front of me. "You could never—you *did* never. I thought you understood. His Majesty explained you would be back soon and we could tell you what we knew. We didn't *want* to keep things from you." She anxiously scanned my face. "You understand, don't you?"

"What—you could tell me what you knew?"

"Caroline remembered you, of course. Both of you. My great-great grandmother remembered the two very tall, very beautiful blondes who dressed strangely and spoke even more strangely.

"She remembered everything the angels—for so she believed you to be—everything the angels said. She went away shaken but grateful. She left Massachusetts and settled farther west, happy to have her life and her wits.

"And she told her daughter what happened to her. How faith can become first a shield, then a club. She told her girl child how the angels saved her from a cruel mob and a crueler death. And her daughter told *her* daughter, who told me. It was my favorite bedtime story, the only one I never tired of." She paused. "It was Erin's favorite as well."

I was still clinging to her hands, still staring up at her and wishing I was human enough to cry real tears. But I wasn't, and never would be again. Instead, what was waiting for me down a tunnel of centuries was the woman who had no friends, only soldiers. The woman who made the Marc-Thing, or allowed the Marc-Thing to be made, and didn't know where her husband was or *if* he was, and didn't care.

"Tina, I shouldn't have. I didn't know, but that's exactly

my point. I *didn't* know, which should have been all the reason I needed to steer clear of another life."

Tina pulled one hand out of my clutches, and I let her. For a second I thought she was going to haul off and give me a well-deserved belt on the jaw. Instead, she carefully turned one of my hands in hers, palm up, and bent forward and kissed it. Then she folded my fingers over her kiss and speared me with her dark gaze. Her long blonde waves had come loose—her hair was everywhere, but I was too busy looking into her eyes to shake it out of my way.

"My dear dark queen," she said, and gifted me with the warmest smile I'd ever seen on her face. "I have always known."

She let me cry on her lap for a long time.

Chapter 75

After an embarrassingly long time, I pulled myself together, accepted a hug from Tina, ran my fingers through my (dirty) hair, and sighed. "Okay. That was cathartic."

"My! Your face is even dirtier now."

"You don't have to sound so happy about it."

"No, I suppose not." She wasn't laughing at me . . . barely. "Would you like a smoothie?"

"I would *love* a smoothie, and then we have to talk. I mean, I have to find Sinclair first and apologize, but then we have to talk. When I left the house? Jessica wasn't pregnant, and Nick hated me."

"Really?" Tina's eyes were wide and curious. "That's . . . difficult to imagine. My. You *do* have stories to tell, don't you?"

Ah . . . some stories, yeah. But not all.

"I'll go get some started . . . Nick left what appears to be three dozen grocery bags in the kitchen. With your permission, Majesty." She wandered off, muttering to herself. "How we'll eat them all without His Majesty finding out or some of the berries going bad I do *not* know . . ."

Okay. Time to get my ass upstairs, take a shower, change my—my—

My letter!

I sank to my knees, clawing open the bag and rummaging through clean panties to find the letter Sinclair had left for me. Since I knew I'd fucked up and wanted to apologize, now would be the time to read it. And since he and Tina seemed to know exactly where I'd gone, and what I'd been up to . . .

I ripped it open with trembling fingers and read it right there on the parlor floor.

My own, my dearest Queen,

You have been gone less than four hours and I can scarcely bear it. I disliked avoiding you and letting you journey through time not knowing you had my support and admiration and, always always, my love. I did not like it, though I know it was necessary to both my past as the son of murdered farmers and brother to a murdered twin, and my future as a reigning monarch.

More: it was necessary to bring you into my life. There is nothing I would not endure a thousand thousand times to be certain that would come about.

My sister would have loved you, as I love you. I will regret to the end of my days that you and she could never meet . . .

again. How well we remembered your visit when we were children! How you enchanted my beloved twin and cast your spell on me!

How grateful I am that you made me strong.

Elizabeth, your charm and your power come from the simple fact that you have no idea how powerful you have always been. This is the sort of thing that makes me love you while fighting the urge to strangle you.

He was right! I knew what that expression looked like. I'd seen it a zillion times in the last few years. Sort of like constipation paired with a sugar rush.

By now many of your questions about my past have likely been answered.

Yeah, you could say that.

But if any questions remain, I will answer them. If you require any information on any topic with which I am familiar, I shall provide you with all you need in the best way I can.

The time to keep secrets from you is over. Your footprints can be found throughout our lives; you have always been in our lives, and at last you can know it, to our gratitude and joy. Knowing this, we have counted the minutes until your return to your proper place in time.

Should this be at all unclear, I shall say it straight out: your place is at my side, and will always be, whether it is sixty years ago or five thousand years from now.

In this, as in all things, I am your devoted husband, servant,
and monarch.

My own, how I miss you.

Sink Lair.

My hand spasmed and the note crumpled in my fist. I
gasped and tried to smooth it out, which would have been
tricky even if I hadn't been crying. The nickname he hated!
He'd signed it with the nickname he hated!

More: he let me go to hell, even though he knew I was
going to be hip deep in all kinds of crap. For a macho control-
freak, old-fashioned chauvinist like my husband, for him to
stand back and let all that happen, let me face all sorts of
danger and bad smells . . . well.

"Ah, I not only heard your dulcet voice but followed the
smell of grime." I looked up. Sinclair was leaning in the doorway, arms crossed over his chest. "Your face is smudged, my
own. And I must apologize for picking such an ugly, pointless
argument to make you think—"

"Shut up!"

He blinked. "As you wish."

"And fuck me!"

He blinked again. Had he developed a nervous twitch
while I was gone? "As you wish."

And just like that, I was in his arms. Just like that, we
went staggering all over the parlor, kissing hungrily, biting, licking, yanking at our clothes, tripping over the end
table (twice) and the couch (once), until we finally realized we
should just stay on the floor.

My shredded leggings were more shredded, and Sinclair
was trying to rip his tie off without strangling himself more

than I accidentally had. I'm not sure why he was bother-
ing, since his white dress shirt was in several pieces on the
carpet . . . force of habit, maybe?

"My own, my dear, my Elizabeth, *my* Elizabeth, how I
missed you."

"Less talk," I panted, levering my hips off the floor to meet
his. "More dick."

He laughed into my mouth. "As you—ah. That's . . .
really quite lovely."

"Gawd, it sounds like a herd of pissed-off jaguars in here.
What the—aw, dammit!"

Marc was in the doorway, arms akimbo. "Oh, come on!
You know how long it's been since I got laid? I've been lugging BabyJon to every Gymboree in town just to meet someone who'll be my favorite bad choice!"

"Out!" Sinclair roared, not even looking.

"It's not fair!" he whined, retreating with both hands over
his eyes. "Bad enough you two are ridiculously hot so we all
assume you're having awesome monkey sex, but that's why
you have a bedroom! So the rest of us don't have to walk in
on scenes like this! Stop it, that table's almost three hundred
years old! Oh, now you're just flaunting your vampire superpowers and sex life." His voice was getting fainter. "The rest
of us get to live here, you know. I mean *have* to. *Have* to live
here. Aw, dammit . . ."

Epilogue

I had just finished checking on my new "ink" and deciding who would rest in peace, and who would be my new gopher, when a familiar doorway made of Hellfire began cutting its way into my office.

I leaned back, opened the top drawer, extracted the pen I'd had made just for this, then smiled as the devil dropped through the door in the ceiling onto my carpet.

"That's dramatic," I commented, "even for you."

Laura Morningstar grinned. "What can I say, big sister? I'm in a flamboyant mood."

"Another of your would-be heirs made it through adolescence?" I asked idly. "Or another dupe allowed himself to be seduced? Or did you think up something even more wonderfully awful to do to our father?"

"All three!" my sister answered, hugging herself with glee. She was, as I was, still a beautiful woman. In fact, at only a thousand-some years old, she was years away from her prime.

Which was fine with me. I didn't need her in her prime, but she needed me in mine.

"I'm glad to see you," I said, and it was nothing but the truth.

"I'm sure." She plopped into the chair opposite my desk. "Relieved they're gone?"

"There are no words," I fervently replied. "What a distasteful business."

"You just don't like remembering how you used to be."

Among other things, yes. But never mind, little sister. Never mind.

"And speaking of the bad old days, I'm finished with your husband."

"Excellent. Because I'm ready to take him back."

"Oooh, sounds kinky. Can I watch?"

"It doesn't, and no, you cannot."

Laura held out her hands. A small circle of Hellfire—even after all these centuries, I still couldn't look at it directly— opened about two feet above her, and an enormous book landed in her hands with a distinctive *whump!*

"Behold, the king of the vampires." Laura dropped the book on my desk. "It took longer than I anticipated to quiet him, skin him, and bind him. I won't lie: I was impressed. He never made a sound. Not once in seventy-five years."

I sighed . . . an unnecessary breath, but old habits were the hardest to break. Case in point: my husband.

I had disliked him at first. Then had become infatuated. Then devoted. And then disappointed. Finally: disenchanted.

He never would have helped me keep things the way they

were, the way I knew, from my travels with the devil, they had to be.

Really, there was only one way he could help me now.

"It'll take a while to get it all down exactly right. There's quite a bit to remember."

Laura yawned. She'd never been one for details.

"But once it's finished, you'll be able to bring it back? It's a trip of more than a thousand years, you'll recall."

"If I recall, why d'you remind me? And a thousand years might as well be six months, after all this time. Or did you forget about practice making perfect?" She smiled. "I got my start schlepping you around Salem, remember?"

"Vividly."

I picked up my pen, flipped open the cover of the blank book, dipped the tip of the pen in blood, and began to write on my husband.

Chapter one, page one.

The Book of the Dead.

Also available in MaryJanice Davidson's wonderful
Undead series, published by Piatkus:

UNDEAD AND UNWORTHY

Having recently lost her dad and stepmother, Betsy Sinclair
(née Taylor) is adjusting to rather more than just married life.
Their untimely deaths have left her and Eric as sole guardians
of her little brother, Jon. Two vampire parents – albeit vampire
royalty – for a decidedly human baby. Still, Betsy is more than
up for the challenge. If only everyone would stop being so
nervous around her, given her sudden recent burst of power.
Betsy most emphatically Does Not Want To Discuss It, and for
the moment, everyone is following her lead.

But then the ghost of Betsy's stepmother turns up at their
house. And as stubborn and insufferable as she was in life, she's
even more annoying in death – especially as she regards her
demise as all Betsy's fault!

978-0-7499-0941-3

UNDEAD AND UNEASY

Betsy Taylor, undead vampire queen, has been given a new nickname by her nearest and dearest: Bridezilla. Because whether you're alive or undead, planning weddings is a bitch. Especially when your groom thinks the whole thing is a waste of time.

Betsy's also dealing with a full house: she lives with a ghost (Cathy), a werewolf (Antonia), a gay physician/human (Marc), her fiancé and vampire king (Eric Sinclair), her best friend (Jessica), a recovering Fiend (Garrett). But when Sinclair disappears and then, one by one, her friends go missing, Betsy begins to get seriously uneasy . . .

978-0-7499-3893-2

UNDEAD AND UNPOPULAR

Betsy Taylor, Vampire Queen, already has plenty on her plate. For one thing, next week is her 31st birthday – and her 1st anniversary of being undead. On top of that, she still has wedding plans to finalise – and it's not helping that the prospective groom is avoiding anything to do with it. And then there's her decision to stop drinking blood – something she has yet to share with Eric Sinclair, her fiancé.

So the last thing she wants to deal with is uninvited guests, even if they happen to be the powerful European vampires who have finally come to pay their respects the week before her birthday. Some of them don't want Betsy as their Queen, and will do anything to get rid of her. As if turning thirty last year (not to mention dying) hadn't been traumatic enough. And trying to give up blood is making her *really* cranky . . .

978-0-7499-3799-7

Watch out for MaryJanice Davidson's fabulously funny
Fred the Mermaid series!

SLEEPING WITH THE FISHES

Fredericka Bimm – Fred – is a mermaid. But she is not the stuff of legends. A marine biologist, she knows what's in the water so chooses not to expose herself to those toxins. She's allergic to shellfish. The sea creatures she can communicate with won't do her bidding. And she doesn't have long blonde hair or a perfect body. And she's definitely not perky!

Fred's life is mostly spent trying to conceal her origins – and lately she's been trying to figure out just why there are weird levels of pollutants in the local seawater. Then two strangers come into her life. Her new colleague is a sexy – if over-curious – hunk with a mermaid fixation. The other claims he is Artur, the high prince of the black seas – and Fred's rightful ruler!

978-0-7499-3801-7